THE BLACK EYED PROPHECY

The Black Eyed Prophecy

C.K. GILMORE

Copyright © 2024 by C.K. Gilmore
All rights reserved. No part of this book may be reproduced in any manner whatsoever without written permission except in the case of brief quotations embodied in critical articles and reviews.
First Printing, 2024

Contents

Dedication		vi
One	The Storm	1
Two	The Knock on the Door	27
Three	Truth and Guilt	45
Four	Promises Made, Laws Broken	61
Five	The Vow	81
Six	Ghosts, Ghouls, and Goblins	99
Seven	The Mystery Package	117
Eight	Echoes of the Past	135
Nine	Winters Cold, Flame Rekindled	155
Ten	The Warehouse	179
Eleven	Valentines and Keystones	197
Twelve	The Lighthouse	209
Thirteen	Death and Discovery	223
Fourteen	The Apporaching Storm	245
Fifteen	Into the Darkness	253
Sixteen	The Truth Revealed	273
Seventeen	Shadows Ascended	287
Eighteen	Rising Light	297
Nineteen	A New Beginning	309

For my family, who taught me that the best stories are written in the quiet moments between heartbeats, and who never once doubted that I could catch stardust with words.
For my friends, who walked beside me through the darkness and the light, laughing at my worst jokes and believing in my best dreams.
And for you, dear reader, who chose to step into this world with me. Welcome to the magic hiding in plain sight.
Special thanks to my parents, who filled our house with books and wonder, and to my brother, who always asked "what happens next?"
Your love lights the way through every story.

Chapter One

The Storm

Salem, Massachusetts wore its history like a well-worn cloak, both comfortable and slightly frayed at the edges. Colonial-era buildings stood shoulder-to-shoulder with modern storefronts, their weathered brick facades telling silent stories of centuries past. October painted the trees in brilliant shades of amber and crimson, and a crisp autumn breeze carried the scent of fallen leaves and wood smoke through narrow streets that hadn't changed their course since the 1600s.

Tourists clutched their phones and snapped photos of the witch-themed gift shops, their excited chatter mixing with the click of their shoes against ancient cobblestones. They came seeking the ghosts of Salem's darkest chapter, never suspecting that real magic coursed through the city's veins like an invisible current, hidden in plain sight behind a veil of mundane reality.

Alex Kingston knew both sides of Salem intimately. At twenty-one, he'd spent his entire life navigating between two worlds: the Salem that everyone could see, and the one that existed in the spaces between heartbeats. With wavy blonde hair that caught the autumn sunlight and sapphire blue eyes that seemed to hold secrets, he looked every bit the part of a young newspaper reporter – khakis, button-down shirt, messenger bag slung across his shoulder. Nothing about his appearance suggested he was anything more than another young professional making his way through the historic downtown.

He had always prided himself on his rationality. At twenty-one, he'd already carved out a comfortable niche for himself in Salem, where he'd lived all his life. His job as a local journalist for the newspaper kept him grounded in facts and reality, or so it seemed.

But like Salem itself, Alex Kingston had depths that few could see. He was a witch, born into one of the city's oldest magical bloodlines. The power that hummed beneath his skin was his birthright, carefully hidden from the world at large by generations of practiced discretion and the watchful eye of the Order of Salem.

He paused outside Derby Square, checking his watch. His lunch break had run longer than intended – he'd lost track of time at his favorite café, poring over an old tome of magical theory disguised as a dog-eared copy of "The Great Gatsby." The brass hands of the Custom House Maritime Museum's clock warned him he had exactly seven minutes to make it back to the Salem Gazette's offices.

The newspaper occupied the second floor of a restored Victorian building on Essex Street. Its brick facade was distinguished from its neighbors only by a modest brass plaque and the faded gold lettering on the front window: "Salem Gazette - Since 1768." What the sign didn't mention was that the paper had been quietly owned by magical families for most of those years, serving as both a legitimate news source and a carefully curated monitor of supernatural activities that might threaten the veil between worlds.

Alex took the stairs two at a time, the wooden steps creaking in familiar places. The newsroom greeted him with its usual cacophony: phones ringing, keyboards clicking, the ancient radiator in the corner hissing like a mechanical cat. The space was organized chaos, with desks arranged in loose clusters and walls covered in framed front pages marking significant moments in Salem's history. To those who knew where to look, certain headlines held double meanings, recording events in both the mundane and magical worlds.

"Cutting it close, Kingston!" Sarah Chen called out from her desk, not looking up from her computer screen. Her long black hair was pulled back in a neat ponytail, and her fingers flew across the keyboard with machine-gun precision. At twenty, fresh out of college, she was the youngest member of the newsroom staff besides Alex himself. She was also possibly the most talented researcher he'd ever met – a fact that sometimes made him nervous, given her knack for digging up obscure details that others might prefer stayed buried.

"Traffic," Alex lied smoothly, dropping into his chair at the desk opposite hers. It wasn't exactly a lie – he had been stuck behind a tour group moving at glacial speed, but that had only accounted for about thirty seconds of his delay.

"Traffic consisting of exactly sixteen tourists in matching red windbreakers, led by a guide with a fake Salem accent?" Sarah raised an eyebrow, finally looking up from her screen. "I saw them from the window. You were at Brews & Books again, weren't you?"

Before Alex could defend himself, a door at the far end of the newsroom opened, and Thomas Marshton emerged from his office. The editor-in-chief's salt-and-pepper hair was slightly disheveled, as if he'd been running his hands through it in frustration, and his thick mustache twitched slightly as he surveyed the newsroom. His brown eyes settled on Alex with the intensity of a hawk spotting a field mouse.

"Kingston! My office, five minutes. Bring whatever you've got on the missing pets story."

Alex nodded, already pulling up files on his computer. The missing pets story had seemed like a fluff piece when Marshton first assigned it to him two weeks ago – the sort of thing you buried on page six when news was slow. But as he'd dug deeper, patterns had emerged that made the hair on the back of his neck stand up. Twelve dogs and seven cats had vanished from their yards in the past month, all within a five-block radius of the old Pioneer Village. No signs of struggle, no bodies found, just pets seemingly evaporating into thin air.

To most people, it would seem like nothing more than a sad coincidence, maybe the work of a coyote or an irresponsible owner leaving gates open. But Alex had grown up learning to spot the patterns that others missed, the subtle signs that something wasn't quite right with the natural order of things. And everything about this story felt wrong in ways he couldn't quite put his finger on.

"Want me to pull up the satellite view of the area again?" Sarah offered, already opening Google Maps. "I marked all the disappearance locations yesterday. There's definitely a pattern, even if I can't figure out what it means."

Alex smiled gratefully at his friend. Sarah might not know about his other life, about the real Salem that existed alongside the one she knew, but her instincts were sharp. Sometimes he wondered if on some level she sensed more than she let on.

"Thanks, but I think I've got everything I need," he said, gathering his notes. He'd made two sets one for Marshton, containing only the facts that would make sense to non-magical eyes, and another in a notebook charmed to look blank to anyone but him, where he'd recorded the more troubling details. The way all the missing animals had been described as acting strangely in the days before their disappearance. The cold spots reported by their owners. The children in the neighborhood talking about new friends who only came out at twilight.

As he headed toward Marshton's office, Alex couldn't shake the feeling that he was missing something important, something that was staring him right in the face. The autumn sunlight streaming through the newsroom's tall windows suddenly felt thin and weak, and for just a moment, he could have sworn he saw his shadow move in a way that didn't match his steps.

But that was ridiculous. Shadows didn't move on their own, not in broad daylight, not in the normal world that existed on this side of the veil. He was letting his imagination run away with him, seeing magic in mundane coincidences. Sometimes a missing pet was just a missing pet.

Wasn't it?

He knocked on Marshton's door, pushing away the nagging doubts. He had a job to do – two jobs, really. And for now, at least, those jobs required him to focus on the ordinary, explainable version of events. The version that wouldn't frighten people. The version that kept the veil intact.

"Come in, Kingston," Marshton called out, his voice muffled by the frosted glass door. "Let's see what you've got."

Alex took a deep breath and turned the handle, not noticing the way the shadows in the corner of the newsroom seemed to gather and whisper as he stepped into his editor's office. He didn't see the way Sarah frowned at her computer screen, rubbing her eyes as if trying to clear them of some strange distortion. And he certainly didn't notice the small figure that watched from the street below, its eyes as black as polished obsidian, its pale face turned up toward the newspaper's windows with an expression of patient, hungry interest.

The day was still perfectly normal, after all. For now.

Tom Marshton's office was a shrine to old-school journalism. The walls were lined with framed front pages and journalism awards, their glass reflecting the afternoon sunlight that filtered through venetian blinds. A massive desk dominated the room, its surface covered in neat stacks of papers and manila folders. The computer monitor seemed almost like an afterthought, tucked into the corner as if Marshton tolerated its presence rather than embraced it.

"Sit down, Kingston," Marshton said, not looking up from whatever he was reading. His reading glasses were perched on the end of his nose, and Alex noted how the editor's thick mustache twitched slightly as he read — a tell that usually meant he was irritated about something.

Alex slid into one of the two chairs facing the desk, fighting the urge to cast a subtle comfort charm on the hard wooden seat. The chairs were notoriously uncomfortable, and office rumor suggested Marshton had chosen them specifically to keep meetings brief. As he waited for his boss to acknowledge him, Alex found himself thinking of at least three different hexes that could make that perfectly groomed mustache fall out. Nothing permanent, of course — just enough to crack that stern facade for a day or two.

But such thoughts were dangerous, even in jest. The Order of Salem's rules were absolute: no magic in front of non-magical people, no matter how tempting the circumstance. Even if Marshton would look significantly improved with purple polka-dotted eyebrows.

"So," Marshton finally said, setting down his papers and fixing Alex with a penetrating stare. "Tell me why I shouldn't kill this story and give you something more substantial to work on. Missing pets? This isn't exactly Pulitzer material, Kingston."

Alex opened his notebook, buying time to organize his thoughts. "There's a pattern here, sir. It's not just random disappearances. All nineteen pets vanished within a five-block radius. No traces, no bodies, nothing to suggest animal attacks or theft. And all within the last month."

"Coyotes," Marshton said dismissively, waving a hand. "Or maybe one of those fisher cats. Natural explanation."

"In broad daylight? In fenced yards? And why haven't any remains been found?" Alex leaned forward slightly, careful to keep his voice level and professional despite his growing frustration.

"There's more here, sir. The temperature readings in the areas where pets disappeared have been consistently lower than the surrounding areas – I checked with weather monitoring stations. And the children in the neighborhood have been reporting—"

"Children?" Marshton's eyebrows rose. "You're basing investigative journalism on playground gossip now?"

Alex bit back a sharp retort, feeling the familiar tingle in his fingertips that came with suppressed magical energy. How easy it would be to make Marshton understand, to show him the patterns that were so clearly supernatural to anyone who knew what to look for. One simple revelation spell would—

But no. That way lay disaster, not to mention severe consequences from the Order. Instead, he took a deep breath and tried again.

"The children's accounts corroborate each other, sir. They're all describing the same thing strange kids they've never seen before, showing up around dusk. Always asking to play with their pets. The timing matches perfectly with the disappearances."

Marshton leaned back in his chair, studying Alex with an expression that was hard to read. The wall clock ticked loudly in the silence, and a car horn honked somewhere on the street below. Finally, the editor sighed.

"Look, Kingston. You're a good reporter. Sharp eye, good instincts. But sometimes a story just isn't there. Write it up if you want – half a column, page six. Then I need you focused on the zoning board meeting next week. That's where the real story is."

The zoning board. Alex managed not to roll his eyes, but it was a close thing. If Marshton only knew that three of the board members were actually shapeshifting fae creatures who'd been maintaining their positions since the 1950s, maybe he'd find that less interesting.

"Yes, sir," Alex said instead, closing his notebook. "I'll have the pet story on your desk tomorrow morning."

"Good man." Marshton was already looking back at his papers, clearly dismissing him. "Close the door on your way out."

Alex stood, tucking his notebook under his arm. He was almost to the door when Marshton spoke again.

"Oh, and Kingston? Stay away from Pioneer Village. That area's not as safe as it used to be. Wouldn't want one of my reporters disappearing like those pets, would we?"

Something in the editor's tone made Alex pause, his hand on the doorknob. When he glanced back, Marshton was focused on his work, looking for all the world like he'd already forgotten Alex was there. But there had been something in those words – a weight to them that seemed out of place for casual concern.

"No, sir," Alex said carefully. "That would be unfortunate."

He stepped out of the office, letting the door click shut behind him. Sarah looked up from her desk with raised eyebrows, clearly hoping for gossip about the meeting, but Alex just shook his head slightly. His mind was already racing, analyzing Marshton's parting words from every angle.

Stay away from Pioneer Village. Not a suggestion – a warning. But why would Tom Marshton, thoroughly mundane newspaper editor, know anything about the dangers gathering in that part of town? And why had his shadow, cast on the office wall by the afternoon sun, seemed to shift and darken when he'd said those words?

Alex returned to his desk, mind churning. He had two stories to write now – the sanitized version for the Salem Gazette, and the real version for the Order of Salem's archives. And he had a growing suspicion that his editor might deserve a chapter in both.

The rest of the afternoon passed in a blur of keyboard clicks and phone calls. Alex wrote and rewrote the pet disappearance story, trying to find the right balance between revealing enough to warn people and concealing the more unsettling details. By the time he saved the final draft, the newsroom had emptied considerably, and the quality of light coming through the windows had changed that particular golden-amber unique to October evenings in New England, when summer's lingering warmth finally surrenders to autumn's embrace.

"Earth to Alex," Sarah's voice cut through his thoughts. She was standing by his desk, her messenger bag already slung over her shoulder, dark eyes studying him with a mixture of amusement and concern. "You've been staring at your screen saver for the past five minutes. Please tell me we're still on for Rosie's? I've been craving their apple pie all day."

Alex blinked, coming back to himself. "Yeah, of course. Seven o'clock, right?"

"Unless you're planning to go chasing after more missing pets," Sarah teased, but there was a hint of genuine curiosity in her voice. "That was weird, what Marshton said about Pioneer Village. Since when does he care about reporter safety? Usually he's trying to send us into active crime scenes."

"You heard that?" Alex began shutting down his computer, trying to keep his voice casual.

"These walls are basically paper," Sarah shrugged. "Plus, I've gotten good at reading your 'Marshton just said something strange' face. You've been wearing it all afternoon."

Alex managed a laugh, but his mind was racing. Sarah was too observant by half – it made her an excellent researcher but sometimes made him nervous about maintaining the veil of secrecy his kind were bound to uphold. "I'm sure he's just being overcautious. You know how he gets when slow news weeks drag on."

The autumn sun was already flirting with the horizon as Alex stepped out onto Essex Street, the cool air carrying hints of woodsmoke and fallen leaves. This was his favorite time of year in Salem, when the shortening days seemed to thin the barriers between worlds, and magic felt closer to the surface of everything. But it was also when the city's darker aspects emerged from whatever shadows had hidden them through the brighter months.

October in New England had its own peculiar rhythm. Darkness fell earlier with each passing day, as if the night was slowly reclaiming territory lost during summer's expansive reign. By month's end, twilight would arrive before most people left their offices, turning the evening commute into a journey through deepening shadows.

Alex pulled his light jacket closer, more out of habit than real need for warmth. The street was still busy with tourists making their way back to hotels and parking garages, their shopping bags emblazoned with logos from various witch-themed gift shops. A group of them passed him, laughing about some ghost tour they'd just finished, and he had to suppress a smile at their excited chatter about EMF readings and orbs in their photos. If they only knew what real magic looked like, how it hummed in the very foundations of the city...

Pioneer Village nagged at his thoughts as he walked, Marshton's warning playing on repeat in his mind. The historical site was less than a mile from where he stood – he could easily swing by before meeting Sarah at Rosie's. But something in his gut told him that might be unwise, at least until he had a better grasp of what he was dealing with.

The missing pets, the strange children, Marshton's cryptic warning – pieces of a puzzle that didn't quite fit together yet. And now the sun was setting, painting the sky in streaks of deep orange and purple, reminding him that some mysteries were better investigated in daylight.

A cold breeze swept down the street, carrying the first real bite of autumn in its teeth. The tourists quickened their pace, pulling jackets tighter and huddling closer together. But it wasn't just the temperature that had changed – there was a weight to the air now, a density that seemed to press against Alex's magical senses like a looming storm front.

He checked his watch – still forty-five minutes until he was supposed to meet Sarah at Rosie's. The diner was in the opposite direction from Pioneer Village, its warm lights and coffee-scented air promising safety and normality. The sensible thing would be to head there early, maybe review his notes while he waited.

But Alex Kingston had never been particularly good at doing the sensible thing.

He hesitated at the corner of Essex and Summer streets, looking first toward the inviting glow of downtown, then in the direction of Pioneer Village, where the gathering darkness seemed somehow deeper, more purposeful. The street lights were already flickering to life, creating pools of artificial daylight that seemed to emphasize the shadows between them rather than dispel them.

"Just a quick look," he muttered to himself, knowing even as he said it that no reconnaissance mission in the history of Salem had ever been "just a quick look." But he had time before meeting Sarah, and Pioneer Village was technically on his way to the diner. Sort of. If you squinted at the map and ignored several more direct routes.

Besides, he reasoned as he turned down Summer Street, if something dangerous really was lurking around Pioneer Village, he had a responsibility to investigate. Not just as a reporter, but as a witch, as someone who understood the true nature of the threats that sometimes slipped through the cracks in reality.

The street grew quieter as he walked, the tourist crowds thinning out to nothing. Above him, the sky deepened from purple to indigo, and the first stars began to pierce the darkening vault of heaven. He didn't notice how his shadow seemed to stretch and twist beneath the street lights, or how the evening breeze carried whispers that sounded almost like children's laughter.

He had a job to do, after all. And he still had plenty of time to meet Sarah for dinner. Probably.

Pioneer Village loomed before him in the gathering darkness, a collection of colonial-era buildings that seemed to huddle together against the encroaching night. During daylight hours, the site served as a living history museum, with costumed interpreters demonstrating 17th- century life to tourists. But now, in the deepening twilight, it looked less like a historical attraction and more like something from a darker page of Salem's past.

The wooden buildings – recreations of the first settlers' homes – stood silent and still, their rough-hewn timbers silver-black in the failing light. Narrow windows gaped like empty eye sockets, and the thatched roofs cast strange shadows that seemed to writhe in the occasional breeze. A split-rail fence marked the property's boundary, its aged wood worn smooth by countless hands.

Alex paused at the entrance, running his fingers over the iron padlock on the gate. A simple unlocking charm would take care of it, but something made him hesitate. The air felt wrong here heavier, as if the darkness had actual weight to it. His magical senses, usually as natural as breathing, felt muffled, like trying to hear underwater.

"You're being ridiculous," he muttered to himself, and with a quick gesture and whispered word, the lock clicked open.

The path through the village was packed dirt, scattered with October leaves that crunched beneath his feet despite his attempts to move quietly. He passed the blacksmith's shop, its cold forge a darker shadow among shadows, and the tiny chapel with its rough-cut cross silhouetted against the darkening sky. The scent of old wood and damp earth filled his nose, along with something else – a subtle wrongness he couldn't quite identify.

Near the center of the village stood the largest structure, a reproduction of the original meetinghouse. Its steep-pitched roof rose like a black triangle against the purple-black sky, and its door hung slightly ajar, swaying almost imperceptibly in a breeze Alex couldn't feel.

A soft scuffing sound came from behind the building.

Alex froze, every magical instinct suddenly screaming at him to leave, to turn around and walk away quickly. But curiosity – his greatest asset as a reporter and his worst fault as a witch, pushed him forward. He moved carefully around the corner of the meetinghouse, one hand raised slightly, ready to cast a defensive spell if needed.

They stood in the small clearing behind the building – two children, a boy and a girl, perfectly still in the growing darkness. They might have been twelve or thirteen, dressed in clothes that seemed oddly formal and pristine – the boy in pressed slacks and a button-up shirt, the girl in a neat pinafore dress that belonged in another decade. Both had straight, dark hair that didn't move in the breeze that stirred the leaves around their feet.

"Hello, mister," they said in perfect unison, their voices carrying an odd echo, as if they were speaking from the bottom of a well. "Would you like to play with us?"

Every magical alarm in Alex's mind went off at once. This close, he could feel the wrongness radiating from them like cold from an open freezer. Their shadows stretched out behind them, far longer than they should have been in the failing light, and seemed to move independently of their bodies.

"We know such wonderful games," the girl said, taking a step forward. "Games from long ago, when this village was real."

"Games of hide and seek," the boy added, also stepping forward. "In places where the seeking never ends."

Alex took an involuntary step backward, his heart hammering against his ribs. In all his years of magical training, all his encounters with the supernatural, he'd never felt fear like this – pure, primal, and absolutely certain. Every fiber of his being screamed that these were not children, had never been children, could never be mistaken for children except in the most superficial way.

They tilted their heads in perfect synchronization, and in the last light of dusk, Alex caught a glimpse of their eyes – solid black, like polished obsidian, with no whites or iris or pupil. Just endless, hungry darkness.

"No, thank you," he managed to say, his voice surprisingly steady despite the terror churning in his gut. "I have somewhere I need to be."

"But it's almost dark," they said together, their smiles too wide, too fixed. "Dark is the best time for playing."

"I'm late," Alex said, backing away slowly. "My friend is waiting for me."

The children's smiles widened further, showing too many teeth. "Friends are good," the girl said.

"We like making new friends," the boy added.

"Goodbye," Alex said firmly, turning away with every ounce of willpower he possessed. It took all his training not to run, to walk at a measured pace back down the path toward the gate. Behind him, he could hear them giggling – a sound like dead leaves scraping against a tombstone.

The walk back to the gate seemed to take hours, though his watch insisted only minutes had passed. He didn't dare look back, but he could feel them watching him, their gaze like ice water trickling down his spine. Only when he was through the gate did he finally break into a run, his feet carrying him swiftly toward the lights of downtown Salem.

He needed to get to Rosie's. He needed to see Sarah, to be surrounded by normal people and fluorescent lights and the smell of coffee and pie. He needed to pretend, just for a little while, that he hadn't seen what he'd seen, hadn't felt what he'd felt.

The street lights created pools of artificial daylight as he hurried toward the diner, but they didn't seem as bright as usual, as if something was dulling their glow. He didn't notice how his shadow sometimes stretched ahead of him and sometimes behind, or how there were moments when he cast no shadow at all. And he certainly didn't notice the two smaller shadows that slid along the edges of the light, keeping pace with him, their movements silent and patient and hungry.

Rosie's Diner blazed with warm light and humanity, its plateglass windows glowing like a beacon in the darkness. The neon sign buzzed cheerfully, casting alternating patterns of red and blue across the wet pavement, and the bell above the door chimed welcomingly as Alex pushed his way inside. The tension in his shoulders began to ease almost immediately, melting away in the face of such aggressive normality.

The diner was a Salem institution, unchanged since the 1950s and proud of it. Chrome and red vinyl gleamed under fluorescent lights, and the air was rich with the smell of coffee, grilled onions, and Rosie's famous apple pie. The steady clatter of plates and silverware mixed with dozen different conversations, creating a symphony of ordinary life that felt like a shield against the wrongness he'd encountered at Pioneer Village.

Behind the counter, Rosie herself held court with the efficiency of a general commanding her troops. At sixty-something (though no one knew the exact number, and no one dared ask), she was a force of nature packed into a five-foot-four frame. Her silver hair was pulled back in its usual tight bun, and her pale blue eyes missed nothing as she directed her waitstaff while simultaneously pouring coffee and ringing up checks.

"Alex Kingston!" she called out as he entered, her voice carrying over the dinner rush noise.

"You're later than usual. Sarah's been waiting, and you know how I feel about keeping a lady waiting."

"Sorry, Rosie," Alex managed a smile, some of the color returning to his face. "Got caught up at work."

Rosie's eyes narrowed slightly as she looked at him, that penetrating gaze that always made him wonder if she saw more than she let on. "You look like you could use some hot chocolate. The real kind, with the mini marshmallows."

"That obvious, huh?"

"Honey, I've been feeding people in this town for forty years. I know shock when I see it walking through my door." She was already reaching for a mug. "Go sit down. I'll bring it over."

"Alex!" Sarah's voice cut through the diner noise, and he spotted her waving from their usual booth in the back corner. The vinyl squeaked as he slid into the seat across from her, and the familiar sensation of being ensconced in this particular booth, in this particular diner, helped ground him further in reality.

Sarah took one look at his face and set down her coffee cup. "Okay, spill it. You look like you've seen a ghost." She paused, then added with a small laugh, "Which, given that this is Salem in October, might actually be literal."

Alex opened his mouth to respond, but was interrupted by Rosie arriving with his hot chocolate –topped with a small mountain of mini marshmallows – and a slice of apple pie he hadn't ordered but suddenly realized he desperately needed.

"On the house," Rosie said firmly, setting them down. "You look like you need it more than my profit margins need the four dollars." She patted his shoulder with grandmotherly affection before heading back to the counter, leaving behind a whiff of floral perfume and no room for argument.

Sarah waited until Rosie was out of earshot before leaning forward. "Seriously, Alex, what happened? Did Marshton give you grief about the story again?"

Alex wrapped his hands around the warm mug, debating how much to tell her. The truth was out of the question – he couldn't explain his magical sensitivities or why they'd gone haywire. But the rest...

"I went by Pioneer Village," he admitted, watching Sarah's eyebrows rise. "After work, before coming here. I know Marshton warned against it, but..."

"But you're you," Sarah finished, nodding. "And?"

"There were these kids there." Alex took a sip of hot chocolate, letting the warmth chase away the last of the cold fear that had followed him from the village. "Behind the meetinghouse. Something was... wrong about them. The way they moved, the way they spoke. They wanted me to play with them."

Sarah's expression sharpened with interest. "Kids hanging around Pioneer Village at dusk? That matches what some of the pet owners told us. Remember Mrs. Rodriguez? She said her daughter kept talking about new friends who wanted to play with their dog. And then the dog disappeared the next day."

"You remember that detail? It wasn't in my notes."

"I remember everything," Sarah said, tapping her temple with a finger. "It's my superpower. And now that you mention it..." She pulled out her phone, fingers flying over the screen. "Three other families mentioned strange children in their statements. I didn't think it was important at the time, but..."

"But now it's starting to look like a pattern," Alex finished, feeling a chill despite the warm diner air.

"More than that." Sarah turned her phone around, showing him a local history website. "I was doing some research while waiting for you. There are records of similar stories going back decades in Salem. Children appearing at twilight, asking to play. Usually right before something or someone goes missing."

Alex felt his mouth go dry. "And no one's connected these incidents before?"

"They're spread out, sometimes years apart. And most people probably wrote them off as urban legends or Halloween stories." Sarah's dark eyes were bright with the thrill of investigation. "But if we cross-reference the dates and locations..."

The bell above the diner door chimed, letting in a gust of cold air that made the lights flicker briefly. Alex found himself tensing, half-expecting to see two small figures in outdated clothes standing in the doorway. But it was just a young couple seeking shelter from the growing chill, their cheeks pink from the wind.

The night had fully claimed Salem by the time Alex left Rosie's, but it was a different darkness than the oppressive shadows of Pioneer Village. Here, the streets pulsed with life and light. College students spilled out of Murphy's Pub, their laughter echoing off colonial-era buildings. Couples lingered over wine at Bella's Italian restaurant, visible through warm-lit windows. Tourism might have ruled Salem's days, but nighttime belonged to the locals.

Alex walked down Essex Street, past shop windows now dark except for small security lights. The air had grown colder, carrying the crisp edge that promised frost by morning. Orange and purple Halloween lights decorated many of the buildings, and a plastic skeleton dangled from the antique lamppost outside the Witch's Brew Coffee Shop, spinning slowly in the breeze.

The noise and activity began to thin as he turned onto his street in the historic district. Here, Victorian-era homes stood like aging dowagers, their gingerbread trim and towers silhouetted against the night sky. Most had been divided into apartments over the years, but Alex's home remained as it had been when his family first bought it in the 1890s – a three-story Victorian painted in historically accurate shades of sage green and cream, with burgundy trim highlighting its architectural features.

Massive oaks lined the street, their nearly-bare branches creating strange patterns against the star-filled sky. Alex's house sat slightly back from the road, protected by an wrought iron fence. The small front yard was neat but not overly manicured, with late-blooming asters adding splashes of purple among the fallenleaves.

A carved pumpkin grinned from the wide front porch – Sarah's contribution to his "sadly neglected Halloween spirit," as she'd put it. The gas-style porch lamp cast warm light over the steps as Alex climbed them, its flame seeming to dance a bit more actively than strictly natural. But that was normal for this house, where even the most mundane objects had absorbed generations of magical energy.

The front door recognized his touch, its multiple locks clicking open without need for a key. The foyer welcomed him with the familiar scent of old wood, beeswax polish, and the countless herbs and magical ingredients stored in his workroom. Small globes of magical light flickered to life along the walls, casting a soft golden glow over polished hardwood floors and antique furnishings.

A loud "mrrp!" announced the arrival of Artemis, his Russian Blue cat, who materialized from the shadows with typical feline dramatics. Her silver-grey coat seemed to shimmer slightly as she wound between his legs, her green eyes bright with intelligence that sometimes seemed more than natural. Which, given that she was a witch's familiar, was probably accurate.

"Yes, yes, I know I'm late," Alex said, bending to scratch behind her ears. "And yes, I'm aware your dinner is exactly twenty-three minutes overdue. The world might end, right?"

Artemis gave him a look that suggested this was, indeed, a possibility.

The kitchen was at the back of the house, its modern appliances coexisting somewhat uneasily with the Victorian architecture. Alex fed his imperious companion, then made his way to the living room, where a plush leather couch beckoned invitingly. The sound, of distant thunder, creating a relaxing environment.

Rain lashed against the windows of Alex's home, creating a constant backdrop of white noise that usually helped him focus. Tonight, however it felt oppressive, as if the storm was trying to claw its way inside. Wind howled through the eaves of the old Victorian houses that lined the street, a mournful sound that carried with it the whispers of hundreds of years of secrets. The ancient maples, that towered over the street swayed dangerously, their nearly bare branches, scraping against weather-worn siding like bony fingers.

Inside his living room, Alex sat on his couch, bathed in the cold, blue glow of his laptop screen. The harsh light accentuated the shadows under his eyes, and the furrows in his brow. He stared at the blinking cursor, on his screen willing the words to come. His mind was still on what he had seen earlier this evening. The half-empty cup of coffee at his elbow had long since gone cold, a film forming on its surface like a murky crystal ball.

A sudden flash of lightning, followed by a deafening crack of thunder, made him jump. The power flickered once, twice, and then plunged the house into darkness. Artemis, meowed and jumped up on the couch, her eyes seeming to glow in the dark.

"Dammit," he said, whispering under his breath. He got up and fumbled through the room, to a table where an oil lamp was sitting. With a quick motion of his hand, the lantern lit, casting its light across the room.

"Its, just the storm," he told the cat as she moved between his feet.

A sudden flash of lightning illuminated the room in a harsh, electric blue, casting strange, elongated shadows across the walls. It was followed almost instantly by a deafening crack of thunder that shook the windows in their frames and sent vibrations through the floorboards. Artemis, jumped at the noise, her hair starting to stand on end. Suddenly the power flickered once, the lights dimming, and brightening like a faltering pulse. Then again, longer this time, plugging the room into momentary darkness, before sputtering back to life. Alex help is breath willing the electricity to stay on, but it was a futile hope. With a final, defeated hum, the power gave out entirely. The room was once again, plunged into darkness, the only light coming from a single oil lamp that Alex held in his hand.

Alex, cursed under his breath again. He sat the oil lantern down on his coffee table, his laptop still casting a blue glow on the couch. He slumped into the sofa, again, closing the lid to his computer. "Well, girl..." he said to Artemis who had jumped into his lap, purring happily. "I guess this means, we will get an early night."

Thats when he heard it.

Chapter Two

The Knock on the Door

The knock, when it came, was so soft it might have been mistaken for a branch tapping against the door. Artemis's purring stopped abruptly, her ears swiveling toward the front of the house.

"Hello?" A child's voice called from the porch. "Can we come in and play?"

Artemis's fur stood on end, her tail puffing to twice its normal size. A low growl rumbled in her throat – a sound Alex had never heard her make before.

Alex sat perfectly still, his heart hammering against his ribs.

"Hello?" Alex called out, his voice sounding strangely thin in the darkness. "Who's there?"

"Alex?" The voices called in unison, sweet and terrible. "Won't you please let us in? It's cold out here. So very cold."

"We followed you home," the girl's voice said, dropping any pretense of childhood innocence. "We always follow our new friends home."

Artemis leaped from Alex's lap and ran to the door, her back arched, every hair standing on end. The temperature in the living room plummeted, frost forming delicate patterns on the inside of the windows.

Against his better judgment, Alex made his way to the door. His hand hesitated on the deadbolt. Something deep in his gut was screaming at him not to open it, a primal instinct that he couldn't explain. With a deep breath, he unlocked the door and pulled it open.

Two children stood on his doorstep, a boy and a girl who couldn't have been older than ten. They were soaked to the bone, their clothes clinging to their small frames. What made his blood run cold, was their eyes. Where there should have been whites and irises, and pupils, there was only an inky, otherworldly blackness.

Alex, recognized the children, as the ones he had seen earlier that night in pioneer village. Those same dark eyes. It was as if someone had taken the night sky, stripped it of stars and poured it into the children's eye sockets. His instincts were urging him to slam the door shut, to run and hide, but he stood frozen, unable to look away from the void, where eyes should be.

The girls pale lips parted, and when she spoke, her voice was eerily calm amidst the raging storm. It was a child's voice, and yet..not. There was an undercurrent to it, a resonance that seemed to bypass his ears and vibrate directly in his mind.

"Please," she said, the word hanging in the air between them like a tangible thing. "Can we come in?"

A gust of wind whipped rain into Alex's face, shocking him back to his senses. He blinked rapidly, droplets clinging to his eyelashes, distorting his vision. For a moment, just a fraction of a second, the children looked... different. Older. Hungrier. But when he focused again, they were just two soaked, pitiable waifs.

This was no longer just a story for the Salem Gazette. This was something else entirely, something that threatened the carefully maintained boundary between the normal world and the darker forces that lurked at its edges.

And somehow, Alex knew, it was only beginning.

The girl tilted her head slightly, an unnaturally fluid motion. "Will you invite us in?" She asked again, her tone carrying just a hint of impatience now. "It's so cold out here."

Alex's hand tightened on the doorknob. Whatever choice he made in the next few seconds would change his life forever. He took a deep breath, the taste of ozone sharp on his tongue, and made his decision. Little did Alex know, but opening that door was just the beginning. The simple act of turning the knob would be like pulling a thread on a sweater—once tugged, the entire fabric of his reality would begin to unravel. The boundaries between the world he knew and the shadows that lurked just beyond the edge of perception would blur, then dissolve entirely.

As the storm raged on outside, as the Black Eyed Children stood expectantly on his threshold, Alex stood poised on the bring of a journey that would transform him forever. The choice he made in this moment would set in motion a chain of events that would not only determine his fate, but the fate of everyone in Salem.

The wind howled, carrying with it the whispers of forgotten gods. The rain, pounded a rhythm like an eldritch heartbeat. And someone in the darkness, something ancient and patient smiled knowing that soon, very soon, the game would begin anew.

Alex took a deep breath, steeling himself for whatever came next. He had always prided himself on his pursuit of truth, on his need to uncover stories others overlooked. Now he was about to become part of a story greater and more terrifying than anything he could have imagined. His fingers tightened around the door knob, his knuckles turning white with the force of his grip. An inexplicable sense of wrong washed over him as he started at the girl on his doorstep. Her voice ostensibly child-like, seemed to reverberate in the air between them, carrying undertones that made his skin crawl. It was as if another, older more sinister voice lurked just beneath the surface of her words, barely contained.

With each syllable she uttered, Alex felt a chill creep up his spine, raising goosebumps along his arms. It was as though tendrils of ice were snaking through his veins, freezing him from the inside out. He swallowed hard, trying to shake off the unnatural dread that gripped him.

Alex forced himself to think past the fear. He was a Kingston, a witch of one of Salem's oldest bloodlines. He had resources, training, power. He just had to stay calm and—

"Dark is better for playing," they said in unison. "Dark is where we belong. Dark is where you'll belong too, once you let us in."

Alex raised his hand, summoning a sphere of magical light. The warm golden glow pushed back the darkness, but the shadows it created seemed deeper, more purposeful. They moved against the walls in ways that shadows shouldn't, stretching and twisting toward the door.

"I don't want to play," he said firmly, trying to inject power into his words. "You're not welcome here."

The girl's gaze intensified, her black eyes seeming to pierce through him, laying bare his deepest fears. Alex felt exposed, vulnerable, as if those eyes could see every secret he'd ever kept.

"LET US IN," she demanded, her tone shifting dramatically. Gone was any pretense of childish innocence. Her voice now carried an unmistakable command, laced with barely contained malice. The words seemed to reverberate in the air, carrying a weight that pressed against Alex's chest, making it hard to breathe.

His hand trembled on the door knob, caught between the instinct to slam the door shut and a strange, almost hypnotic compulsion to obey. The girl's eyes never left his face, and in their depths, Alex thought he saw something move---a flicker of something ancient and hungry. His fingers curled around the door knob, his knuckles white with tension. The metal felt ice-cold against his clammy skin, a stark contrast to the feverish heat coursing through his body. His heart hammered in his chest, each beat a thunderous roar in his ears.

"NO!" The word tore from his throat, primal and raw. It wasn't a conscious decision---some deep, instinctual part of him had seized control, desperate to shield him from whatever lurked on the other side of the door. With a sudden burst of strength, Alex slammed the door shut. The sound reverberated through his living room, echoing the frantic rhythm of his pulse. For a moment, time seemed to stand still, the world narrowing to nothing but Alex and the closed door before him.

More frost crept across the windows, forming patterns that looked disturbingly like childish handprints. The wood of the door creaked, ancient timber protesting against a pressure that had nothing to do with physical force. Artemis's growl deepened, taking on a resonance that seemed impossible from a normal cat's throat.

Who were those children? Why had their presence filled him with such inexplicable dread? Their eyes... those pitch-black orbs that seemed to swallow all light. Just the memory sent a fresh shiver down Alex's spine.

BANG... BANG... BANG...

The door shuddered in its frame. One of the frosted glass panels cracked, a thin line appearing like a spider's web across its surface. Through it, Alex caught a glimpse of their eyes –

endless black pools that seemed to drink in what little light remained.

Artemis suddenly leaped onto the small table by the door, her green eyes blazing with an inner light. She opened her mouth and let out a sound that was definitely not catlike – a deep, resonant tone that made the air itself vibrate.

"A guardian," the children said, something like surprise in their unified voices. "How...interesting. We haven't seen one of those in a very long time."

Alex stared at his cat – no, his familiar, he corrected mentally – as she continued her otherworldly song. He'd always known she was more than she appeared, but this was beyond anything he'd imagined. The temperature in the house began to rise slightly, warmth returning wherever her strange music reached.

"The old magics," the girl's voice said, showing the first hint of uncertainty. "They're not supposed to be here anymore. Not in this age."

"They're supposed to be forgotten," the boy agreed. "Like we were forgotten. Until now."

Artemis's song grew louder, and the runes brighter, until the entire door frame blazed with blue fire. The shadows on the walls retreated, drawing back from that ancient light like waves from a shore. The crack in the glass panel stopped spreading.

"This isn't over," they said together, their voices fading slightly. "The game is just beginning, Alex Kingston. We have so many new friends to make. So many games to play."

Their laughter echoed one final time, growing distant until it faded into the normal sounds of the night. The porch light sputtered back to life, and through the cracked glass panel, Alex could see that they were gone. The other lights in the house came back on as well, humming with ordinary electrical current as if nothing unusual had happened.

Artemis's song faded to a normal purr, though her eyes still gleamed with that strange inner light. She looked up at Alex and gave a small "mrrp" that somehow managed to convey both "you're welcome" and "we need to talk about this" simultaneously.

Alex sagged against the wall, his knees threatening to buckle beneath him. Though the encounter had lasted mere minutes, it had hollowed him out, leaving him as exhausted as if he'd run for miles. His magical senses – usually as natural as breathing – felt scraped and tender, like a nerve exposed to open air. The children had brought something with them, an energy that still lingered like frost on glass: ancient as forgotten graves, hungry as the void between stars, and patient as mountains. It waited, he realized with a shudder. Whatever it was, it simply waited.

Alex scrambled to his feet, rushing to the window. He yanked the curtains aside, fully expecting to see the black-eyed children staring up at him from the street. But the road was empty, bathed in the orange glow of streetlights. There was no sign of the strange visitors.

With shaking hands, he reached for his phone. He needed to talk to someone, to hear a friendly voice that could anchor him to reality. His finger hovered over Sarah's contact, but he hesitated. What would he say? How could he explain what had just happened without sounding completely insane, or worse telling her the truth about himself.

The phone rang once, twice, three times.

"Come on, Sarah," he muttered. "Pick up. Please pick up."

A fourth ring. A fifth.

And then, instead of Sarah's voice or her voicemail, he heard children laughing.

The sixth ring cut off mid-tone, replaced by Sarah's familiar voice. "Alex? Everything okay?"

The normality of her tone – slightly distracted, as if he'd interrupted her reading – made his knees weak with relief.

"Yeah, I just..." He hesitated, unsure how to ask if she'd noticed any strange children without sounding completely unhinged. "I wanted to make sure you got home alright."

"Aww, worried about me?" He could hear the smile in her voice. "I'm fine. Just going through some old newspaper archives I found online. Did you know there was another rash of pet disappearances in Salem back in 1952? And again in 1973? I'm starting to see a pattern, but..." She stifled a yawn. "Sorry. I should probably get some sleep. Real investigating can wait until morning."

"Have you noticed anything... unusual? Outside your windows, maybe? Or heard any strange noises?"

Sarah laughed. "Okay, those ghost stories at Pioneer Village really got to you, didn't they? I'm fine, Alex. My doors are locked, my pepper spray is handy, and the scariest thing outside my window is Mrs. Sullivan's Halloween decorations next door." She paused. "You should get some sleep too. You sound exhausted."

"Yeah, you're probably right." The normalcy of their conversation was gradually easing the tight knot of fear in his chest. "See you tomorrow?"

"Bright and early. And Alex? Try not to let your imagination run wild. Salem's spooky enough without adding to it."

After they hung up, Alex made a careful circuit of the house, checking every window and door. The familiar followed at his heels, her tail held high, occasionally pausing to sniff at the air with an expression of feline concentration. Satisfied that the house was secure, Alex climbed the curved wooden staircase to the second floor. His bedroom was at the back of the house, occupying what had originally been the master suite. Like the rest of the house, it balanced the old with the new – a king-sized bed with a heavy wooden headboard carved with subtle protective symbols shared space with a modern desk.

Bookshelves lined one wall, filled with an eclectic mix of journalism texts, magical theory books disguised as classic literature, and actual classic literature. A large bay window overlooked the back garden, its window seat scattered with comfortable cushions and more books. The hardwood floor was softened by a thick Persian rug that had been in the family for generations.

Alex changed into sleep pants and an old Salem State t-shirt, his movements automatic as exhaustion began to catch up with him. The events of the evening felt almost dreamlike now, viewed through the lens of ordinary routine. Maybe Sarah was right – maybe he was letting the season, the stories, get to him.

Artemis jumped onto the bed, turning three precise circles before settling into her usual spot near the pillows. Her green eyes tracked Alex as he moved around the room, still carrying that hint of otherworldly awareness that he could no longer pretend not to notice.

"We're going to have a long talk about your hidden talents tomorrow," he told her as he climbed into bed. She responded with a purr that managed to sound both noncommittal and slightly smug.

The bedside lamp clicked off with a gesture, leaving only the faint silver of starlight filtering through the bay window.

Outside the Kingston house, in the deeper shadows beneath the oak trees, two small figures stood perfectly still. Their black eyes reflected no light, seeming instead to absorb what little illumination reached them, creating tiny voids in the darkness. They watched the second-floor window where the light had just gone out, their faces wearing identical expressions of patient hunger.

"Sleep well, Alex Kingston," they whispered in unison, their voices carrying on a wind that touched nothing else.

The girl's head tilted at an impossible angle. "Dream while you can."

"Before the real games begin," the boy finished.

A car turned onto the street, its headlights sweeping across the scene. In that brief moment of illumination, the space beneath the trees was empty, as if the children had never been there at all. Only the frost on the grass marked where they had stood, two small patches of ice that somehow refused to melt, even as the night grew warmer.

Morning light filtered through the kitchen windows of the Kingston house, casting long rectangles of autumn sunshine across the antique oak table. Alex sat nursing his second cup of coffee, watching steam rise in lazy spirals from the dark liquid. The events of the previous night felt almost dreamlike in the crisp morning air, though the cracked glass panel in his front door served as a tangible reminder that it had all been very real.

Artemis perched on her favorite windowsill, tail twitching as she watched a cardinal hop along the frost-covered garden path. After last night's revelation of her abilities, Alex found himself studying his familiar more closely, noting the subtle shimmer in her grey fur and the knowing gleam in her green eyes. She had yet to repeat her otherworldly performance, acting for all the world like any ordinary cat more interested in breakfast than supernatural phenomena.

The floorboards creaked as Alex pushed himself up from the chair, his muscles aching from a night of fitful sleep. Something pulled at him, an unsettling whisper in the back of his mind that drew him toward the front door. His feet carried him forward almost of their own accord. The deadbolt remained secure, just as he'd left it – but as he leaned in closer, his breath caught in his throat. There, stark against the white paint, were smudges that made his skin crawl. Dark, sooty marks that formed unmistakable shapes: small handprints pressed against the wood, as if tiny fingers had been reaching, grasping, trying to get in.

Alex bolted to the kitchen, his heart hammering against his ribs as he snatched a sponge and drenched it under the faucet. Water dripped down his forearms as he attacked the door, scrubbing with desperate intensity. But the marks refused to fade – if anything, the water seemed to make them darker, more defined, as if the very essence of those small, sinister prints had seeped into the wood itself. Each futile swipe of the sponge only served to remind him that some things couldn't be erased, couldn't be wished away in the light of morning. The handprints remained, a dark testament to what had come calling in the night.

His shoulders slumped in defeat as he trudged back to the kitchen, the weight of his failed attempt pressing down on him like a physical thing. The sudden knock at the door sent a jolt through his system – coffee splashing over the rim of his cup as his muscles instinctively tensed. But this sound carried none of last night's otherworldly menace. Instead, it rang with purpose and normality, the kind of knock that belonged to the daylight world. Artemis confirmed his assessment; rather than bristling with supernatural warning, she chirped with familiar delight. Her sleek form bounded from her perch, tail raised like a banner of welcome as she pranced toward the door, transforming from mystical familiar to ordinary housecat in the span of heartbeat.

Sarah Chen stood on his porch, wrapped in a navy wool peacoat and an oversized burgundy scarf that nearly swallowed her chin. Her long black hair was pulled back in a neat ponytail, and her cheeks were pink from the unexpected cold. Frost still clung to the grass and trees, unusual for this early in autumn.

"Okay," she said without preamble, "spill it. What really happened last night? And don't give me that 'just checking if you got home safe' line again. I know your worried voice, and that was definitely it."

Alex stepped back to let her in, watching as she immediately crouched to give Artemis her expected morning greeting. The cat rubbed against Sarah's legs, purring loudly enough to sound almost like a small motor.

"Coffee?" he offered, trying to buy time to organize his thoughts, to figure out how to explain the inexplicable without revealing too much.

"Already had two cups. Stop stalling." Sarah straightened up, unwinding her scarf. "Does this have something to do with those kids you saw at Pioneer Village? Because I did some more digging after you called, and—"

"You said you were going to sleep!"

"And you said you were just checking if I got home okay." She raised an eyebrow. "We both lie sometimes. Now talk." Alex opened his mouth, closed it, then opened it again. Where could he even begin?

Alex led her into the kitchen, where the morning light and the lingering smell of coffee created an atmosphere of normalcy that made the previous night's events seem even more surreal. Sarah settled into one of the kitchen chairs, while Artemis resumed her windowsill perch, though her attention seemed more focused on their conversation than the birds outside.

"They showed up here last night," Alex finally said, watching Sarah's expression carefully. "The children from Pioneer Village."

Sarah leaned forward, her reporter's instincts visibly engaging. "Here? At your house? What time? What did they do?"

"It was around ten, maybe ten-thirty. They..." He paused, considering how to describe the encounter without mentioning the supernatural elements. "They followed me home. Knew my name somehow. They wanted to come in, kept asking me to let them in to play. There was something wrong about them, Sarah. Something..." He struggled to find words that wouldn't sound completely insane. "Something not right."

"Not right how?"

"Their voices, for one thing. They didn't sound like children, not really. And their eyes..." He suppressed a shudder at the memory of those black voids.

Sarah had pulled out her reporter's notebook and was writing rapidly. "And this was after they approached you at Pioneer Village, asking similar questions about playing?" At Alex's nod, she continued, "Did they threaten you?"

"Not exactly," Alex said, carefully measuring each word. He shifted in his seat, fingers absently tracing the rim of his coffee cup as he searched for the right way to explain. There was an art to revealing just enough while holding back the darker truths, a balance he'd learned from years of straddling two worlds. After a moment, he lifted his gaze, meeting Sarah's eyes with a mix of reluctance and resolution that spoke volumes beyond his simple words.

Sarah's expression shifted from fascination to determination. "Don't you see? This confirms everything I found last night. These sightings, these children – they're connected to every major disappearance in Salem's history. Not just pets, but people too. I found records going back decades, all with the same pattern."

"Which is exactly why we should be careful," Alex insisted. "If these kids really are responsible for disappearances—"

"Kids?" Sarah shook her head. "I don't think they're kids at all. I think they're something else, something using the appearance of children to... I don't know, lure people? Gain trust?" She flipped through her notebook. "Every account describes them the same way – outdated clothes, strange voices, always asking to be invited in to play. And their eyes..." She looked up at Alex. "Every single account mentions their eyes."

Alex felt a chill that had nothing to do with the morning frost. How much had Sarah already pieced together? How close was she to stumbling onto truths that the Order of Salem had worked for centuries to keep hidden?

Artemis suddenly tensed on her windowsill, her tail puffing slightly. She let out a small warning trill – nothing like last night's otherworldly song, but enough to make Alex turn toward the window. For just a moment, he thought he saw two small shadows move across the frost-covered garden. But when he blinked, they were gone.

"Alex?" Sarah's voice brought him back to the conversation. "There's something you're not telling me, isn't there? Something you know about what's really going on?"

He met her gaze, seeing the intelligence and determination there, and made a decision that he hoped he wouldn't regret. "Yes," he said quietly. "But I'm not sure you're ready to hear it."

"Try me."

Outside, the cardinal that Artemis had been watching suddenly took flight, as if startled by something neither of them could see. The morning suddenly seemed colder, despite the bright sunshine streaming through the windows.

Chapter Three

Truth and Guilt

Alex took a deep breath, his heart hammering against his ribs. Everything he'd been taught since childhood screamed against what he was about to do. The Order's rules were absolute, handed down through generations: magic must remain hidden, the veil between worlds maintained at all costs.

"I'm a witch," he said simply.

Sarah stared at him for a long beat before barking out a laugh that dripped with sarcasm. "Right. And I'm secretly the Queen of England having a holiday in Massachusetts." She rolled her eyes and leaned back, crossing her arms with the kind of practiced skepticism that came from years of chasing down sources for the paper. "Look, I know you're creative, Alex, but you'll have to do better than that. What's actually going on here?" Her smile held a mix of amusement and concern, the kind reserved for friends who might be losing their grip on reality.

"I'm serious, Sarah."

"Sure you are." Sarah rolled her eyes, her reporter's skepticism in full force. "Look, if you don't want to tell me what's really going on, that's your choice, but don't expect me to swallow this ridiculous—" She broke off mid-sentence, her practiced cynicism crumbling as reality shifted before her eyes.

Alex raised his hand, interrupting her mid-sentence. The morning sunlight streaming through the kitchen windows suddenly gathered, coalescing into golden spheres that danced through the air like soap bubbles made of pure light. They circled Sarah's head, casting warm reflections across her suddenly slack-jawed face.

"That's... that's just some kind of trick," she managed, though her voice had lost its certainty. "Mirrors, or..."

Alex gestured again, and the spheres of light merged into a miniature galaxy that spun slowly above the kitchen table, casting star-patterns across the ceiling. With another movement, he transformed it into a shimmering butterfly that fluttered around Sarah's head before dissolving into sparks that vanished like falling snow.

"Holy shit," Sarah whispered. She reached out, trying to catch one of the disappearing sparks. "Holy actual shit."

Artemis chose that moment to leap onto the table, fixing Sarah with a knowing green-eyed stare. The cat's fur shimmered with that subtle otherworldly gleam that Alex now recognized as barely contained magic.

"And Artemis," Alex added, "isn't exactly a normal cat."

As if on cue, Artemis's purr deepened into that otherworldly resonance from the previous night, sending tremors through the coffee cups until they danced against their saucers. Sarah stared, transfixed, as the ordinary morning transformed into something extraordinary before her eyes. Her mouth worked silently, trying to form questions that her mind wasn't ready to ask. The comfortable world she'd known just moments ago was dissolving, replaced by one where cats could shake reality and her best friend wielded powers from ancient bloodlines. The silence that followed wasn't just awkward – it was heavy with the weight of shattered perceptions and endless possibilities.

"How... how long?" she managed finally. "Have you always...?"

"Since birth," Alex said quietly, a weight in his voice that spoke of generations. "Magic flows through certain bloodlines, and the Kingstons have been part of Salem's true history for centuries. Not the staged shows and gift shop trinkets - but real, ancient power."

"The tourist stuff," Sarah echoed, her voice barely a whisper. Her spine suddenly stiffened and her eyes widened as the pieces clicked into place. "The witch trials... all of it... it wasn't just hysteria, was it? It was real?" Her expression transformed rapidly – horror dawning in her widened eyes, shock parting her lips, and beneath it all, an unmistakable spark of fascination lighting up her face.

"Yes and no." Alex settled into the chair across from her. "The trials themselves were mostly hysteria, innocent people accused by frightened neighbors. But they happened because people knew, deep down, that real magic existed. They just targeted the wrong people."

"And that's why..." Sarah's reporter brain was visibly connecting dots. "That's why you were so interested in the missing pets case. You knew it wasn't normal."

Alex nodded. "There's an organization – the Order of Salem. They formed during the witch trials to protect both magical and non-magical people. They created a separation between the two worlds, a kind of veil that helps ordinary people rationalize away anything too obviously magical."

"A conspiracy," Sarah breathed, her eyes bright with the thrill of discovery. "A centuries-old conspiracy right here in Salem, and I never..." She paused. "Wait. How many others are there? Other witches?"

"I can't tell you that," Alex said quickly. "I shouldn't even be telling you this much. The Order has strict rules about revealing magic to outsiders. If they find out I've told you..."

"What? They'll turn you into a toad?" Sarah's attempt at humor faded when she saw his expression. "They would actually do that?"

"No, but they might bind my powers. Or worse, modify your memories so you forget everything you've learned." He leaned forward, his expression deadly serious. "Sarah, you have to understand – this isn't just about me. The separation between magical and non-magical worlds exists for a reason. The last time they overlapped freely, it led to the witch trials. People died."

Sarah was quiet for a moment, absently reaching out to stroke Artemis, who had moved closer to her. "Is that why you're telling me now? Because of those children? Are they... are they something magical?"

"They're..." Alex's voice trailed off, his expression darkening as he searched for words to capture the wrongness he'd sensed. "I don't know exactly what they are. But they radiate something ancient – the kind of old that makes my magic recoil. And they're dangerous, Sarah. That much I know in my bones." He leaned forward, his eyes intense with barely contained fear.

Sarah opened her mouth to argue, then closed it again. She looked around the kitchen, taking in details she must have seen dozens of times before but never really noticed – the strange symbols carved subtly into the window frames, the herbs drying in bunches from the ceiling beams, the way Artemis's eyes seemed to glow slightly in the morning light.

"Okay," she said finally. "Show me everything."

"Sarah—"

"No, listen." She leaned forward, her expression intense. "You've already broken the rules by telling me this much. And those things, those children – they're hurting people, taking pets, maybe worse. You need help investigating this, someone who can move in the normal world without raising suspicions. Someone who knows how to dig up information." A slight smile crossed her face. "And let's be honest, I'm the best researcher you know."

A wry smile tugged at Alex's lips before blossoming into a genuine laugh, the sound carrying equal parts amusement and resignation. "Can't argue with that. Not even if I wanted to."

"So?" She raised an eyebrow. "Partners? For real this time, no more secrets?"

Alex stared at her outstretched hand, his mind racing through a dozen scenarios, each worse than the last. The Order's laws weren't just rules – they were boundaries carved in stone through centuries of sacrifice and secrecy. Breaking them meant risking everything: his magic, his heritage, his place in a world few ever glimpsed. The weight of generations of Kingstons seemed to press down on his shoulders, warning him away from this precipice. Yet here he stood, on the edge of that very cliff.

But Sarah was right – he needed help. And more importantly, she needed to understand what she was really dealing with if she was going to stay safe.

Artemis made a small chirping sound that somehow managed to convey approval.

"Partners," Alex agreed, taking her hand. "But Sarah? This isn't a game. What we're dealing with–those children – they're more dangerous than anything you've ever encountered."

"I know," she said, her grip firm. "That's what makes it the story of a lifetime."

The autumn sun climbed higher, its warmth gradually erasing the morning frost from grass and concrete. Nature's ordinary rhythm of thaw and renewal touched everything – almost everything. Beneath the kitchen window, two small patches of ice defied the growing warmth, refusing to surrender their form. They remained stark against the dark earth: perfect impressions of child-sized footprints, their edges crystalline and sharp despite the sun's insistence. The unnatural cold they radiated seemed to whisper of things that had no place in daylight hours, of visitors who left marks that neither sun nor time could easily erase.

"We need to go to the library," Alex announced, standing up from the kitchen table.

Sarah blinked at the sudden change of topic.

"The library? Alex, you just told me magic is real, here are evil children stalking the town, and you want to check out books? I mean, I love research as much as the next journalist, but—"

Just—" Alex snagged his keys from the counter, cutting off her questions with a knowing half-smile. "Trust me on this one. It'll make sense when we get there." He paused at the door, giving her an appraising look. "Though you might want to hang onto that scarf. Nathan's got this thing about keeping the place practically arctic. Pretty sure he thinks books hibernate or something."

"Nathan? The librarian?" Sarah's eyes widened. "Wait, is he—"

"Not here," Alex said, his voice dropping to barely above a whisper. His eyes darted to the windows, then back to Sarah, carrying the weight of secrets that seemed to press against the very air of the room.

The familiar drive to Salem Public Library had transformed into something altogether different, as if Sarah had slipped into a parallel reality where everything looked the same but hummed with new possibility. She pressed her forehead against the cool glass of the passenger window, watching her hometown reshape itself through a lens of newfound knowledge. Each passing figure now carried a question mark: the sharp-suited businesswoman clutching her morning coffee like a lifeline – did real magic lurk beneath her corporate facade? The elderly man on his usual bench, newspaper spread across his lap like wings, his weathered hands perhaps hiding centuries of secrets.

A jogger and her golden retriever loped past, and Sarah wondered if the dog could sense what its owner might be. Even the barista, visible through the steamy window of her favorite coffee shop, moved with a grace that suddenly seemed suspect. How many of them walked between worlds? How long had she been surrounded by magic without ever knowing it? The Salem she'd known since childhood was dissolving, pixel by pixel, revealing something far more intricate beneath its surface.

"You're staring," Alex noted, amusement coloring his voice.

"Can you blame me?" Sarah turned to face him. "It's like... like finding out there's been a whole parallel universe running alongside ours this entire time. That guy who just crossed the street – is he...?"

"Mr. Peterson? No, he's completely normal. Just really into model trains." Alex paused at a red light. "Though his neighbor Mrs. Sullivan? The one with all the Halloween decorations?"

"No way."

"Way. Those jack-o'-lanterns of hers? They actually float when no one's looking."

The Salem Public Library stood proudly on Essex Street, its Victorian architecture a testament to the city's long history. The red brick facade was adorned with intricate stonework that, Sarah now realized, probably contained more than just decorative patterns. The morning sun caught the tall windows, making them gleam like amber.

"Okay," Alex said as he parked, "when we go in, let me do the talking at first. Nathan... well, he can be a bit intense about protocols. And finding out I've told you about all this?" He winced. "Let's just say it'll go better if I handle the initial conversation."

"You want me, Sarah Chen, investigative journalist, to keep quiet while you explain something potentially explosive?" She raised an eyebrow.

"Yes?"

"Just checking." She mimed zipping her lips. "Lead the way, Mr. Magic."

Alex rolled his eyes at the nickname but led them up the library's stone steps. The heavy wooden doors swung open with barely a touch, and Sarah could have sworn she heard them whisper as they passed through.

The library's interior was exactly as Sarah remembered it – warm wood paneling, towering shelves, the perpetual quiet broken only by the soft sounds of pages turning and keyboards clicking. The morning light streamed through high windows, creating pools of golden illumination between the stacks. Everything looked perfectly normal.

Nathan Holloway sat behind the circulation desk, his light brown crew cut and professional attire making him look every bit the serious librarian. But there was something about his dark green eyes as they looked up at Alex's approach – a weight, a knowing that Sarah had never noticed before.

"Alex," Nathan said, his voice carrying that particular library whisper that somehow traveled further than normal speech. "Bit early for..." He trailed off as he spotted Sarah, his eyes narrowing slightly. "And Ms. Chen. How... unexpected."

Alex cleared his throat. "Nathan, we need to talk. About the special collection."

Nathan's expression didn't change, but the temperature around the circulation desk seemed to drop several degrees. "The special collection is closed for inventory."

"It's important," Alex insisted. "And she knows."

Those final words seemed to crystallize in the air between them, heavy with unspoken meaning. Nathan's green eyes darted from Alex to Sarah and back again, and in that moment, she caught something impossible – tiny emerald sparks dancing in his irises like lightning trapped in bottles.

"She... knows." Nathan's voice was very, very quiet. "Alexander Davenport Kingston, please tell me you didn't—"

THE BLACK EYED PROPHECY ~ 55

"Full naming? Really?" Alex sighed. "Can we have this conversation somewhere more private? Unless you'd prefer to discuss it here in front of..." He gestured to a nearby elderly woman, who was very obviously trying to eavesdrop while pretending to read a magazine.

Nathan's jaw worked for a moment, then he stood with mechanical precision. "My office. Now!" He paused, glancing at Sarah. "Both of you!"

Alex could tell, that Nathan was angry, he'd only every seen him like this once before, he could fill a tightness in his stomach, he hated when he was upset with him, and this time was different than any other, as sense of dread filled him, as they walked to the office.

As they followed Nathan toward the back of the library, Sarah leaned close to Alex and whispered, "Davenport?"

"Not a word," Alex muttered back. "Not one word."

Nathan's office defied the normal constraints of the library's architecture. The room seemed impossibly large for the building's floor plan, its walls lined with leather-bound books that Sarah was certain weren't part of the public collection. A massive oak desk dominated the space, its surface covered in ancient texts and scrolls that appeared to be written in languages that definitely weren't taught at Salem State.

A glass-fronted cabinet behind the desk held objects that made Sarah's eyes hurt if she looked at them too directly – crystals that seemed to contain galaxies, a clock whose hands moved in impossible directions, what appeared to be a living shadow contained in a bell jar.

"Sit," Nathan said, gesturing to two leather armchairs that Sarah could have sworn weren't there a moment ago. As they sat, he remained standing, pacing behind his desk with controlled agitation. His movements were precise, economical, but Sarah could sense the tension radiating from him.

"Do you have any idea," he began, his voice deceptively calm, "what the Order will do if they find out about this? The protocols exist for a reason, Alex. The law exists for a reason Alex, how could you be so careless, so....so....arrogant?"

"Nathan," Alex interrupted. "Its not like, I had any intention of this happening." He could feel the guilt building into him. Nathan was obviously upset with him, and he hated the way he looked at him, a look of pure disappointment, not anger...which was worse.

Sarah watched the exchange with growing fascination. Beyond the gravity of their words, there was something else happening here – a current of unspoken tension that had nothing to do with magical protocols. The way Nathan's gaze lingered on Alex's face a fraction too long, how Alex's fingers drummed nervously on his chair's armrest whenever Nathan moved closer.

"Tell me everything," Nathan said, finally sinking into his desk chair. As Alex recounted the previous night's events, Sarah noticed how they unconsciously mirrored each other's posture, leaning forward when the other spoke, their bodies oriented toward each other like flowers turning toward the sun.

"And Artemis?" Nathan asked when Alex finished. "She manifested guardian abilities?"

"Full resonant harmonics," Alex confirmed. "I've never seen anything like it. Heard anything like it."

"That's... concerning." Nathan ran a hand through his short hair, a gesture that seemed to catch Alex's attention more than it warranted. "Guardian manifestation usually only occurs in response to primordial threats. If your familiar felt the need to access those powers..."

"These Black Eyed Children," Alex's voice dropped to barely above a whisper, the words heavy with dread, "they're something ancient. The kind of old that makes time itself feel young." His gaze drifted to Nathan's, finding himself caught in those remarkable eyes. The emerald depths held him there.

Nathan held Alex's gaze for a long moment, and Sarah had to resist the urge to fan herself. The tension between them was practically visible now, like heat waves rising from summer pavement.

"The Order won't see it that way," Nathan finally said, his voice softer. "You know how they are about outsiders, Alex. Especially after what happened with your mother."

Alex flinched slightly at that, and Nathan immediately looked regretful, as if he'd crossed some unspoken line.

The silence that followed was heavy with unspoken words. Nathan absently traced a pattern on his desk with one finger, leaving brief trails of golden light that faded like dying sparks.

Alex watched the movement with an intensity that suggested he was deliberately avoiding looking at Nathan's face.

"We'll need access to the restricted archives," Alex finally said, breaking the tension. "If theres anything about these children, it has to be in one of the books in there."

"Alex—"

"She's already involved, Nathan. We can't change that now. "

Nathan's jaw worked for a moment, then he sighed. "Your grandmother is going to kill me for this," he muttered, then raised his voice slightly. "Ms. Chen?"

Sarah sat up straighter. "Yes?"

"What you're about to see..." He paused, choosing his words carefully. "The restricted archives contain knowledge that most of humanity isn't ready to handle. Knowledge that could shatter the careful balance we've maintained for centuries. Are you prepared to accept that responsibility? To keep these secrets, even if they would make the story of your career?"

Sarah glanced at Alex, who gave her an encouraging nod, then back to Nathan. "Yes," she said firmly. "Whatever it takes to understand what we're dealing with."

Nathan studied her face for a moment, then nodded. He stood and moved to the glass cabinet behind his desk. As he reached for what appeared to be an ordinary brass key, Sarah noticed how Alex's eyes followed his movement, lingering on the line of his shoulders beneath his crisp shirt.

Oh yes, she thought with an internal smile, there was definitely more than magic brewing in this library. And somehow, she suspected that unraveling the mystery of the Black Eyed Children might not be the only revelation this investigation would bring to light.

"Follow me," Nathan said, moving toward what had appeared to be a solid wall but now showed the outline of a door. "And Ms. Chen? Try not to scream. The books don't like it."

The door opened into... impossibility.

Chapter Four

Promises Made, Laws Broken

Sarah stopped dead in her tracks, her mouth falling open. The chamber before them soared upward for at least five stories, its walls lined with endless shelves that seemed to stretch into infinity. Wrought iron spiral staircases connected multiple levels, their railings decorated with intricate metalwork that shifted and moved when viewed directly. Floating globes of warm light drifted between the stacks like lazy fireflies, casting golden illumination across leather-bound spines and ancient scrolls.

"This is..." Sarah turned in a complete circle, trying to process what she was seeing. "This can't... the library is only two stories tall. I've seen it from the outside!"

"Space isn't always what it seems," Nathan said, a hint of pride creeping into his professional tone. "The Salem Public Library exists in both worlds - the one everyone sees, and the one hidden behind the veil. This chamber occupies what we call a fold in reality."

"A fold in..." Sarah shook her head, laughing slightly. "Of course it does. Why not? We've already established magic is real, might as well throw spatial physics out the window too."

Above them, books floated between shelves of their own accord, re-shelving themselves with precise movements. A scroll unrolled as it passed overhead, its text glowing faintly in a language that seemed to move and change as Sarah tried to read it.

"How do you ever get anything done in here?" she wondered aloud. "I'd spend all day just watching the books move."

"You get used to it," Alex said, but his fond smile suggested he still found it magical too. He turned to Nathan, his expression softening slightly. "How's Margaret doing?"

The tension in Nathan's shoulders eased slightly at the mention of his grandmother. "She's... being Margaret. Terrorizing her garden club with suspiciously perfect roses, teaching advanced magical theory to her cats, insisting she's 'not that old' while casually mentioning events from the 1930s in conversation."

"So she's feeling better then?"

"Much. The healing ritual you suggested..." Nathan paused, something vulnerable flickering across his face. "It helped. A lot. I should have thanked you properly for that."

"You don't need to—"

"I do." Nathan's green eyes held Alex's for a moment too long. "You didn't have to help, especially after... everything. But you did."

Sarah glanced between them, fascinated by the layers of unspoken history in their exchange.

"Margaret asked about you, actually," Nathan continued, turning to lead them deeper into the chamber. "Said something about how 'that Kingston boy needs to stop by for tea before I decide to be offended.'" His impression of his grandmother's voice was surprisingly good.

Alex laughed. "Complete with the raised eyebrow and meaningful pause?"

"And the thing where she pretends to be more interested in her knitting than the answer? Yes." Nathan's smile was genuine now, the earlier tension mostly dissolved. "You know how she is. I think she misses having someone to debate magical theory with who actually challenges her ideas."

"You mean someone who argues with her?"

"That too."

They passed through narrow canyons of bookshelves, their footsteps echoing strangely on the marble floor. Sarah noticed that some of the books seemed to watch them pass, their spines turning slightly to track their movement. Others whispered among themselves in languages she'd never heard before, their voices like the rustling of ancient pages.

"Your grandmother's gardens are still the talk of the town," Alex said as they walked. "Those roses of hers won another prize last month, didn't they?"

"Three prizes," Nathan corrected with obvious pride. "Though I'm pretty sure she's breaking about fifteen regulations about magical enhancement of non-magical plants. The Order's Agricultural Committee keeps trying to investigate, but somehow their inspection appointments always get mysteriously rescheduled."

"Imagine that."

"Yes, very mysterious how they all suddenly remember urgent appointments elsewhere right before they arrive." Nathan's deadpan delivery was perfect. "Complete coincidence, I'm sure, that they all develop sudden cravings for her special lavender tea right before they're supposed to inspect the roses."

Sarah watched Alex's face as he laughed at Nathan's story. There was something wistful in his expression, a sort of quiet longing that suggested these moments of easy conversation were rare between them now. Whatever had happened in their past — this "everything" they kept dancing around — it had clearly left marks on them both.

The chamber seemed to respond to Nathan's improved mood, the floating lights burning a bit brighter, the whispers of the books becoming more like contented sighs than suspicious murmurs. Even the metalwork on the staircases seemed to flow more smoothly, creating patterns that reminded Sarah of flowing water.

"Here we are," Nathan announced, stopping before a section of shelving that looked identical to all the others. "The historical records of supernatural entities and their manifestations in Salem." He paused, glancing at Sarah. "I should warn you – some of these texts can be a bit... intense. The Order's archivists don't believe in sanitizing history."

"I graduated with honors from the Columbia University School of Journalism," Sarah said with pride. "I can handle intense."

"We'll see," Nathan murmured, reaching for a large black volume whose spine seemed to absorb light rather than reflect it. "We'll see."

Hours melted away in the impossible chamber, marked only by the shifting of shadows cast by the floating lights. Books and scrolls accumulated around them like academic snowdrifts as they worked, forming precarious towers on the massive oak table Nathan had somehow summoned with a casual wave of his hand.

Sarah had long since abandoned her scarf, though she occasionally caught herself shivering – not from cold, but from the contents of the texts she was studying. The Order's archivists, she'd discovered, had indeed been thorough in their documentation of Salem's darker history. Perhaps too thorough.

Alex and Nathan had settled into a rhythm of careful avoidance, each hyperaware of the other's movements but studiously maintaining their distance. When their hands accidentally brushed reaching for the same book, they both jumped as if shocked, mumbling apologies and retreating to opposite ends of the table.

"Got something," Sarah announced, breaking the tension. She was bent over a leather-bound volume whose pages seemed to exhale a faint mist as she turned them. "Listen to this:

'From the personal accounts of Reverend Isaiah Hampton, 1847:

The children appeared first at twilight, as they always do. Two of them, a boy and girl of perhaps twelve summers, though age sits strangely upon them, like ill-fitting clothes. They came to my door three nights in succession, always with the same request – to be invited in to play.

Their clothing was peculiar, not of any current fashion, yet pristine as new-fallen snow. Their voices carried echoes of something ancient, something that had never been young. But it was their eyes that revealed their true nature – black as the space between stars, consuming light rather than reflecting it.

I have documented seventeen disappearances in the past month alone – nine children, five adults, and three animals. All vanished after reporting similar visitations. Those who disappeared had one thing in common – they had invited the children in, had agreed to play their games.

Most troubling is their knowledge of things they cannot possibly know. They speak of events long past as if they were present, recall secrets told only in confession, know the names of those they have never met. They appear immune to all conventional wards and protections, though they cannot enter a dwelling without invitation.

The Order's attempts to track or capture these entities have proven futile. They appear and vanish at will, leaving only frost in their wake, even in the height of summer. Their true nature remains a mystery, though certain texts suggest they may be neither demon nor spirit, but something older – echoes perhaps of what existed before order was imposed upon chaos.'"

Sarah looked up from the text. "There's more. Notes about their patterns, their behaviors. And look at this" – she turned the page – "a sketch."

The illustration, though nearly two centuries old, was unnervingly precise. The children stood exactly as Alex had described them from Pioneer Village, their posture too still, their smiles too wide. The artist had captured something wrong in their proportions, subtle distortions that became apparent only after studying the image for a moment. Their eyes were rendered in what appeared to be pure black ink that somehow seemed darker than the rest of the page.

"That's them," Alex said quietly. "Exactly as they appeared last night."

"There's a notation here in the margin," Nathan leaned closer, his shoulder brushing against Alex's. Neither of them moved away this time, their usual careful distance forgotten in the moment of discovery. "'They speak of games, but their true purpose appears to be collection. They gather not just bodies but experiences, memories, the very essence of their victims. Each disappearance adds to their power, their knowledge.'"

"Collection?" Sarah frowned. "What do they do with what they... collect?"

"Here," Nathan pointed to another passage. "'Those few who have encountered them and survived report sensing an enormous hunger from these entities – not for flesh or blood, but for life itself. They seem to feed on the vital essence of their victims, adding each new experience to their own. This may explain their preference for children, whose life force burns brightest.'"

"But they take adults too," Sarah noted. "And animals. The pets that have been disappearing..."

"Practice," Alex said grimly. "They're starting small, working their way up. Testing the boundaries."

"Testing for what?"

Before Alex could answer, the lights in the chamber flickered, the floating globes dimming momentarily. A cold draft swept through the stacks, causing the books to whisper more urgently among themselves. Even the illustration seemed to shift slightly on the page, the children's endless black eyes appearing to focus on their observers.

"We should go," Nathan said abruptly, closing the book with more force than necessary. "It's not safe to discuss them too directly in places of power like this. The archives... they can sometimes act as conduits."

As if in response to his words, frost began to form on the marble floor around their table, spreading in delicate patterns that looked disturbingly like small footprints.

"Take the book," Nathan added, pushing it toward Sarah. "But be careful with it. Some texts attract attention when they're read too closely."

"Attention?" Sarah asked, but she already knew the answer. The temperature in the chamber had dropped further, and the whispers from the stacks had taken on a different tone – higher, sweeter, like children's voices carried on a cold wind.

"Time to go," Alex agreed, gathering their notes. "We've learned enough for now."

As they hurried toward the exit, Sarah could have sworn she heard giggling from somewhere in the depths of the stacks, and the sound of small feet running on marble floors. But when she turned to look, she saw only shadows moving between the shelves – shadows that seemed to dance and play like children in an endless game.

The mid-afternoon sun felt almost aggressively normal after the otherworldly atmosphere of the restricted archives. Sarah squinted in the bright light, clutching the ancient book to her chest as they descended the library steps. Around them, Salem continued its ordinary routines – tourists taking photos, locals running errands, a group of children playing hopscotch on the sidewalk. The sight of the children made Sarah shiver slightly, despite the warmth of the day.

"So," she said as they reached Alex's car, deliberately lightening her tone, "you and Nathan..."

"Don't start," Alex warned, fumbling with his keys longer than necessary.

"Start what? I'm just saying there was enough tension in that office to power the entire East Coast." She slid into the passenger seat, turning to face him. "How long have you known each other?"

Alex kept his eyes firmly on the steering wheel. "Pretty much forever. Our families are both old Salem lines, we grew up together, went to the same magical training classes—"

"Magical training classes?" Sarah's eyes lit up. "Like Hogwarts?"

"Not exactly," Alex said, fighting a smile. "More like... magical Sunday school? But that's not the point. Nathan and I are just... it's complicated."

"Complicated how?"

"Sarah..."

"The way you both keep almost looking at each other but not quite? The weird tension whenever you accidentally touch? The fact that he obviously still cares about your opinion when it comes to his grandmother's health?" She raised an eyebrow. "That kind of complicated?"

Alex sighed, finally starting the car. "It was a long time ago. Things... happened. Didn't work out."

"Things?"

"Can we talk about something else? Like Margaret?" The relief in his voice at changing the subject was palpable. "She's actually someone you should know about, given everything that's happening."

Sarah allowed the deflection, but filed away Alex's reaction for future reference. "Okay, tell me about Margaret."

"Margaret Holloway is... well, she's a force of nature," Alex said, pulling away from the library. "She's one of the most powerful witches in New England, though you'd never know it from talking to her. She'd rather discuss her prize-winning roses or her latest charity project than the fact that she once redirected a hurricane to protect Salem."

"She did what?"

"1991, Hurricane Bob. The weather service called it a 'miraculous shift in the storm's path.' Margaret called it 'a bit of gardening weather management.' She didn't want it damaging her late-blooming hydrangeas."

Sarah tried to reconcile this information with what she knew of Margaret Holloway – the elegant older woman she occasionally saw at community events, always impeccably dressed, usually fussing over flower arrangements or organizing fundraisers.

"You mean the one who hosts that huge Christmas charity gala every year at the old Hawthorne Hotel?" Sarah asked. "With the ice sculptures that never seem to melt and those impossibly perfect decorations?"

"That's her." Alex smiled. "Though the ice sculptures don't melt because they're not actually ice, and those 'perfect decorations' are usually fairy lights. Actual fairies, I mean, not the electric kind."

"Of course they are," Sarah muttered. "And let me guess – that punch that everyone raves about, the one that makes you feel all warm and happy..."

"Enchanted nectar. Very mild euphoria spell, completely safe for non-magical folks. She says it 'helps open their hearts and their wallets for charity.'"

Sarah shook her head, remembering last year's gala. She'd written a piece about it for the paper – the record-breaking donations, the mysterious aurora borealis that had appeared over Salem that night (despite being geographically impossible), the way everyone had left feeling inexplicably joyful and generous.

"She sounds amazing," Sarah said. "Why haven't you mentioned her before?"

Alex was quiet for a moment, his fingers tapping an irregular pattern on the steering wheel. "Margaret was... is... she was kind of my mentor, in a lot of ways. After my mom left and my dad..." He trailed off. "She helped me understand my magic, control it.

She and Nathan's grandfather took me in during school breaks sometimes, when things at home were rough."

"And then something happened between you and Nathan," Sarah guessed softly.

"Something like that." Alex's voice was carefully neutral. "Margaret still tries to get us to reconcile. Hence the not-so-subtle hints about tea visits and magical theory debates."

"Is that why you haven't been to see her lately?"

"Partly. It's... complicated."

"You say that a lot," Sarah observed. "Maybe it's less complicated than you think."

Alex shot her a look. "Weren't you the one who, four hours ago, was freaking out about magic being real? How are you already trying to fix my love life?"

"So you admit it was a love life?"

"I admit nothing." But there was a slight smile playing around his mouth. "And anyway, we have bigger problems right now than my personal life. Like what we're going to do about our friends from Pioneer Village."

Sarah clutched the ancient book in her lap a little tighter, remembering the frost spreading across the archive floor, the whispers in the stacks. "Right. The murder children who may or may not be ancient chaos entities that collect people's essences. Much more important than your obvious unresolved feelings for the hot librarian."

"He's not..." Alex stopped himself. "Can we focus?"

"Fine, fine." Sarah held up her hands in surrender. "But this conversation isn't over. And something tells me Margaret would be very interested in helping move it along."

"Margaret needs to stay out of it," Alex muttered, but there was affection in his voice. "She's got enough on her plate with the Christmas gala coming up. Did you know she's planning to top last year's aurora borealis?"

They drove in comfortable silence for a moment, the late afternoon sun painting Salem's streets in warm gold. Everything looked so normal, so ordinary. But Sarah knew she'd never see the town the same way again.

The late afternoon sun cast long shadows through the front windows of the Kingston house as Alex and Sarah entered. Alex dropped his keys on the entry table with a tired sigh, carefully placing the ancient tome beside them. The events of the day felt almost dreamlike now, back in the familiar confines of his home.

"I should probably make copies of our notes before—" Alex stopped mid-sentence as they entered the living room. His whole body tensed, and Sarah heard him mutter something that sounded suspiciously like a magic-enhanced curse word.

Two women sat on his couch, looking for all the world like they'd been there for hours. The first was Eleanore Kingston,

Alex's grandmother, her silver hair swept up in an elegant chignon, her posture perfect as she delicately held a teacup that definitely hadn't come from Alex's kitchen. She wore a tailored navy suit that probably cost more than Sarah's monthly rent, and her blue eyes – so like Alex's – held a sharp intelligence that made Sarah want to stand up straighter.

Beside her sat a woman Sarah recognized from newspaper photos of charity events and city council meetings – Adrianna Cromwell. Her dark skin seemed to glow with an inner light, and her perfectly pressed charcoal grey suit somehow managed to look both businesslike and vaguely mystical. Her presence filled the room like a gathering storm, power radiating from her in almost visible waves.

"Alexander," Eleanore said, her voice carrying that particular tone that only disappointed grandmothers can achieve, "would you care to explain why there's a non-magical person standing in your living room who, we received word earlier today knows about our world?"

Alex let out a long groan. "Grandmother, I can explain—"

"Oh, this should be fascinating," Adrianna Cromwell interjected, her voice rich with barely suppressed irony. "Please, do tell us how a Kingston has once again decided that the Order's most fundamental law is more of a suggestion than a rule."

Sarah watched Alex's face flush with anger. "That's not fair. This isn't anything like what happened with my father."

"No?" Adrianna raised one perfectly shaped eyebrow. "A Kingston revealing our world to an outsider, putting everything we've worked to protect at risk?"

Alex then began to recant everything that had happened yesterday, and last night. He talked about the Children at Pioneer Village, and the visitors at his door.

Both older women stiffened at the mention of the Black Eyed Children. Eleanore's teacup clinked sharply against its saucer, and the temperature in the room seemed to drop several degrees.

"Black Eyed Children?" Eleanore's voice was very quiet. "You're certain?"

A heavy silence fell over the room. Adrianna and Eleanore exchanged a look that seemed to carry an entire conversation.

"The situation is more complex than we initially assumed," Adrianna finally said, her tone marginally softer. "Though, I must ask Mr. Kingston, why did you not find it pertinent enough to come to the council about this alarming new?"

Alex, sighed, "I wasn't thinking, I just want to figure out what the hell is going on, I've never seen anything like those children before, nor had I known of their existence until today, when we found this in the archives" Alex, showed the book in his hand to the two older women.

"Not, thinking," Adrianna added, "that sounds typical of a man, reminds me a lot of your father."

"My, son was the same way," Eleanore chimed in as she sipped her tea. "Never thinking about the potential consequences of his actions."

Adrianna turned her penetrating gaze to Sarah. "You understand, Ms. Chen, that knowledge of our world carries tremendous responsibility? That exposure could lead to consequences similar to those your profession often reports on – panic, violence, persecution?"

Sarah straightened her spine. "I understand. I'm a journalist – I know how to keep sources confidential, how to protect sensitive information."

"This goes beyond professional ethics," Eleanore said. "The veil between worlds must be maintained. The alternative..." She glanced at Alex, something sad passing across her face. "We've seen the cost of exposure."

"There might be a way," Adrianna said slowly, "to make an exception in this case. The Kingston line is one of our oldest, most respected families." Her mouth twisted slightly. "Despite certain... previous indiscretions."

Alex flinched at the obvious reference to his father, but held his ground. "What are you suggesting?"

"A magical vow," Adrianna said. "Binding and unbreakable. Ms. Chen would swear to maintain our secrets, and the magic itself would ensure compliance."

"You want me to take a magical oath?" Sarah asked, trying to keep the excitement out of her voice and probably failing. "That's... possible?"

"With witnesses of sufficient power, yes." Eleanore gestured to herself and Adrianna. "It would need to be done properly, with full understanding of the consequences."

"What consequences?" Alex asked sharply.

"Nothing fatal," Adrianna assured them, though her smile didn't quite reach her eyes. "Simply... insurance against indiscretion. The magic would prevent any unauthorized revelation of our world."

"And in return?" Sarah asked, earning an approving look from both older women.

"In return, you may retain your knowledge, assist in the current situation, and continue your... association with the Kingston family." Adrianna rose smoothly to her feet. "Though I suggest you consider carefully before accepting. Such vows are not entered into lightly."

"I'll do it," Sarah said immediately.

"Sarah—" Alex started, but she cut him off.

"No, listen. You trusted me with this secret now I'm choosing to protect it too." She turned to Adrianna and Eleanore. "What do I need to do?"

Eleanore smiled for the first time, and Sarah was struck by how much she looked like Alex in that moment. "Well, for starters, dear, we'll need better tea than whatever my grandson has in his kitchen. And perhaps..." She glanced meaningfully at Adrianna, "we should invite Margaret? She does so love a good ceremony."

"Margaret knows about this?" Alex asked, sounding betrayed.

"Alexander, darling," Eleanore sighed, "Margaret knows everything. It's really quite annoying." She paused. "Though not as annoying as watching you and her grandson dance around each other for the past three years."

Sarah couldn't quite suppress her snort of laughter, which she quickly turned into an unconvincing cough under Alex's glare.

"Right then," Adrianna said, rising gracefully. "Shall we begin?"

Chapter Five

The Vow

Outside, the sun was setting over Salem, painting the sky in shades of purple and gold. And somewhere in the gathering darkness, two children who were not children at all watched and waited, their endless black eyes fixed on the Kingston house, their ancient patience unmarked by the passage of time.

The knock at the door was pure Margaret Holloway – three precise taps followed by a musical chime that definitely didn't come from any physical doorbell. Alex opened the door to find his former mentor standing on the porch, elegant as ever in a dove-grey dress suit, her silver-streaked black hair swept up in a sophisticated twist. Her green eyes – so like Nathan's – sparkled with barely contained mischief.

"Alexander Kingston," she said, pulling him into a warm embrace before he could protest, "if you'd waited any longer to bring me into this drama, I would have been seriously offended." She stepped back, holding him at arm's length to study his face. "You look tired, dear. Have you been eating properly? And don't tell me coffee counts as a food group."

"Margaret," Alex started, but she was already sweeping past him into the house, trailing the scent of roses and what he recognized as serious magical energy.

"Adrianna, Eleanore," Margaret greeted the other women like old friends, which, Alex supposed, they were. "Shall we do this properly then? And you must be Sarah Chen." She turned to Sarah with a warm smile. "I've read your articles. Excellent investigative work, though I suppose now you'll have to be a bit more... selective about what you investigate."

Sarah blinked, clearly caught between intimidation and delight. "Thank you, Mrs. Holloway. Your Christmas galas are legendary."

"Margaret, please. And this year's will be even better – assuming certain people," she shot a meaningful look at Alex, "stop avoiding my invitations. Now then, shall we begin?"

The ceremony itself was both simpler and more profound than Sarah had expected. The four witches formed a circle around her in Alex's living room, their power making the air thick with potential. Margaret produced a silver chord from nowhere, its strands seeming to catch and reflect light that wasn't there.

"The words must come from your heart," Margaret explained, wrapping one end of the cord around Sarah's wrist. "The magic will know if you're sincere."

Sarah took a deep breath, feeling the weight of the moment. "I, Sarah Chen, swear to protect the secrets of the magical world, to maintain the veil between realms, and to use any knowledge gained for the protection and preservation of both worlds." She paused, then added, "I swear this freely and without reservation, understanding the responsibility this knowledge carries."

The silver cord began to glow, wrapped itself around her wrist in an intricate pattern, then seemed to sink into her skin, leaving behind a faint mark like a delicate bracelet tattoo.

"Well done," Adrianna said, sounding genuinely impressed. "The magic has accepted your oath."

"Rather eloquent, actually," Eleanore added. "Most people just stumble through the basic promises."

"She's a writer," Margaret said proudly, as if she'd had anything to do with it. "Words matter to her." She turned to Alex. "Now then, dear, you and I need to have a proper visit soon. There are things we should discuss."

Her tone was light, but Alex caught the serious undertone. "Margaret, if this is about Nathan—".

"This is about many things, Alexander Kingston, not all of them involving my grandson's broken heart." She patted his cheek affectionately. "Though we might discuss that too, over tea. Tomorrow afternoon?"

It wasn't really a question. "Yes, Margaret," Alex sighed, knowing resistance was futile.

The three older witches departed as dramatically as they'd arrived, Margaret's rosescented magic lingering in the air like a favorite perfume. Sarah stood in the middle of Alex's living room, absently touching the silver mark on her wrist.

"So," she said finally, "that just happened."

"Welcome to the magical world," Alex replied dryly. "Where even a simple oath requires three of the most powerful witches in New England and my former mentor playing matchmaker."

"Speaking of matchmaking..."

"Don't start."

"I'm just saying, if Margaret herself is trying to get you and Nathan to—"

"Good night, Sarah."

She laughed, gathering her things. "Fine, fine. But tomorrow you're telling me everything about this 'broken heart' Margaret mentioned."

After Sarah left, Alex stood in his quiet house, feeling the residual magic from the ceremony still humming in the air. Artemis appeared from wherever she'd been hiding during the proceedings, winding around his legs with a questioning trill.

"Yes, I know I have to go see Margaret tomorrow," he told her. "Yes, I know she probably has ulterior motives. And no, I don't want to talk about Nathan."

Artemis gave him a look that suggested she, like everyone else in his life apparently, had opinions about his love life.

"Not you too," he groaned.

But as he prepared for bed that night, Alex couldn't help wondering what Margaret wanted to discuss. She'd had that look in her eyes – the one that meant she knew something important, something that couldn't wait.

The silver mark on Sarah's wrist would protect her now, binding her to their world's greatest secret. But as Alex drifted off to sleep, he couldn't shake the feeling that they were all bound up in something much larger, much older, than mere secrets.

And somewhere in Salem, two children who were not children at all continued their eternal game, patient as the darkness between stars, hungry as the void itself.

The Salem Gazette's office hummed with pre-Halloween energy. Orange and black decorations festooned the desks, and someone had hung paper ghosts from the fluorescent lights, making them dance in the air conditioning's artificial breeze. The usual newsroom chaos had taken on an almost manic quality as reporters rushed to file their stories before the city's biggest celebration kicked into high gear.

Alex sat at his desk, trying to focus on editing his latest article while simultaneously monitoring the growing stack of reports about strange occurrences around town – mysterious cold spots, electronics malfunctioning, and an increasing number of missing pet cases.

The harsh fluorescent lights of the newsroom did little to dispel the shadows under Alex's eyes as he made his way to his desk. He'd managed a few hours of fitful sleep after Sarah left, but his dreams had been plagued by black-eyed children and ominous knocks at the door.

As he booted up his computer, he couldn't shake the feeling that he was being watched. He glanced around the office, but everything seemed normal. His colleagues were engrossed in their work, the familiar buzz of a busy newsroom filling the air.

"Kingston! My office, now!"

Alex jumped at the sound of his editor's voice. Tom Evans was a gruff man in his fifties, known for his no-nonsense attitude and razor-sharp instincts for a good story. As Alex made his way to Tom's office.

"I've got your Halloween assignment," Tom grunted dropping a folder onto his desk. "You and Chen will be covering tomorrow night's festivities. I want everything – interviews with local business owners, tourists' reactions, coverage of the parade, the costume contest, all of it."

"The whole festival?" Alex tried to keep his voice neutral, though his stomach had already started to knot. The Halloween festival meant crowds, chaos, and plenty of opportunities for their unwanted visitors to cause trouble.

"Salem's biggest night of the year!" Tom's smile widened. "When the veil between worlds is at its thinnest, or so they say." Something in his tone made Alex look up sharply, but Tom's expression remained blandly enthusiastic. "I want you both there from the opening ceremony at sunset through the midnight revelries. Get pictures of the jack-o'-lantern display in Salem Common, interviews with the street performers, reactions to the ghost tours."

"Both of us?" Alex asked carefully. "All night?"

"Problem?" Tom's eyes gleamed with something that might have been amusement – or might have been something else entirely. "I thought you and Ms. Chen made quite the investigative team. The way you've been working together lately, heads bent over old books, having intense conversations in corners..."

Alex forced himself to maintain a casual expression. "Just thorough research."

"Of course, of course." Tom nodded, though his smile didn't quite reach his eyes. "Speaking of research – fascinating reading material you've been consulting lately. That volume you brought back from the library the other day looked particularly... enlightening."

Alex's hand twitched toward his messenger bag, where the ancient tome about the Black Eyed Children was carefully hidden under a glamour that made it appear to be "The Complete History of New England Architecture."

"Just background reading," he said lightly. "For context."

"Context is important," Tom agreed, his voice taking on an odd resonance. "Understanding the true nature of things, the patterns beneath the surface. I'm sure tomorrow night will provide plenty of opportunity for... observation."

Sarah chose that moment to appear at Alex's desk, carrying two coffee cups from the shop down the street.

"Ah, Ms. Chen!" Tom turned that too-wide smile on her. "Perfect timing. I was just telling Kingston about your Halloween assignment. I trust you'll both give it the attention it deserves? Really dig deep into Salem's... darker history?"

"Of course," Sarah said, matching his tone with professional enthusiasm. "We'll leave no stone unturned."

"Excellent." Tom's gaze lingered on them both for a moment longer than comfortable. "I look forward to reading your coverage. Who knows? Maybe you'll uncover something... unexpected." He turned to leave, then paused. "Oh, and Kingston? Do be careful tomorrow night. Halloween can be dangerous in Salem. So many strange things happening in the shadows. So many games being played."

"Did he seem..." Sarah, said as they made their way to Alex's desk.

"Creepier than usual?" Alex finished. "Yeah."

"The way he emphasized certain words..." Sarah lowered her voice. "And that thing about games? Do you think he knows something?"

Alex glanced at Tom's office, where their editor was visible through the glass, staring at his computer screen with unnatural intensity. "I think a lot of people in Salem know more than they're letting on. The question is, whose side are they really on?"

Sarah took a sip of her coffee, grimacing at how cold it had gotten during their conversation. "So, Halloween night coverage, huh? Think we'll see any real supernatural activity, or just the usual tourist stuff?"

"Sarah, it's Halloween in Salem, during a prophecy crisis, with ancient evil children running around, and we've been specifically assigned to be out all night by an editor who may or may not be involved in something sinister." Alex ran a hand through his hair. "What do you think?"

"I think," she said, pulling out her reporter's notebook, "that we're going to need a better plan than just showing up with cameras and hoping for the best."

Tomorrow was Halloween in Salem, when the veil between worlds grew thin, and ancient powers stirred in the darkness. And somewhere in town, two children who were not children at all prepared their own celebrations, their eternal game moving into its final phases.

The real question was: who else was playing games in the shadows of Salem? And what would it cost to win?

Margaret Holloway's Victorian mansion stood like a grand dame at the end of Chestnut Street, its gingerbread trim and sweeping verandas a testament to Salem's golden age. Unlike the other historic homes in the neighborhood, Margaret's house seemed to shimmer slightly in the autumn sunlight, as if the very air around it was charged with magic – which, Alex knew, it absolutely was.

The famous gardens that surrounded the house defied both nature and logic. Roses bloomed in impossible colors, their petals shimmering with subtle iridescence that no natural flower could achieve. Late-blooming hydrangeas formed perfect spheres of blue and purple, while chrysanthemums the size of dinner plates nodded in a breeze that seemed to affect only them. Even the grass appeared to have been individually arranged, each blade perfectly aligned with its neighbors.

The stone path to the front door wound between beds of flowers that definitely weren't in season and shouldn't have been able to grow in New England's climate. Alex recognized night-blooming jasmine, tropical orchids, and what appeared to be a small patch of singing violets – their gentle humming just barely audible as he passed.

He'd barely raised his hand to knock when the door swung open, releasing a wave of warm air scented with cinnamon, vanilla, and that particular mix of herbs that always meant serious magic was brewing.

"You're late," Margaret announced, though Alex knew for a fact he was exactly on time. She wore an elegant emerald green dress that complemented her eyes, her silver-streaked black hair arranged in its usual perfect twist. "Come in, come in. The tea's getting cold, and the scones are entirely too fresh."

Alex found himself swept into the house with Margaret's usual efficiency, barely having time to note the shifting patterns in the wallpaper – actual moving vines and flowers that formed and reformed as he watched. The entrance hall opened into a sunny conservatory that somehow managed to be larger than the house's external dimensions should have allowed.

"Sit," Margaret commanded, gesturing to a comfortable armchair near a table already set for tea. "And tell me everything. How are you? Have you heard from your mother? That last postcard from Peru was terribly vague – 'Found something interesting, more soon' indeed. As if that's any kind of proper communication."

Alex settled into the chair, accepting the delicate teacup Margaret pressed into his hands. "I'm fine, and no, I haven't heard from Mom since that postcard three months ago. You know how she gets when she's on a dig."

"Hmph." Margaret's disapproval was clear as she arranged herself in the opposite chair. "Diana always did get too caught up in her work. Even before she knew about magic. Though I suppose that's what attracted James to her in the first place – that intensity of focus."

The mention of his father made Alex tense slightly. Margaret, naturally, noticed.

"And how are you really, dear? Not just the polite answer you give everyone else."

"I'm..." Alex paused, considering his words carefully. Margaret had always been able to tell when he was less than truthful. "I'm managing. The Black Eyed Children are concerning, obviously. And now with Sarah knowing about our world..."

"Yes, about that." Margaret fixed him with her penetrating gaze. "Quite a risk you took there. Though not an unwise one, given the circumstances." She sipped her tea thoughtfully. "She has good instincts, that one. Strong mind, stronger spirit. Rather like your mother in that way."

For the next hour, Margaret led him through what felt like an interrogation disguised as a casual tea party. She asked about his work at the newspaper, his magical studies, whether he was eating properly, if he'd considered getting a familiar other than Artemis ("One can never have too many magical allies, dear"), and his thoughts on the upcoming winter solstice celebrations.

Finally, just as Alex was beginning to hope he might escape without the conversation he'd been dreading, Margaret set down her teacup with a decisive clink.

"Now then," she said, her tone shifting to something more serious, "we need to discuss something rather important. And yes," she added as Alex suppressed a groan, "it does concern Nathan."

"Margaret—"

"Don't 'Margaret' me in that tone, Alexander Kingston. This is more important than your mutual stubbornness." She waved her hand, and a scroll materialized on the table between them. It looked ancient, its parchment yellowed with age, sealed with wax that seemed to shimmer with its own inner light.

"What is that?"

"A prophecy," Margaret said simply. "One that's been in my family's keeping for generations. One that I believe concerns you and Nathan specifically."

Alex felt his stomach drop. In his experience, prophecies were never good news – they tended to be cryptic, dangerous, and frustratingly inevitable.

"The Prophecy of Converging Bloodlines," Margaret continued, breaking the seal with a touch.

"Made by the Blind Seer Amarantha Vale in 1847. Margaret unrolled the scroll, revealing text that seemed to move slightly on the page, as if the words were reluctant to be pinned down to any one meaning. "It speaks of two ancient magical lines – Kingston and Holloway – and a choice that could either save or doom us all."

"Margaret, please tell me you're not suggesting—"

"That you and Nathan are the subjects of a prophecy that might be the key to stopping an ancient evil that's once again stirring in Salem?" Margaret's eyes twinkled despite the seriousness of her words.

Outside in the magical gardens, the roses turned their blooms toward the conservatory windows, as if listening. A chill breeze stirred their petals, carrying with it the faint sound of children's laughter.

The familiar warmth of Rosie's Diner felt like a refuge after the intense magical atmosphere of Margaret's house. The lunch rush was just winding down, the clatter of plates and murmur of conversations creating a comforting backdrop of normality.

Sarah sat in their usual booth, a half-eaten club sandwich and a notebook covered in her distinctive scrawl in front of her.

Alex slid into the booth, still clutching the two gilt-edged invitations Margaret had pressed into his hands as he left – elegant cards that somehow managed to sparkle without actually having any glitter on them. He'd tried to refuse, but Margaret had simply smiled that knowing smile of hers and said, "The prophecy isn't the only thing that needs a little nudge, dear."

"Let me get this straight," Sarah said in a low voice, leaning forward over her coffee cup. "Margaret Holloway, who is apparently some kind of magical powerhouse disguised as a garden club enthusiast, thinks you and Nathan are the subjects of a centuries-old prophecy about 'converging bloodlines' that could either save or destroy everything?"

"That's the simplified version, yes."

"And this prophecy just happens to surface now, when we've got ancient evil children running around stealing pets and threatening people?"

Alex glanced around the diner, then leaned closer, lowering his voice further. "'When silver tears fall from a moonless sky, And ravens perch where doves once made their nest, Two streams of power, ancient and blessed, Shall merge where fallen stars now rest.'"

"That's... actually pretty poetic," Sarah said, scribbling in her notebook. "Go on."

"'From Kingston's line of twilight born, Where magic flows like morning dew, And Holloway's flame, since ages sworn To guard the veil between worlds two.'" Alex paused, taking a sip of coffee. "'One child of storm, one child of flame, When joined shall break or mend the chain, That binds the realms of light and shade— Upon their choice, all fates are laid.'"

"And Margaret thinks this refers to you and Nathan specifically?"

"The firstborn of each line in this generation," Alex confirmed. "Me and Nathan are both only children, both direct descendants of the original magical families."

"And you both have the worst timing in romantic history," Sarah added. "What happened between you two anyway? Margaret mentioned something about a broken heart?"

Alex stared into his coffee cup as if it might contain answers. "It was three years ago. We were...everything was..." He sighed. "Then my mother disappeared in Peru, and my magic started acting up – grief does weird things to magical control. Nathan wanted to help, but I pushed him away. Said some things I shouldn't have. He took a position at the library's magical archives in London for a year, and when he came back..."

"You both decided it was easier to avoid each other than deal with your feelings?"

"Something like that."

Sarah sat back, considering. "And now there's a prophecy saying you two need to work together to save the world? Talk about your forced proximity tropes."

"This isn't one of your romance novels, Sarah."

"No, it's better. It's a magical prophecy about two people who clearly still have feelings for each other being destined to either save or destroy the world." She paused. "Though I'm a little concerned about that 'break or mend' part. Sounds like it could go either way."

Before Alex could respond, a cold draft swept through the diner, making the lights flicker briefly. Through the window, Alex caught a glimpse of two small figures standing on the sidewalk outside, their faces turned toward the diner with unnatural stillness. By the time he blinked, they were gone.

"Speaking of Margaret..." Sarah picked up one of the invitations Alex had set on the table, admiring the way it seemed to catch light that wasn't there. "A Christmas gala, huh? With actual fairies and enchanted punch?"

"She insisted I bring you. Said something about you needing to see 'how we do things properly in magical society.'" Alex managed a smile. "Fair warning – Margaret's parties tend to be intense."

Outside, the autumn day continued its normal patterns, but the shadows seemed a little deeper, the air a little colder. And somewhere in Salem, two children who were not children at all played their eternal games, waiting for the pieces to align, for the prophecy to unfold.

Chapter Six

Ghosts, Ghouls, and Goblins

Salem Common had transformed into a Halloween wonderland, though Alex couldnt help noticing how the cheerful decorations cast unusually dark shadows in the late afternoon light. Orange and purple lights festooned every tree, and elaborate cobweb decorations stretched between lampposts, glittering with artificial dew. The scent of caramel apples, cotton candy, and warm cider filled the air, mixing with the smoke from food vendors' grills.

"Your phone isn't going to suddenly show a message if you check it every thirty seconds," Sarah said, not looking up from her notebook where she was recording impressions of the festival.

"I'm not..." Alex stuffed his phone back in his pocket.

"Uh-huh." Sarah's tone made it clear she wasn't buying it.

Before Alex could defend himself, a group of children ran past, their Halloween costumes already on despite the early hour. Two of them wore ghost sheets with eye holes, and Alex found himself tensing before realizing they were just normal kids, their laughter genuine and childlike.

"Over there," Sarah pointed toward a particularly elaborate booth decorated with authentic-looking grimoires and crystal balls. "Madame Zelda's Authentic Salem Magic. Want to bet how 'authentic' she really is?"

The woman running the booth looked exactly like what tourists expected a Salem witch to be in flowing black robes, dramatic makeup, and enough crystal jewelry to open a new age shop. She was currently reading tarot cards for an enthusiastic group of college students.

"Actually," Alex said quietly as they approached, "that's Zelda Blackwood ,She's technically retired now, but she used to teach advanced magical theory to Order initiates. The fortune telling is just her way of hiding in plain sight."

Sarah's eyes widened. "Seriously? So those readings are real?"

"As real as she wants them to be. Though she usually keeps things vague enough to pass as entertainment." He paused. "The crystals are genuine too, but they're mostly for show. She doesn't need tools for actual divination."

They spent the next hour interviewing vendors and festival-goers, collecting quotes and color for their article. Sarah's notebook filled with details about the elaborate decorations, the various attractions, and the growing crowd of tourists in increasingly creative costumes.

"The jack-o'-lantern display is particularly impressive this year," commented Mary Sullivan, owner of the local bakery and, Alex knew, a minor weather witch who specialized in creating perfectly atmospheric conditions for outdoor events. "Though I do hope the temperature stays warm enough for the evening activities." She gave Alex a meaningful look that suggested she'd be doing her part to ensure exactly that.

"And the ghost tours are already sold out," added Peter Holmes, who ran Salem Historical Tours. "People can't get enough of Salem's spooky history, especially on Halloween night."

Alex checked his phone again.

They wound their way past Salem's historic buildings, now transformed into seasonal haunted houses that straddled the line between tourist entertainment and magical camouflage. Victorian mansions loomed above them, their windows flickering with what visitors would dismiss as clever LED effects but Sarah now recognized as contained spellwork. Wisps of mist curled around doorways – not from hidden machines, but from actual enchantments carefully crafted to seem artificial.

Alex's trained eye picked out the Order members woven through the crowds: the woman in a tour guide's colonial dress whose hand occasionally traced warning sigils in the air, the street vendor whose cart's position perfectly maintained the boundary between mundane and magical sectors, the photographer whose camera captured more than just tourist snapshots. They moved with practiced casualness, their eyes constantly scanning for any ripple of genuine supernatural disturbance in the sea of manufactured scares. Even the position of the food carts and souvenir stands, Alex noted, formed a subtle pattern – a protective circle hidden within the chaos of the festival.

A group of teenagers shrieked with delight as an "animatronic" ghost floated past them – a minor spirit actually earning its keep by playing along with the Halloween festivities. Above it all, real witchlight danced along the rooflines, disguised as simple string lights, while authentic protection wards sparkled beneath fake plastic decorations.

"Cotton candy?" Sarah offered, holding out a massive cloud of pink sugar she'd bought from a nearby vendor. "You look like you need the sugar boost. And maybe a distraction from whatever worst-case scenarios you're imagining."

"I'm not—" Alex's protest was interrupted by the sound of children laughing. He spun around, scanning the crowd, but saw only normal families enjoying the festival.

"Okay, that's it." Sarah grabbed his arm and steered him toward an empty bench. "Sit. Talk. What's really going on? And don't say nothing, because you're wound tighter than my grandmother's antique watch."

Alex sank onto the bench, dragging a hand through his already disheveled hair. "Something's not adding up. I texted Nathan earlier and he still hasn't gotten back to me, which isn't like him at all." His fingers absently traced the outline of his phone in his pocket, as if willing it to buzz with a response. "And then there's Tom suddenly assigning us this coverage out of nowhere." He trailed off, his expression growing more troubled.

Sarah watched as he seemed to wrestle with something, his shoulders tense with the weight of unspoken words. Finally, he leaned closer, his voice dropping to barely above a whisper. "There's something else. Something Margaret showed me about the prophecy that I haven't told you yet." He glanced around before continuing, "'When silver tears fall from a moonless sky.' That's how it starts. ..."

"Is a new moon," Sarah finished, her eyes widening.

"Exactly. It's like all the pieces are lining up, but we don't know what picture they're supposed to form." He pulled out his phone again, thumb hovering over Nathan's number.

The afternoon light began to soften, casting long shadows across the cobblestones as they continued their interviews. Each conversation seemed to add another piece to an increasingly unsettling puzzle.

Most festival attendees bubbled with enthusiasm about the haunted houses and psychic readings, their voices bright with the artificial spookiness of the season. But the moment Alex or Sarah steered the conversation toward the disappearances, a familiar change would come over their subjects – shoulders tensing, eyes darting away, voices dropping to whispers before falling silent altogether.

Yet some couldn't help but let fragments of truth slip through:

There was the elderly man on Essex Street, his weathered hands trembling slightly as he spoke of "dark times" that had plagued Salem throughout its history. "Always followed by years of prosperity," he'd added, his rheumy eyes suddenly sharp with meaning. "As if the town itself demands a price for its blessings." He'd shuffled away before they could press further, leaving behind words that hung in the air like frost.

Near the witch museum, they met a teenage girl with bright blue hair and too many bracelets. She'd started talking about the festival before suddenly grabbing Sarah's arm. "My little brother," she'd whispered, glancing over her shoulder, "he saw them last week. Children standing outside his window, just... watching. Their eyes were wrong." She'd released Sarah's grip and melted into the crowd before they could ask what she meant by 'wrong.'

The local history buff they found in the library's research section had seemed eager to help at first. He'd pulled out stacks of old town records, pointing out patterns that stretched back centuries. "Every twenty years," he'd muttered, flipping through brittle pages. "Like clockwork. Disappearances, strange sightings, unexplained events – all on the same cycle." But when they'd asked to see the records themselves, he'd suddenly remembered an urgent appointment, hastily returning the documents to their restricted section.

Around them, the festival was getting busier as sunset approached. More elaborate costumes appeared in the crowd – vampires, werewolves, and witches that made Alex want to laugh at how far they missed the mark. The food vendors' grills sent up clouds of fragrant smoke, and somewhere nearby, a band was setting up for the evening's entertainment.

Everything looked perfectly normal, perfectly festive. Which was exactly what worried him.

The sun was sinking behind Salem's historic rooftops when Alex saw it. There, where festival lights faded into autumn shadows, stood a small figure. It wore a plastic Halloween mask – some mass-produced cartoon character's grinning face – but the disguise only made its presence more unsettling. Because behind the mask's cheerful eyeholes, Alex could see nothing but darkness. No white, no iris, no reflection of the nearby festival lights. Just two pools of absolute black, ancient and hungry, staring back at him from behind a child's costume.

The figure raised one small hand with unnatural grace, pointing directly at Alex with a deliberation that made his blood run cold. A group of trick-or-treaters bounced past, their excited chatter and rustling candy bags seeming obscene against the moment's horror. When they cleared his line of sight, the figure had vanished – but Alex could still feel the weight of those bottomless eyes, could still sense the silent message in that pointed finger.

"Alex?" Sarah's voice seemed to come from very far away, filtering through layers of dread. She touched his arm, and he flinched. "Hey, you look like you've seen a..." She stopped herself, her reporter's instincts picking up on his tension. Her voice dropped lower, more urgent. "What is it? What did you just see?"

"Well," Alex said quietly, "I guess we don't have to wonder where they are anymore."

The words had barely left Alex's lips when a scream sliced through the carnival atmosphere – a sound that didn't belong among the laughter and music, a cry that spoke of primal terror rather than Halloween thrills. Alex's eyes met Sarah's, and in that split-second glance, he saw his own dread reflected back at him. The moment they'd been dreading had arrived.

"No, no, no," Alex muttered as they pushed through the crowd. The festival's cheerful facade was crumbling as panic rippled outward like a stone dropped in still water. The press of bodies around them felt suffocating – tourists stumbling backward, parents clutching their children closer, faces transforming from festive joy to confused fear.

Sarah grabbed his sleeve, pointing. "There!"

They burst through the final wall of onlookers into a small clearing that had formed naturally, like animals instinctively backing away from a predator. In its center, a young boy trembled in his mother's arms, his Spider-Man costume torn at the shoulder. Tears cut clean trails through the face paint on his cheeks, and his small body shook with sobs that seemed to come from somewhere deep and primal.

"Tommy, baby, you need to tell me what happened," his mother was saying, her voice tight with barely controlled panic as she ran her hands over him, checking for injuries. Her eyes darted around the crowd, searching for threats or answers.

"It was right here!" Tommy choked out between sobs, pointing at the empty air with a shaking finger. "The monster was right here! It... it wasn't wearing a costume. Its eyes..." His voice cracked, dissolving into fresh tears as he buried his face in his mother's shoulder.

The festival lights seemed dimmer somehow, the autumn air carrying a chill that hadn't been there moments before. Above them, a string of decorative lanterns swayed without a breeze, casting shifting shadows that seemed to reach toward the boy with dark fingers.

Alex approached slowly, reaching for his press badge with deliberate care to appear as unthreatening as possible. "Hi there," he kept his voice gentle, steady.

"I'm Alex Kingston with the Salem Gazette. Would you mind telling me what happened?"

The mother's arm tightened around her son, her eyes narrowing with the protective instinct of a parent whose child has just been scared senseless. "This really isn't the time for—"

"It wasn't pretend!" Tommy burst out, his voice raw with desperation to be believed. "Everyone thinks it's just Halloween stuff, but it wasn't!" His small hands clutched at his mother's jacket. "It looked like a kid at first, like maybe they were trick-or-treating too, but then..." He swallowed hard, fresh tears welling up. "Their eyes were wrong. All black, like... like looking into nothing." His voice dropped to a whisper. "It reached for me."

Alex felt the temperature around them seem to drop several degrees. Behind him, he heard Sarah's sharp intake of breath. Their eyes met in a fraction of a second – both recognizing that this was exactly what they'd been afraid of.

Sarah crouched down to Tommy's level, her reporter's notebook conspicuously absent. "Hey, Tommy," she said softly, as if sharing a secret. "I believe you. Can you tell me which way they went?"

Tommy's free hand rose, pointing toward the old cemetery that bordered the town square. The evening fog had begun rolling in early, unusual for this time of day, curling around the weathered headstones like ghostly fingers. "They just... stepped back into the fog. But—" his voice caught. "It smiled at me first. Not like a normal smile."

The nearby street lamp flickered once, briefly, and somewhere in the distance, a church bell tolled out of schedule.

The fog rolled in with unnatural speed, thick coils of mist slithering between carnival booths and around people's feet. The temperature plummeted so suddenly that nearby drinks began to frost over, breath turning visible in wispy clouds. The festival lights took on an eerie, diffused glow through the gathering murk.

The sharp click of boots on cobblestones announced the arrival of a police officer – Alex recognized Officer Mendez from previous stories. As the officer began taking statements, Alex gently tugged Sarah's elbow, drawing her a few steps away from the growing crowd of onlookers.

"That cemetery," he murmured, keeping his voice low. His eyes darted to where the iron gates were becoming increasingly obscured by mist. "We can't let them get away this time."

Sarah pulled her jacket tighter, but Alex knew the shiver that ran through her wasn't just from the cold. "Yeah," she whispered back, her reporter's determination warring with newfound caution. "But Alex..." She caught his arm as he started to move. "If those things are really out there in force, we need a plan. We can't just go charging in like it's another corruption exposé at City Hall."

The fog continued its steady advance, and somewhere in its depths, a child laughed – the sound neither near nor far, and not quite human.

They picked their way toward the cemetery, each step taking them further from the festival's warmth and light. The cheerful carnival music grew distorted in the thickening fog, transforming from merry melodies into something discordant and wrong. Ancient oak trees loomed above them, their nearly bare branches clawing at the darkening sky like gnarled fingers.

The cemetery's wrought-iron gates rose before them, Victorian scrollwork barely visible through the mist. Decades of weather had eaten away at the black paint, leaving rust-red wounds that looked almost fresh in the fading light. As Alex pressed his hand against the cold metal, the hinges protested with a sound like a dying breath. Sarah winced at the noise, the gate's metallic keen seeming to echo far longer than it should have.

Beyond the threshold, worn headstones emerged from the fog like ancient teeth, their weathered faces bearing silent witness to centuries of Salem's secrets. Dead leaves skittered across the path before them, their dry rustle somehow more unsettling than complete silence would have been. The air here felt older, heavier, as if they'd stepped through more than just a physical gateway.

The cemetery air hung thick and heavy, like breathing through wet silk. Fog writhed between the tombstones in impossible patterns, as if guided by unseen hands. Colonial-era headstones rose from the mist like ancient sentinels, their carved faces worn to haunting approximations of their original designs by centuries of weather. The few jack-o'-lanterns that lined the cobblestone path seemed to pulse with an unhealthy light, their carved grins more rictus than revelry. Their flames cast wild shadows that danced across lichen-covered marble and weathered granite – shadows that moved just a fraction too slowly, that twisted in ways that didn't quite match their source.

"Alex." Sarah's voice was barely a breath, her fingers digging into his arm. The fog parted for a moment, like a curtain drawn back on a nightmare.

There, between a crumbling angel monument and an ancient oak, stood a small figure. It was child-sized, perfectly still in a way no living child could manage. As they watched, it began to turn – not with the natural movement of a person, but with the deliberate precision of a music box ballerina, each degree of rotation measured and mechanical. Its face emerged from shadow, and Sarah bit back a gasp. Where there should have been eyes, two bottomless pools of darkness caught the jack-o'-lantern light and seemed to swallow it whole.

"Sarah." Alex's voice was barely audible above the whisper of dead leaves. "Remember what the book warned us about." His hand found her arm, a steadying gesture for them both. "Don't meet their gaze directly. And no matter what they say, what they ask..." He swallowed hard. "Don't invite them closer. Don't invite them to do anything."

They moved forward with measured steps, fallen leaves crackling beneath their feet like tiny bones. The figure remained motionless, watching them with that terrible stillness that spoke of infinite patience. Something about its posture suggested amusement, as if their caution was a game it had watched played out countless times before.

The sharp crack of a branch splitting shattered the cemetery's hollow quiet. Alex and Sarah spun around, hearts hammering, to find Tom Evans looming from the fog like some film noir detective. Their editor's bulky frame blocked the path back to the gate, his face half-hidden in shadow.

"Well, well." Tom's familiar growl carried an edge they'd never heard before. "If it isn't my star reporters." He stepped forward, and something about his movement seemed wrong, too fluid for his usual bear-like gait. "Want to tell me what you're doing poking around a cemetery after hours?" His eyes caught the light strangely, like polished glass. "Besides working on that Halloween festival piece I assigned you?"

"Tom!" Alex's voice cracked slightly, his mind scrambling for a plausible explanation. "This isn't— we were just following up on some local folklore. You know, spice up the festival coverage with some historical color." Even to his own ears, the lie sounded paper-thin.

Their editor stepped closer, moonlight catching the silver at his temples. Something lurked behind his usual gruff exterior – an emotion Alex couldn't quite place. "Don't insult both our intelligences, Kingston." Tom's voice was quieter than usual, more controlled. "You and Chen have been poking around places you shouldn't, asking questions that are drawing the wrong kind of attention." His eyes flickered between them, carrying a weight that felt like more than simple editorial concern. "What are you really chasing here?"

The laughter came before Alex could answer – a sound that slithered through the fog like ice down their spines. It mimicked childhood joy the way a corpse mimics sleep: a hollow approximation that only emphasized the wrongness beneath. The sound seemed to come from everywhere and nowhere, echoing off centuries-old headstones with unnatural resonance.

Tom's reaction was subtle but immediate. His shoulders tensed, and something like recognition flashed across his face before he masked it. "What the hell was that?" he demanded, but there was a tremor in his voice that betrayed him – not the confusion of someone encountering something unknown, but the fear of someone confronting something grimly familiar.

Alex spun back toward the angel monument, but the small figure had vanished. The fog churned thicker, as if responding to some unseen signal. More laughter rippled through the cemetery, a chorus of ancient voices wearing children's sounds like ill-fitting masks. The jack-o'-lanterns' flames guttered, casting wild shadows that danced like eager audiences to this macabre performance.

"We're leaving. Right now." Sarah's voice held the kind of forced calm that barely contained rising panic. Her fingers found Alex's sleeve, tugging with urgent insistence.

They stumbled toward the gate through fog that seemed to cling to their legs, trying to slow them. Tom's footsteps followed close behind, his questions cutting through the mist like bullets.

"What exactly have you two gotten yourselves into? Who else have you talked to about this?"

Alex's foot caught on an exposed root, and Sarah steadied him. The cheerful glow of the festival beckoned beyond the cemetery walls, seeming impossibly far away. At the gate, he couldn't help himself – he looked back one final time.

What he saw froze the breath in his lungs. Dark figures stood scattered among the headstones, small silhouettes that should have been innocent but weren't. Their eyes, dozens of black pools of ancient darkness, stared back at him with terrible purpose. Their whispers came in unison, a sound like dead leaves scraping across stone: "Soon, Alex Kingston. Very soon."

They burst through the gate and into the festival's warmth, the sudden assault of carnival music and laughing crowds feeling like a slap of unreality. Before Alex could catch his breath, Tom's hand clamped down on his shoulder with surprising strength.

"Listen carefully," Tom's voice dropped low, carrying an edge that didn't match his usual editorial bluster. "Some doors aren't meant to be opened. Some stories aren't meant to be told." His eyes held Alex's with unsettling intensity. "Drop this now, both of you. Before you draw attention from things that can't be reasoned with, can't be investigated, can't be stopped." He released his grip and stepped back, straightening his jacket. "Consider that a friendly warning... while warnings can still help."

Tom's footsteps faded into the carnival chaos, leaving Alex and Sarah in an island of uneasy silence amid the festival's forced cheer. Before they could process his veiled threat, something caught Alex's eye – a weathered angel statue near the cemetery gate he could have sworn wasn't there before.

"Sarah," he breathed, taking an involuntary step closer. "Look."

The marble angel's face was lifted toward the darkening sky, its features worn smooth by centuries of weather. But there, catching the festival lights, were trails of moisture running from its eyes. The droplets gleamed with an impossible silvery sheen, too bright and metallic to be ordinary rain or dew.

"Silver tears fall from a moonless sky," Alex whispered, his voice hoarse. The words of the prophecy seemed to hang in the air between them. Sarah followed his gaze upward, where the evening sky stretched vast and empty above them – no moon, no stars, just an endless void that seemed to watch them with the same patient malice as those children's black eyes.

"Alex?" Sarah's voice wavered slightly. "Please tell me that statue was here when we came in."

A single silver tear dripped from the angel's chin, hitting the ground with an audible ping that shouldn't have been possible. Behind them, the festival lights flickered in unison, just for a moment, and somewhere in the distance, children laughed.

"What do we do now?" Sarah's voice carried the slightly hysterical edge of someone trying very hard to maintain their reporter's composure. She ran her hands through her hair, a nervous habit Alex had noticed whenever a story veered into unexpected territory. "Because I've got to tell you, Alex, this is way beyond anything they covered in Journalism school."

Alex tore his gaze away from the weeping angel, his mind racing through the implications. "This isn't random," he said, pulling Margaret's copied prophecy from his jacket pocket. The paper seemed to hum with a subtle energy in the presence of those silver tears. "Margaret showed me this for a reason. 'Silver tears fall from a moonless sky' – those exact words. And now here we are, with..." He gestured at the statue, its metallic tears still catching the carnival lights like liquid mercury.

"You're telling me that some centuries-old prophecy is just... what? Coming true? Right now?" Sarah's skepticism warred with what she'd just witnessed. "And Tom... did you notice how he—"

"Exactly." Alex cut her off, glancing around to ensure they weren't being overheard. "We need to decode the rest of this prophecy, and fast. Because if this part is already happening..." He left the thought unfinished, but they both felt the weight of it.

The ancient clock tower began to toll, each deep, resonant strike echoing through Salem's streets like a prophecy of its own. One... two... three... With each hollow boom, the festival lights flickered and dimmed, as if something was slowly drinking the warmth from the night. Shadows lengthened across the cobblestones, stretching into shapes that didn't quite match the objects casting them.

Alex watched the darkness pool between the carnival booths, remembering Margaret's words about the time when veils grew thin. Around them, the festival-goers began their exodus, parents shepherding tired children home, couples walking arm in arm, all of them blissfully unaware. They were living in a world where the greatest fear was running out of candy, where black eyes belonged to face paint and plastic masks, where silver tears were just tricks of the light.

The final toll faded into the autumn night, leaving behind a silence that felt expectant, hungry. Halloween's mask of playful frights was slipping away, revealing something far older and darker beneath. As Sarah's hand found his in the growing dark, Alex knew with bone-deep certainty that their investigation had crossed a line. The real horrors – the ones that had stalked Salem's streets long before tourist shops and haunted houses – were stirring from their slumber.

The night might be ending, but their nightmare was just beginning to unfold.

Chapter Seven

The Mystery Package

The Salem Gazette's morning editorial meeting had taken on a grim tone in recent weeks. What had started as isolated incidents had become an undeniable pattern – children vanishing without a trace, leaving behind only frost-covered rooms and terrified families.

"That's the fifth child in three weeks!" Mike Reynolds, the crime beat reporter, slapped another missing person report onto the growing pile on the conference room table. "Emily Rowan age eight. Disappeared from her bedroom Saturday night. Parents say the room was freezing cold, even though the heat was on full blast."

Alex's hand tightened around his coffee cup.

"And still no leads," Tom Marshton mused from the head of the table, his expression unreadable.

"No signs of forced entry, no evidence of foul play. Just empty rooms and broken families." His eyes met Alex's briefly, and that now-familiar gleam of something not quite right flickered in their depths. "Fascinating pattern, wouldn't you say, Kingston?"

After the meeting, Sarah cornered Alex by the coffee machine. "We need to do something," she whispered. "These families – they have no idea what they're really dealing with. Maybe if we could warn them somehow..."

"Without breaking your magical vow or exposing the whole supernatural world?" Alex shook his head. "The Order's already doing what they can – setting up protective wards around schools, distributing enchanted tokens disguised as safety whistles. But until we understand what the Black Eyed Children are really planning..."

The rest of his workday passed in a blur of worried conversations and mounting evidence that something dark was moving through Salem. Every new report carried the same hallmarks unusual cold, children speaking of new friends who wanted to play, rooms empty except for a light dusting of frost.

The early November darkness had already settled over Salem as Alex and Sarah pushed through Rosie's Diner's door, the little bell overhead chiming a welcome. Warmth and the rich scent of coffee wrapped around them like a familiar blanket, a sharp contrast to the bitter wind that had dogged their steps through the streets. The usual evening crowd had dwindled to barely a handful of patrons, their quiet conversations echoing in the unusual emptiness.

Rosie appeared at their usual booth before they'd even shed their coats, her perpetual smile carrying a strain that hadn't been there a month ago. "You two look half frozen," she said, fidgeting with her order pad. "Though can't say I blame anyone for hurrying home these days. Getting dark so early now..." She glanced at the windows, where night pressed against the glass like a physical thing. "What with everything that's been happening, folks are scared. Not that I blame them."

She returned moments later with two steaming mugs of hot cocoa, topped with a generous swirl of whipped cream – her standard comfort offering for troubled times. As she moved away to tend to one of the few occupied tables, Alex watched her normally bouncing step seem heavier, weighted down by unspoken worries.

"I've never seen it this empty," Sarah murmured, wrapping her cold hands around the warm mug. Her reporter's eyes scanned the nearly vacant diner. "Not even during that blizzard last winter."

Alex stirred his cocoa absently, watching the whipped cream dissolve into swirls. "It's not just the early darkness keeping people inside," he said quietly. "Did you notice how Rosie couldn't quite bring herself to say the word 'disappearances'? Like saying it might make it more real?"

"Can you blame her?" Sarah leaned closer, her voice dropping. "Three kids in the past month. No bodies, no evidence, just..." She made a vanishing gesture with her fingers. "Gone. And now with what we saw in the cemetery—"

After finishing their meals – Alex's half-eaten pot roast a testament to his distracted mind – they stepped back into the night. The warmth of Rosie's Diner clung to them briefly before surrendering to November's bite. Though Alex's house sat just a few blocks away, the familiar route felt altered, twisted into something less welcoming by the premature darkness.

The street lay too quiet for this hour, marked only by the occasional sweep of headlights that made their shadows dance grotesquely against brick buildings. Shop windows that should have glowed with evening commerce stood dark, CLOSED signs turned hours too early, as if the businesses themselves were huddling away from the night. The few stores still lit seemed like lonely beacons in a darkening sea, their lights serving only to emphasize the growing shadows between them.

"Remember when this street used to be packed, even at this hour?" Sarah's voice carried unnaturally in the stillness, her breath forming ghost-like whispers in the cold air.

Alex nodded, noting how their footsteps echoed off the colonial-era buildings that loomed above them. The historic charm of Salem's downtown had taken on a more sinister cast these past weeks, its centuries of history seeming less like tourist appeal and more like layers of accumulated secrets. Even the brass door knockers and weathered shutters appeared to watch their passage with ancient, knowing eyes.

A lonely wind whispered down the street, carrying dead leaves that scraped across the cobblestones like skeletal fingers. Somewhere in the distance, a dog barked once and fell silent, as if regretting drawing attention to itself in the gathering dark.

The porch light cast a weak glow over something that definitely hadn't been there when Alex left that morning: a wooden box, small enough to cradle in two hands, that seemed to absorb the light rather than reflect it. The wood was ancient oak, darkened by centuries, its surface covered in intricate carvings that appeared to shift when viewed directly – Celtic knots that wound into protective sigils, that transformed into what might have been words in a language too old to name.

"Alex?" Sarah's voice carried a note of warning. "Please tell me you don't make a habit of getting creepy mystery boxes delivered to your doorstep."

He crouched down to examine it closer, careful not to touch. The carvings seemed deeper than they should be, as if they continued into the very heart of the wood. A folded piece of parchment – not paper, but actual parchment – was secured to the lid with a blob of dark red wax, unmarked by any seal. The message, written in an elegant hand that somehow managed to suggest age despite its clarity, made Alex's breath catch:

> "The answers you seek lie within, but beware the cost of knowledge. Some truths are best left buried. - J"

"J?" Sarah whispered, leaning over his shoulder. "You don't think..." She left the question hanging, but Alex could hear the unspoken name they were both thinking: James. His father.

"That's not possible," Alex said, but his voice lacked conviction. His hand hovered over the box, and he could have sworn he felt it pulse with a subtle energy, like a heartbeat trapped in wood. "He's been gone for ten years."

"Yeah, well, a week ago I thought black-eyed children were just creepy internet stories, so maybe we should expand our definition of 'possible.'" Sarah hugged her arms against a chill that had nothing to do with the November air. "Are you going to open it?"

The porch light flickered once, and in that brief moment of darkness, both could have sworn they saw the carvings on the box writhe like living things.

The porch light cast their shadows across the weathered boards as Alex and Sarah stared at the box, neither quite willing to be the first to touch it. A distant church bell tolled, its sound muffled by the thick November air, marking a moment that felt suspiciously like a point of no return.

"You know," Sarah said softly, her reporter's confidence wavering, "we could just pretend we never saw this. Go inside, make coffee, convince ourselves this is all some elaborate Halloween prank." But even as she spoke, they both knew that option had vanished the moment they'd seen those black eyes in the cemetery.

Alex drew in a deep breath, the cold air sharp in his lungs. His hand moved toward the box with the slow inevitability of fate itself. The wood felt alive beneath his fingers, thrumming with a subtle energy that might have been magic, might have been fear, might have been both. The carvings seemed to respond to his touch, the ancient symbols warming beneath his fingertips like awakening creatures.

"Here goes everything," he murmured. The lid opened with a sound like a long-held sigh.

Darkness deeper than velvet lined the interior, cradling three objects that seemed to glow with their own subtle light: a brass key, its surface etched with symbols that matched the box's carvings; a piece of parchment, yellow with age, folded with precise creases; and a book bound in leather so dark it seemed to swallow the porch light. The leather was cracked with age, yet the binding remained intact, as if time itself had been afraid to completely claim it.

"Oh god," Sarah breathed, leaning closer despite herself. The streetlight caught her profile, illuminating the mix of dread and fascination in her expression. "Alex, that book... I've seen something like it before, in the restricted section of the library archives. But Nathan said those texts were just myths, stories about—"

"About the first families of Salem," Alex finished, his mouth dry. His fingers hovered over the book, feeling heat radiating from its ancient pages.

The porch light flickered again, and somewhere down the street, a cat yowled – a sound too similar to a child's cry. The night seemed to press closer, as if drawn by the box's opening, eager to witness what happened next.

They carried the box into Alex's living room with the careful reverence usually reserved for explosive devices. Artemis materialized from the shadows, her green eyes fixed on the box with an intensity that seemed more than mere feline curiosity. She leaped onto the coffee table, her tail twitching as she watched them arrange the objects on its surface.

The brass key caught the lamp light, casting strange shadows on the wall. The leather book seemed to drink in the room's warmth. But as Alex lifted these items, something shifted in the velvet lining – another piece of parchment, folded differently than the first, as if it had been hidden beneath the others with deliberate care.

"There's more," Alex murmured, easing the document free. The parchment felt alive beneath his fingers, crackling with age yet surprisingly supple, as if preserved by something more than mere careful storage. As he unfolded it, the paper seemed to sigh – a sound that made Artemis's ears twitch forward.

"It's a map," Sarah breathed, leaning closer. Her reporter's notebook lay forgotten on the table as she traced the air above the document, not quite daring to touch it. "But look at these markings..."

The map showed Salem, but not the Salem they knew. Ancient ley lines crossed the familiar streets like veins of power. Symbols clustered around certain locations – the cemetery, the witch museum, places they passed every day without understanding their true significance. Delicate script in faded ink noted things that shouldn't exist: "Threshold of Whispers," "Gate of Autumn's End," "The Crossing Place."

But it was the marking in the forest that drew their eyes and held them. Deep in the woods where hiking trails gave way to older paths, a symbol had been drawn with such force it had nearly torn the parchment: a stylized eye, rendered in ink so black it seemed to absorb the lamplight. Unlike the other markings, this one appeared recent, its edges still sharp and clean.

Artemis growled low in her throat, a sound Alex had never heard her make before. The cat's fur stood on end as she stared at the eye, her own eyes glowing with an increasingly bright emerald light.

Alex lifted the book with reverent care, the leather binding warm against his palms despite the room's chill. As he eased the cover open, centuries exhaled onto his skin – the rich, complex scent of aged paper, forgotten ink, and something else, something that made Artemis's whiskers twitch. The pages were surprisingly supple, as if whatever magic had preserved them was still active after all these years.

Spidery handwriting filled each page, the ink shifting from faded brown to midnight black, suggesting multiple authors over multiple eras. Intricate diagrams bloomed across the yellowed paper: spiraling patterns that hurt his eyes if he looked too long, symbols that seemed to pulse with their own inner light, and incantations in languages that felt ancient before Latin was young.

"This is..." Sarah leaned closer, her reporter's instincts warring with awe. "God, Alex, this is like finding an instruction manual for all the things that go bump in the night. Look at these notes in the margins – different handwriting, different centuries, all adding to it."

He turned another page, and a phrase leaped out at him, the words so dark they might have been written yesterday. His breath caught. "Sarah." His finger traced beneath the text, careful not to touch it directly. "The Shepherds of the Dark?"

"Who are they?" Sarah asked, curiosity getting the better of her.

"Never heard of them," Alex added. "

"According to this, they're not just keeping secrets – they're working towards something specific." Alex's voice dropped lower as he read. "They're not protecting the old ways; they're trying to break them. It says here they're actively working to 'hasten the great awakening,' to 'return chaos to its rightful place.'"

The lamp light seemed to dim as he spoke the words, and Artemis pressed against his leg, her fur standing on end. A diagram on the facing page showed a circle of thirteen figures, their faces obscured, standing around what looked like a cauldron. But something about the way it was drawn suggested this was no mere historical record – it was a blueprint.

"The Great Awakening," Sarah rolled the words around like they might reveal their meaning through sound alone. Her reporter's notepad sat neglected on her knee, her usual compulsion to document everything forgotten in the weight of the moment. "That's not ominous at all. Any idea what we're talking about here? End of the world? Zombie apocalypse? Really unpleasant Tuesday?"

Alex ran a hand through his already disheveled hair, exhaustion warring with the night's revelations. "I wish I knew. Margaret might, though." He closed the book carefully, its pages seeming to resist being shut. "I'll head over to her place first thing tomorrow. If anyone knows what this means, it'll be her."

Their attention turned to the final item – the key. It lay on the coffee table, its tarnished brass somehow managing to look both ancient and dangerous. The metal caught the lamp light oddly, throwing shadows that didn't quite match its shape. At its head, worked into the intricate metalwork, that same eye stared back at them – the one from the map, the one that shouldn't exist.

"Well, that's not terrifying at all," Sarah muttered, leaning closer but not touching. "What are the odds this opens something we really don't want to open?"

Artemis padded over to sniff at the key, then backed away with a low growl, her tail puffed to twice its normal size. The cat's reaction made the hair on the back of Alex's neck rise.

"Knowing our luck?" He reached for the key, then hesitated, his fingers hovering above its worn surface. "It probably opens exactly what we don't want it to. The question is – do we have a choice anymore?"

A sudden crash shattered the night's quiet, making Artemis leap straight up, her fur bristling. The cat's ears swiveled toward the window, her growl deepening into something almost supernatural. Alex and Sarah exchanged quick glances before moving to the window, the key and its mysteries momentarily forgotten.

The streetlight cast pools of sickly yellow across Mrs. Kourtier's Victorian home opposite, its gingerbread trim throwing strange shadows. Another sound split the darkness – glass breaking, followed by what might have been a struggle, might have been furniture being overturned, might have been something worse.

"That's coming from Mrs. Kourtier's," Alex's voice tightened with concern. The elderly woman had lived there as long as he could remember, her cookie-scented kitchen a sanctuary during his troubled teenage years. "She lives alone since Mr. Kourtier passed."

"Alex—" Sarah grabbed his arm, pointing. The front door stood wide open, swaying slightly in a wind that shouldn't have been able to reach it. No lights showed from within – just darkness that seemed deeper than natural, as if something had sucked all illumination from the house.

They burst out of Alex's front door, the forgotten key glowing faintly warmer on the coffee table behind them. The street felt longer than usual, each step carrying them toward that gaping doorway that waited like an open mouth. Their footsteps echoed off centuries-old buildings, too loud in the artificial quiet that had fallen over the neighborhood.

The closer they got, the more wrong everything felt. No car alarms had been triggered. No neighbors peered out their windows at the disturbance. Even the crickets had fallen silent, as if nature itself was holding its breath.

They stood at the threshold, the darkness from within seeming to reach for them like grasping fingers. The porch boards creaked beneath their feet, the sound unnaturally loud in the strange silence that had fallen over the street.

"Mrs. Kourtier?" Alex's voice carried a forced calm. "It's Alex Kingston from across the street. Are you okay in there?" The darkness swallowed his words without even the courtesy of an echo.

Sarah shifted uneasily beside him. "We should check inside," she whispered, though her voice suggested she'd rather do anything else. "But I left my phone at your place, and it's darker than—" She broke off as Alex raised his hand, palm up.

Light bloomed between his fingers, a soft blue-white glow that pulsed like a captured star. Sarah let out a startled laugh that carried a hint of hysteria. "Right. Of course. Magical flashlight. Because that's just a thing you can do. Any other useful tricks you've been keeping to yourself?"

The light revealed Mrs. Kourtier's living room, usually a sanctuary of academic comfort, transformed into something out of a nightmare. Books that had survived centuries lined the walls, their spines a testament to Martha's lifelong obsession with Salem's true history. Papers carpeted every surface, covered in her distinctive handwriting – notes about local legends, folklore, and things that weren't supposed to exist.

But violence had invaded this scholarly haven. A Victorian reading chair lay on its side, one leg splintered as if thrown. Shards of what had been an antique Tiffany lamp glittered on the carpet like fallen stars. And there, leading toward the kitchen's darkness, drag marks scarred the Persian rug – parallel lines that spoke of resistance, of someone being pulled against their will.

"Alex," Sarah's voice shook slightly as she pointed to a notebook lying open near the marks. "The page it's open to... look at the symbol she was drawing."

There, sketched repeatedly across the paper with increasing urgency, was the same eye that marked their map, that adorned their key. The final drawing was unfinished, the pen's stroke trailing off violently across the page.

The magical light in Alex's palm flickered, as if something in the house was trying to swallow it too.

"Sarah." Alex's voice barely carried above a whisper, but its urgency made her spin around. His magical light cast strange shadows over the scattered papers as he crouched down, pointing to something that made his blood run cold.

There, drawn with the desperate precision of someone racing against time, was that same haunting eye. But this version was different – more complete somehow. Concentric circles radiated out from it like ripples in dark water, each ring covered in symbols that seemed to shift when viewed directly. The eye itself had been sketched over a map of Salem's oldest district, its pupil centered precisely on a location that made Alex's magical senses hum with recognition.

"Another map," Sarah breathed, kneeling beside him. Her reporter's instincts warred with growing dread as she studied the markings. "But these circles... they look almost like—"

"Like wards," Alex finished. "Or boundaries." His finger traced the outermost ring, and he could have sworn he felt energy spark against his skin. "And look where the eye is centered."

"The old shipping warehouse district," Sarah murmured. "Where all those homeless people reported seeing..." She trailed off, neither of them needing to finish the thought.

"I think we just found what that key opens." Alex's light flickered again, and somewhere deeper in the house, something that shouldn't have been able to move shifted in the darkness. "And I think whatever took Mrs. Kourtier knew she'd found it too."

For a moment, they just stared at each other, the weight of understanding passing between them without words. The magical light caught the gleam in Sarah's eyes – equal parts journalistic fire and primal fear. They were pulling at threads now, and something ancient was unraveling. Alex could feel it in the air, taste it in the gathering darkness.

The crash exploded through the silence like a gunshot, making them both lurch upright. Sarah's hand found Alex's arm, her fingers digging in with unexpected strength. Through Mrs. Kourtier's bay window, they could see her metal garbage can lying on its side, its contents strewn across her normally immaculate lawn like the aftermath of a tiny tornado. But there, at the edge of Alex's magical light, something moved – a small silhouette that shouldn't have been there, its movements too precise, too deliberate for any child. As it slipped into the deeper shadows between houses, Alex caught a glimpse of eyes that reflected his light like polished obsidian.

The magical light in his palm guttered like a candle in a draft, and somewhere in the house behind them, floorboards creaked beneath feet too small to belong to Mrs. Kourtier.

"Alex." Sarah's voice cracked with barely contained panic. "We need to go. Now."

They fled Mrs. Kourtier's house, trying not to run but not quite managing to walk, the weight of unseen eyes pressing against their backs. The street between the houses seemed to stretch like taffy, each step taking them both too long and not long enough to reach Alex's door. Only when they were inside, locks clicking into place, did they let themselves breathe again.

Sarah's hands shook slightly as she finished her call to the police, her reporter's skill for crafting narratives coming in handy as she described hearing a disturbance, finding an open door — nothing about small figures in the shadows or eyes that shouldn't exist. Nothing about symbols that seemed to watch them from the pages of ancient maps.

The sharp chirp of Alex's phone cut through the room's tension like a knife, making them both jump. Sarah's nervous laugh died in her throat as she saw Alex's face drain of color, his eyes fixed on the screen's glow.

"Who is it?" she started to ask, but the words faded as she leaned in to read the message. The number was unfamiliar, but the words carried a weight that seemed to press against their skin:

"The hour grows late. The Shepherds prepare the way. Find the door, stop the ritual. The fate of Salem hangs in the balance. - J"

The signature hung there, that single letter somehow more ominous than all the words that came before it.

The autumn night pressed against the windows, thick with promises and threats, with mysteries begging to be unraveled. Alex stood there, the phone still warm in his hand, its message burning behind his eyes. For the first time since black eyes had appeared at his door, since silver tears had fallen from a moonless sky, he felt something stir beneath the dread – a dangerous spark of hope.

They were close now. He could feel it in his bones, in the way his magical senses hummed like plucked strings. The truth lay scattered before them in ancient maps and prophecies, in coded warnings and brass keys that waited to unlock doors that perhaps should stay sealed. Salem's fate balanced on a knife's edge, teetering between salvation and an darkness older than the town itself.

Sarah caught his eye, and he saw his own determination reflected there. Whatever waited in the shadows, whatever the Shepherds had planned, whatever door needed to be found – they would face it together. The night might be dark and full of horrors, but they had something the darkness didn't: they had purpose, they had each other, and most dangerous of all, they had nothing left to lose.

Artemis purred, the sound carrying that strange resonance that spoke of magic and warning both, as somewhere in Salem's darkness, children who weren't children at all began to gather.

Chapter Eight

Echoes of the Past

The path to Margaret Holloway's mansion felt different today. The magical gardens that usually burst with supernatural vitality lay subdued beneath a crystalline sheen of early winter frost. Even the singing violets, Margaret's pride and joy, seemed to whisper melancholic harmonies into the bitter morning air.

Alex pulled his coat tighter as he climbed the marble steps, his breath visible in the growing cold. The brass griffin knocker felt like ice against his knuckles. Behind him, dead leaves skittered across the garden path like nature's warning signs.

The door opened to reveal Margaret Holloway, resplendent in a deep purple velvet dress that seemed to shimmer with barely contained magic. Her silver hair was elegantly coiled atop her head, held in place by what looked suspiciously like enchanted hairpins.

"Alex!" Her face lit up with genuine warmth, though something knowing lurked behind her smile. "What perfect timing, darling. We were just discussing you."

Alex's steps faltered. "We?"

"Come along," Margaret gestured him forward, her bangles chiming like tiny bells. "Into the sitting room."

"Margaret, please tell me you haven't—" Alex's words died in his throat as they rounded the corner. There, perched on the Victorian settee like a queen holding court, sat Adrianna Cromwell. Her silver dress caught the morning light like liquid moonlight, creating a striking contrast against her dark skin. Those eyes that had seen centuries regarded him with amused interest.

"Alex Kingston." Her voice carried the weight of ages, smooth as aged bourbon and twice as potent. "How fascinating to find you at the center of things once again."

"Madame Cromwell." Alex fought the urge to bow – an instinct her presence tended to inspire. "I'm sorry, I didn't mean to interrupt. Margaret, I can come back—"

"Nonsense, dear boy." Margaret's tone brooked no argument as she gestured to a high-backed chair. "You're exactly where you need to be, exactly when you need to be here." She smiled, but it didn't quite reach her eyes. "Please, sit. We have much to discuss."

The grandfather clock in the corner ticked ominously, its hands suggesting a time that didn't quite match any watch in Salem.

Alex spent the next hour recounting the previous night's events, the words spilling out like water breaking through a dam. When he finished, the sitting room fell into a heavy silence, broken only by the irregular ticking of that peculiar grandfather clock.

"The Shepherds of the Dark?" Adrianna's voice carried a weight Alex hadn't expected, as if the mere mention of the name had aged her centuries in moments.

Margaret's fingers tightened around her teacup. "Alex, darling, you're absolutely certain that's what you read? The exact words?"

In response, Alex pulled out his phone, showing them the cryptic message. Then, with careful movements, he retrieved the wooden box from his messenger bag. The carvings seemed to writhe more actively in the presence of such powerful witches.

"Adrianna..." Margaret's voice held a warning.

"I know, Margaret." Adrianna cut her off, her usual diplomatic poise cracking slightly. "If they truly seek the awakening, the Council must be informed immediately." She rose from her seat, the silver dress catching the light like liquid mercury.

"Wait," Alex leaned forward, frustration evident in his voice. "What exactly is this awakening everyone keeps dancing around? What are we really dealing with here?"

The two women exchanged looks heavy with centuries of shared knowledge. Finally, Adrianna settled back into her seat, smoothing her dress with practiced grace.

"Before there was light," she began, her voice taking on the cadence of ancient storytelling, "before there was dark, before there was anything at all, there was the void. And from that void emerged Balor."

"Not emerged," Margaret corrected gently. "Balor was the void given form, chaos incarnate. Neither good nor evil, simply... endless possibility without purpose."

"From this chaos," Adrianna continued, "rose Cerridwen, she who sought to bring order to endless possibility. She saw that without structure, without pattern, all of existence would eventually collapse back into the void."

"The stories say," Margaret added, her voice dropping to barely above a whisper, "that their battle lasted an eternity and no time at all. Reality itself was their battlefield, forming and un-forming with each exchange."

"In the end," Adrianna's eyes grew distant, "Cerridwen realized she couldn't destroy chaos without destroying creation itself. So she bound Balor, using thirteen seals forged from the very fabric of reality."

"And the awakening?" Alex prompted, though part of him dreaded the answer.

"Is what happens," Margaret said grimly, "if those seals ever break."

"So who exactly are these Shepherds of the Dark?" Alex leaned forward, hands clasped together. "Beyond cryptic messages and ancient symbols."

Adrianna's expression darkened, her fingers tracing patterns in the air that made the light bend strangely. "They've been a thorn in the Council's side for centuries. Thirteen members, always thirteen, though their identities remain frustratingly elusive." She paused, considering her next words carefully. "They believe Balor to be the one true god, that Cerridwen's binding was an act of cosmic tyranny rather than salvation. They seek to 'free' him." Her lip curled slightly at the word. "To return all existence to blessed chaos, as they see it."

"Alex." Margaret's voice drew his attention. Her eyes held that particular intensity he'd come to recognize as prelude to uncomfortable revelations. "The prophecy I showed you – I wasn't entirely forthcoming about its subject. It speaks of Balor's awakening, yes, but also of its prevention. The convergence of Kingston and Holloway bloodlines isn't just possibility – it's necessity."

"Wait." Alex's mind raced to keep up. "What makes our families so special? Why Kingston and Holloway specifically?"

"Oh, my dear boy." Adrianna's voice softened with something like maternal affection, though her eyes remained ancient and knowing. "Every witch walking this earth is a child of Cerridwen. She is the mother of all magic, the source from which our power flows." She gestured, and the air between them shimmered with illustrations of her words. "When she created the Cauldron Born – what we now call witches – she began with five families: Cromwell, Blackwood, Brighton, Kingston, and Holloway."

"And of those five," Margaret added, her voice carrying both pride and concern, "the Kingston and Holloway lines reach back furthest. Our families were the first to drink from her cauldron, the first to accept the duty of maintaining balance between order and chaos." She reached for Alex's hand. "Which makes you and Nathan uniquely positioned to either prevent catastrophe..."

"Or inadvertently help cause it," Adrianna finished grimly.

The fluorescent lights hummed overhead like restless spirits, casting harsh shadows across the collage of headlines and photographs that wallpapered the Salem Gazette's office. Old stories stared back at Alex from their frames – local triumphs, minor scandals, all seeming trivial now compared to the weight of what he'd learned that morning. His coffee had gone cold hours ago, forgotten as his mind turned Margaret and Adrianna's words over and over like worry stones.

The familiar symphony of the newsroom – keyboards clacking, phones ringing, the ancient printer's asthmatic wheeze – felt oddly distant, as if he were hearing it all through water. Around him, reporters chased their deadlines, blissfully unaware that the fate of reality itself might hinge on a prophecy involving him and—

"Earth to Alex?" Sarah's voice cut through his reverie as she perched on the edge of his desk, nearly knocking over his untouched coffee. Her usual energetic demeanor seemed subdued, dark circles under her eyes suggesting she'd slept about as well as he had. "You've been staring at that same paragraph for twenty minutes. What did Margaret—"

The newsroom's scanner crackled to life, its usual static-filled chatter suddenly focusing into sharp clarity. "All units respond... missing person reported at 156 Essex Street... juvenile female, approximately age twelve..."

The world seemed to stop. Sarah's hand found Alex's shoulder, gripping tight enough to hurt. Around them, the newsroom continued its normal bustle, but all they could hear was the dispatcher's voice listing details that felt horrifyingly familiar.

"Dark hair, last seen wearing a blue coat... witness reports... unusual circumstances..."

"Alex," Sarah's voice dropped to barely above a whisper. "That's right around the corner from where Mrs. Kourtier—"

The overhead lights flickered once, and for just a moment, Alex could have sworn he saw small handprints appear in the frost forming on his office window – handprints that disappeared when he blinked, leaving only the impression of dark eyes watching from somewhere just out of sight.

Tom Marshton materialized from his office like a storm front, his bulk casting strange shadows under the fluorescent lights. Something about his movement seemed too fluid today, too calculated for his usual bearlike gait. He stopped at Alex's desk, his eyes holding an intensity that didn't quite match his casual tone.

"Kingston." Tom's voice carried its usual gruffness, but there was an undercurrent of something else – something that made Alex's magical senses prickle with warning. "Got a lead for you." He glanced at Sarah, then back to Alex, his eyes lingering just a fraction too long. "There's a woman at Danvers State Hospital. Been there fifteen years."

He placed a manila folder on Alex's desk with deliberate care. "Interesting story. Claims she had an... encounter with these 'children' everyone's whispering about lately." The way he said 'children' made the air temperature seem to drop several degrees. "My source says she's the only known survivor of whatever happened that night. Well, the only one who kept her sanity, anyway."

Tom's fingers drummed against the folder, and Alex noticed his editor's usually impeccable manicure was ragged, as if he'd been chewing his nails. "Funny thing is," he continued, his casual tone belied by the tension in his shoulders, "nobody seems to remember how she got to the hospital in the first place. The admitting paperwork is... incomplete."

Sarah opened her mouth to ask a question, but Tom was already turning away, his movements just a bit too precise. "Check it out," he called over his shoulder. "Could be nothing. Could be everything." The light caught his eyes strangely as he glanced back one final time. "Just... watch yourselves. Some stories don't want to be told."

"Is it just me, or is Tom getting weirder by the day?" Sarah's voice followed their editor's retreating form. "Like he's trying too hard to seem normal."

"Listen," Alex gathered his coat, lowering his voice. "Come by my place tonight. You need to hear what Margaret told me this morning. It's..." He glanced around the newsroom. "It's bigger than we thought. Way bigger."

The transition from Salem's autumn-painted streets to Danvers State Hospital's institutional sterility hit like a physical wall. Gone were the warm oranges and reds of falling leaves, replaced by endless corridors of mint green and stark white. The air itself felt different here – processed, recycled, carrying that particular blend of disinfectant and despair unique to psychiatric facilities.

Dr. Eliza Foster's heels clicked against the linoleum like a metronome, the sound bouncing off walls that had witnessed decades of human suffering. Her silver hair was pulled back in a severe bun that somehow softened her sharp features rather than emphasizing them.

"Thank you for making time to see me, Dr. Foster," Alex kept his voice low as they passed rooms with small windows – some dark, some occupied by shadows that might have been people.

"Mr. Marshton can be quite..." she paused, selecting her words with clinical precision, "persuasive when he wants something." She glanced sideways at Alex, her grey eyes carrying years of carefully catalogued observations. "Though I must admit, your interest in Mrs. Abernathy intrigues me. Her case is rather... unique in my experience."

Something in her tone made Alex's magical senses stir uneasily. Through a nearby window, he caught a glimpse of a patient drawing on the wall with what looked like charcoal – perfect circles, over and over, each with a dark center that might have been an eye.

Dr. Foster followed his gaze and quickly steered him down another corridor. "This way, Mr. Kingston. Mrs. Abernathy's room is just ahead. Though I should warn you – she hasn't spoken to anyone in nearly three years. Not since the last time the children visited."

Dr. Foster paused outside a set of double doors marked 'Recreation Room B,' her hand hovering over the handle. The institutional lighting caught the silver threads in her hair as she turned to Alex, her professional demeanor softening slightly.

"Before we go in, Mr. Kingston," her voice dropped to barely above a whisper, "I need you to understand something about Mrs. Abernathy." She glanced through the door's wire-reinforced window. "Fifteen years is a long time to live with trauma. The woman you're about to meet... reality bends differently for her now." A slight furrow appeared between her brows. "Some days are better than others. Today seems good, but please – tread carefully."

Alex nodded, trying to project a reassurance he didn't quite feel. The weight of Tom's manila folder seemed to burn in his jacket pocket.

The recreation room struck him as almost aggressively cheerful, with its butter-yellow walls and large windows that faced the hospital's maple-lined grounds. Sunlight streamed in, creating pools of warmth on the institutional carpet. Patients drifted through these sunshine islands like quiet ghosts – some reading dog-eared paperbacks, others engaged in endless games of solitaire, a few simply swaying to music only they could hear.

In the far corner, partially sheltered by a large potted fern, sat a woman who seemed to have faded like an old photograph. Her white hair caught the sunlight like spider silk, her thin fingers methodically sorting through puzzle pieces spread before her. The puzzle, Alex noticed with a chill, appeared to be entirely black.

"Clara?" Dr. Foster's voice carried the gentle authority of long practice. "Clara Abernathy? There's someone here who'd like to speak with you."

The elderly woman's hands stilled over her puzzle. When she looked up, Alex felt his breath catch – her eyes held a clarity that seemed almost painful in its intensity, like looking directly into a bright light.

"The reporter," she said, her voice surprisingly strong. "The one who sees them too." Her fingers resumed their movement through the puzzle pieces, but her eyes never left Alex's face. "I've been waiting for you to come ask about the children."

Behind them, the recreation room's door clicked shut with a finality that made Alex's skin prickle.

"Emily." Mrs. Abernathy breathed the name like a prayer, like something precious and fragile that might shatter if spoken too loudly. "No one's mentioned my Emily in years." Her fingers traced the edge of a puzzle piece, over and over, a nervous habit born from years of institutional routine. "They all think I'm crazy, you see. Easier to believe that than to admit what really happened. But you..." Her eyes found Alex's with unsettling clarity. "You've seen them too, haven't you? The children who aren't children at all."

Alex settled into the chair across from her, the plastic squeaking in protest. The memory of Halloween night rose unbidden – that jack-o'-lantern appearing in his locked apartment, its eyes carved impossibly deep, gleaming with a darkness that swallowed light. He pushed the thought away, focusing on the woman before him.

"Please," he said softly. "Tell me what happened that night."

Mrs. Abernathy's gaze drifted to the window, where autumn leaves danced against a sky that suddenly seemed too bright, too normal for the story she was about to tell. "It was such an ordinary evening. That's what I remember most – how ordinary it all was. Emily was eight." A smile touched her lips, brief but genuine. "She had just lost her front tooth, was so proud of the gap in her smile. I was tucking her in when..." Her hands stilled on the puzzle. "When we heard the knock."

She drew a shaky breath, and Alex noticed the room had grown quieter, as if the other patients sensed the weight of what was coming. "Emily was always trying to help. 'I'll get it, Mommy!' she said. I can still hear her little feet on the hardwood, running to answer..." Her voice cracked slightly. "I heard her giggling at first, talking to someone. But then... then her laugh changed. It became something else. Something scared."

Mrs. Abernathy's fingers began moving again, faster now, sorting black puzzle pieces with growing agitation. "I ran to the door. There they stood – a boy and girl, maybe Emily's age. But wrong. All wrong. Their clothes were old, like from a photograph I once saw of children in the 1940s. And their eyes..." She shuddered, and Alex felt the temperature in the room seem to drop. "Their eyes were like looking into empty space. Not just black – but endless. Like falling into nothing forever."

"What happened then?" Alex barely recognized his own voice, rough with tension.

The puzzle piece in Mrs. Abernathy's hand snapped in two, but she didn't seem to notice. Outside, a cloud passed over the sun, and for just a moment, all the shadows in the room seemed to point toward them like accusing fingers.

"They asked to come in," Mrs. Abernathy's voice dropped to a hoarse whisper, her fingers white-knuckled around the broken puzzle piece. "Their voices... they weren't child voices at all. Like something ancient wearing a child's words like an ill-fitting mask. Emily started backing away – my brave, helpful Emily, suddenly terrified. I tried to close the door, but..." She swallowed hard. "It was like trying to push against the ocean."

Tears carved silent paths down her weathered cheeks. "Then Emily just... changed. The fear drained from her face. She walked toward them like a marionette, strings pulled by something I couldn't see. I screamed her name, lunged for her, but—" Her hands made a helpless gesture. "There was nothing there. Just air where my daughter should have been. Then they were gone, all three of them, leaving nothing but empty night and my screams."

"The police said I must have..." Her voice cracked. "That I had to have... my own Emily..." Fresh tears welled up. "Fifteen years they've kept me here, waiting for a confession I'll never give, because it's not what happened."

Alex reached across the table, covering her trembling hand with his own. "I believe you, Mrs. Abernathy."

Her head snapped up, eyes suddenly sharp as cut glass. "Because you've seen them, haven't you? The ones with void-dark eyes?"

A commotion erupted by the windows before Alex could respond. A young man in hospital whites stood rigid with terror, pointing at something beyond the glass. "They're here!" His scream shattered the room's artificial calm. "The dark-eyed ones are watching!"

Alex bolted to the window, heart thundering against his ribs. There, at the edge of the hospital grounds where autumn light seemed to fade into unnatural shadow, stood two small figures. Even at this distance, their eyes were visible – perfect circles of absolute darkness that seemed to pull at his soul. He blinked, and they vanished like smoke in wind, leaving only bare trees swaying in a breeze that hadn't been there moments before.

"Mr. Kingston." Mrs. Abernathy's voice behind him made him jump. Her grip on his arm was like iron, belying her frail appearance. "They've chosen you now." Her words carried the weight of prophecy. "Just like they chose Emily. Just like they chose James."

The world seemed to tilt sideways. "My father? How could you possibly—"

But the clarity had already fled from her eyes, replaced by the vacant stare of someone lost in memories too painful to fully remember. "Emily?" she called softly to the empty air. "Sweetheart, is that you? Mommy's been waiting so long..."

Outside, the maple leaves began to fall, though there was no wind to dislodge them.

Dr. Foster swept in with practiced efficiency, her voice carrying the soothing tones reserved for agitated patients. But Alex barely registered her presence, his mind spinning like a compass near a lodestone. The mention of his father's name had cracked something open inside him – a door he'd kept firmly shut for ten years. How could this woman, locked away in an institution for fifteen years, know anything about James Kingston's disappearance?

The recreation room's cheerful yellow walls suddenly felt suffocating, the autumn sunlight too harsh against his eyes. Other patients had gathered at the windows now, their faces pressed against the glass like pale moths drawn to light. But they weren't looking out – they were looking up, at something Alex couldn't quite bring himself to see.

His phone vibrated against his chest, the sensation jolting him back to reality. Sarah's name flashed on the screen, along with words that made his stomach drop: "Alex, you need to see this."

The drive from Danvers State felt endless, Mrs. Abernathy's words echoing in Alex's mind like a broken record. The autumn afternoon had taken on a strange quality, as if reality itself was holding its breath. When he finally pulled up to Sarah's building, she was already on the steps, her usual energetic presence subdued by something that made his magical senses hum with warning.

Then he saw it. Sitting innocently beside her like some kind of macabre welcome gift – another carved pumpkin. Its eyes caught the fading daylight wrong, seeming to swallow it rather than reflect it. As Alex approached, those dark hollows appeared to track his movement, like the eyes in old portraits that follow you across a room.

"Sarah?" The tension in his voice matched the rigid set of her shoulders.

"You're not going to believe this," she said, but her attempt at her usual reporter's excitement fell flat, undermined by the tremor in her hands as she reached for something beneath the pumpkin. "It was here when I got home. Just... waiting."

The pumpkin's surface bore an inscription, the letters carved with unsettling precision: "The past holds the key. Time is a circle." The words seemed to shift slightly when viewed directly, as if trying to rearrange themselves into other messages.

Sarah pulled out an aged envelope, its paper the color of old bones. "There's more."

The photograph inside made Alex's world tilt sideways. The image showed the old Salem Library, its Victorian architecture barely changed from today. But it was the people in the photograph that made his breath catch – faces from different times converging impossibly in one moment. His father, James Kingston, young and vital, stood near the center. And beside him...

"That's her." The words came out as barely more than breath. "That's Mrs. Abernathy. But this picture... it can't be more than ten years old. She looks exactly the same as she did today."

The crack split the autumn air like a gunshot, making them both jump. The pumpkin had split perfectly down its center, as if cleaved by an invisible blade. Where pale flesh and seeds should have been, a small key nestled in darkness — ancient brass that seemed to drink in what little daylight remained.

"It's identical," Sarah breathed, pulling the key from the box out of her pocket. The two pieces of metal seemed to resonate with each other, creating a subtle hum that made Alex's magical senses prickle.

"Who's orchestrating this?" Alex ran a hand through his hair, frustration evident in every movement. "The box, the messages, the photo — it's like someone's laying out breadcrumbs, but to what?"

"Alex." Sarah's voice carried that particular tone she used when approaching a difficult story angle. "What if... what if it's James? Your father?"

The suggestion hit him like a physical blow. "Sarah, don't." His voice came out rougher than intended. "He's gone. Dead. Everyone says so — Margaret, the Council, even my mother."

"Yeah?" Sarah's eyebrows rose in that familiar challenging arch. "And a month ago, everyone would have said magic was impossible. Yet here we are, with carved pumpkins that split themselves open and keys that hum with power." She gestured at the photograph. "Time clearly isn't working the way we thought it did."

"Sarah." Alex's voice dropped low, weighted with years of painful acceptance. "There's no such thing as time magic. It's one of the fundamental laws – even Margaret says it's impossible. The past is past. Dead is dead." But even as he spoke the words, he couldn't help noticing how the two keys seemed to pulse in sync, like twin hearts beating to a rhythm older than time itself.

The setting sun cast long shadows across Sarah's steps, and in their darkness, small footprints appeared and disappeared, leading nowhere.

November bled into December, carrying with it the weight of uncovered secrets and growing dread. While Alex and Sarah pieced together fragments of an ancient threat, Salem wrapped itself in holiday cheer, seemingly deaf to the whispers of darkness beneath its cobblestones.

The town square had undergone its annual transformation overnight, as if trying to ward off shadows with pure festivity. Twinkling lights draped the colonial-era buildings like strings of captured stars. A massive Christmas tree dominated the center, its ornaments catching the winter sun in brief flashes of gold and red. Wreaths adorned every lamppost, their ribbons dancing in the December wind, while fresh snow blanketed the ground in deceptive innocence.

Alex sat at his desk in the newsroom, fingers hovering over his keyboard as he tried to inject appropriate holiday enthusiasm into his parade coverage. How did you write about Christmas floats and marching bands when you knew what lurked in the spaces between normality?

The newsroom door crashed open with enough force to rattle the framed headlines on the wall. Tom Marshton stormed through like a gathering storm, his usual bearlike presence twisted into something darker. His movements were jerky, almost mechanical, as if his body wasn't quite under his control. Without acknowledging anyone, he vanished into his office. The slam of his door made the blinds rattle.

"Jesus!" Alex nearly knocked over his coffee as Sarah materialized beside his desk.

"Did you see that? Tom looks like he's about to explode." She lowered her voice, leaning closer. "And did you notice his eyes? For a second there, they almost looked..."

She didn't finish the thought. She didn't need to.

Through Tom's office blinds, they could see their editor's silhouette pacing, his shadow sometimes seeming to move independently of his body.

Alex drifted to the newsroom's window, drawn by some instinct he couldn't name. Salem lay beneath its fresh blanket of snow like a picture postcard come to life. Christmas lights winked from every eave and window, their multicolored glow reflecting off the pristine white ground. Wreaths and garlands transformed colonial facades into gingerbread houses, while ribbon-wrapped lampposts cast pools of warm light onto empty sidewalks.

It should have been beautiful. Instead, the holiday cheer felt like a thin veneer, a bright disguise stretched over something ancient and hungry. Each twinkling light seemed to cast twice as many shadows, and in those shadows...

He shook his head, trying to focus on the familiar sight of his hometown in winter. But his magical senses hummed a warning, like the vibration of a plucked string. There, across the street, between the pools of lamplight, stood a small figure. Snow gathered on its shoulders but didn't melt, and the cheerful holiday lights reflected in its eyes like stars drowning in infinite darkness.

As Alex watched, unable to look away, it raised one small hand in greeting – a child's gesture made horrifying by its mechanical precision. Then a delivery truck passed between them, and when it cleared, the figure had vanished. But the prints it left in the snow didn't lead anywhere, as if their maker had simply ceased to exist.

Behind him, in Tom's office, something that wasn't quite a shadow moved against the blinds.

Chapter Nine

Winters Cold, Flame Rekindled

December crawled forward with glacial inevitability, each day a blur of ancient texts and false leads. The upcoming Gala loomed over Alex, another night he had to face Nathan, who he thought was still angry with him. The thought alone, made Alex feel a bit of guilt deep in the pit of his stomach.

Alex stood before his bathroom mirror, fighting a losing battle with his tie. The reflection that stared back seemed to belong to a stranger – shadows under his eyes that hadn't been there a month ago, new lines etched around his mouth from too many nights of worried frowning. His phone chirped with Sarah's message: "On my way! Can't believe I'm finally going to one of Margaret's famous galas!!!"

He couldn't help but smile at her enthusiasm, even as his stomach twisted. If she only knew what really gathered at Margaret's celebrations, the ancient powers that danced beneath crystal chandeliers...

His front door opened with its familiar creak, but the woman who stepped through it made him do a double-take. Sarah Chen had transformed herself into something out of a fashion magazine. Her usually practical dark hair was swept up in an elegant twist that emphasized her high cheekbones. She'd traded her reporter's notebook for a clutch that sparkled like captured starlight. The dress – deep emerald silk that seemed to flow like water – made her look less like a determined journalist and more like a dangerous secret wrapped in expensive fabric.

Her triumphant entrance stuttered to a halt as she took in his appearance. "Alexander Kingston." Her voice carried the same tone she used when grilling corrupt officials. "Please tell me you're not wearing jeans and a hoodie to Margaret Holloway's Christmas Gala." She gestured at his casual attire with elegant fingers that sparkled with borrowed jewelry. "Tell me this is just some weird pre-party outfit and you have a tux hidden somewhere."

"I was going to change," he protested weakly, but Sarah was already pushing past him toward his bedroom, muttering something that sounded suspiciously like "magical powers but no fashion sense" under her breath.

"Fine." Alex's patience finally snapped along with his fingers. Magic shimmered around him like heat waves, transforming his casual wear into elegant evening attire. The black suit fit perfectly, each line crisp and precise, while the sapphire vest and bow tie made his blue eyes practically glow. His usually unruly blonde hair smoothed itself into a stylish sweep that looked effortlessly sophisticated. "Better?" He turned to Sarah with a hint of smugness, straightening his newly manifested cuffs.

Sarah's jaw dropped, outrage warring with disbelief on her perfectly made-up face. "Are you kidding me?" She gestured wildly at herself, nearly dropping her clutch. "I spent THREE HOURS on this look! Do you know how long it took to get this twist right? The YouTube tutorial alone was forty-five minutes!" Her eyes narrowed dangerously. "You mean to tell me you could have just..." She mimicked his finger snap with considerably less magical effect. "...and POOF, instant glamour?"

Twenty minutes later, as Alex navigated his car through Salem's snow-dusted streets, Sarah was still going strong. "I had to watch five different videos just to figure out this smoky eye effect." She jabbed an accusatory finger at him. "And don't even get me started on the dress alterations. Do you know how hard it is to find a tailor on short notice?"

"The dress looks amazing," Alex offered diplomatically, trying not to laugh.

"Don't you dare compliment me right now, Alexander Kingston. I'm still processing the fact that you let me struggle with false eyelashes when you could have just..." Another indignant finger snap punctuated the winter air.

A group of carolers on the corner turned to stare as they passed, Sarah's voice carrying clearly through the closed car windows: "THREE HOURS, ALEX. THREE!"

The Hawthorne Hotel stood like a glittering jewel in Salem's winter night, its Georgian architecture enhanced by what appeared to be normal holiday decorations but were, to magical eyes, far more spectacular. Icicles that never melted adorned every window, catching and reflecting light in impossible patterns. Wreaths made from ever-blooming winter roses released subtle enchantments designed to create feelings of warmth and welcome. Even the snow falling around the hotel seemed choreographed, each flake performing its part in an intricate dance.

The grand ballroom had transformed itself into a midwinter dream. Elaborate crown moldings concealed protective runes within their swooping designs, while what appeared to be elegant fairy lights were actually tiny luminous beings that occasionally winked at passing guests. Crystal chandeliers drifted overhead like graceful jellyfish, casting ever-shifting patterns that spelled out ancient words of protection across the marble floor.

In one corner, an ice sculpture of Perseus and Medusa seemed to be playing an endless game of magical freeze-tag, each figure moving when the other was still. The serpents in Medusa's hair occasionally hissed at passing guests who looked too closely.

"Last chance to run," Alex muttered, fidgeting with his bow tie. The magical fabric kept trying to readjust itself into what it considered a more aesthetically pleasing shape.

Sarah smoothed down her emerald silk dress, journalist's determination warring with normal-human nervousness. "After everything we've seen, you think a fancy party's going to scare me off?"

"Just... stick close to Margaret," Alex advised. "And try not to stare at the chandelier sprites. They're terrible flirts."

"Darlings!" Margaret Holloway's voice chimed like crystal as she materialized beside them in a sweep of midnight blue silk. Her gown seemed to have captured the entire night sky within its folds – constellations drifted across the fabric, occasionally rearranging themselves into messages that made Alex's magical senses tingle. Her silver-streaked hair had been woven with what looked suspiciously like captured moonbeams, creating a corona effect that made her seem more ethereal than usual.

"You both look absolutely perfect," she beamed, though her eyes held a sharpness that belied her social butterfly act. "Come along now – simply everyone has been asking about you." She linked arms with them both, her grip surprisingly firm. "And do try to avoid the punch bowl for the next few minutes, dears. I believe it's about to recite poetry."

Above them, a chandelier sprite blew Sarah a tiny kiss that left sparkles floating in the air.

Margaret glided through her ballroom like a ship cutting through silk waters, expertly navigating the social currents. "Georgina, darling!" Her voice carried just the right note of delighted surprise as she steered them toward a woman in a dramatic scarlet gown, her flame-red hair teased into a style that suggested she'd taken 'vintage' as a personal challenge.

"You simply must chat with Alex Kingston." Margaret's gentle push was so smooth, Alex found himself beside Georgina before he could protest. "His recent articles have been quite... illuminating about our local situation." The slight emphasis transformed 'local situation' into something far more significant than tourist statistics.

"Oh yes." Georgina extended her hand with theatrical grace, rings glittering with more than mere diamonds. "I was particularly intrigued by your piece on the unusual cold spots around town. Such... precise observations."

Alex brushed his lips against her knuckles, feeling the protective enchantments humming beneath her skin. "You're too kind."

"And Sarah Chen!" Margaret pivoted smoothly as another couple approached, their matching gray formal wear somehow suggesting storm clouds rather than silver. "Richard, Elizabeth – from our historical society. Sarah's one of the Gazette's finest."

The ballroom filled like a champagne flute, bubbling with magical energy barely contained beneath society manners. In the corner, a string quartet created music that seemed to bypass the ears entirely and speak directly to the soul. The violin, Alex noticed, played with passionate precision despite its empty chair, while the cellist's bow left trails of golden notes hanging in the air.

Waiters wove through the crowd with practiced grace, their silver trays etched with patterns that looked decorative but felt watchful. The champagne flutes they carried clinked with a sound that might have been crystal, might have been warning bells. Each server's uniform bore subtle symbols worked into the embroidery – protective sigils disguised as fancy monograms.

Sarah leaned close, pitching her voice below the magical music. "Is that waiter's bow tie actually watching us?"

"Welcome," Alex murmured back, "to high society's magical security system. Try the crab puffs – they're enchanted to detect poisoning attempts."

A passing server winked at them with eyes that shifted color like opals.

"Is that..." Sarah whispered, nodding toward a regal-looking woman in a green velvet gown who seemed to be slightly transparent around the edges.

"Elisabeth Proctor's ghost is a regular guest," Nathan's voice materialized behind them, carrying that particular warmth that always made Alex's magical senses flutter. "Grandmother insists on inviting her. Founding member privileges and all that."

Alex turned and felt his carefully maintained composure slip sideways. Nathan stood there in a jade green tuxedo that shouldn't have worked but somehow did, the crimson vest and bow tie creating a holiday combination that looked less Christmas cliché and more timeless elegance. He'd styled his hair differently, swept back in a way that emphasized his cheekbones and made his green eyes seem even more intense.

That familiar ache bloomed in Alex's chest – the one he'd been trying to ignore for years. The one that made his magic hum like a plucked string whenever Nathan was near. Their eyes met for a moment too long, and Alex felt the weight of everything unsaid between them press against his ribs like a physical thing.

"The ghost is actually quite charming," Nathan continued, his voice carrying a slight tremor that suggested he felt the tension too. "Though she does tend to get a bit passionate about modern witch rights legislation after her third spectral champagne."

Sarah glanced between them, her reporter's instincts picking up on the charged atmosphere. Even the fairy lights seemed to dim slightly, as if giving them privacy in the crowded room.

Above them, a chandelier sprite nudged its neighbor and pointed, clearly gossiping about the obvious tension below.

"Over there," Alex nodded subtly toward a statuesque woman in shimmering purple robes. "That's the real Madame Zelda. Quite different from her tourist-season persona."

Sarah watched, entranced, as the woman lifted her champagne flute in an elegant gesture. The liquid inside twisted into spiraling patterns of prophecy before settling back into ordinary bubbles. "Wait – you mean the fortune teller from the Halloween festival? The one with all the scarves and fake crystal balls?"

"Funny thing about Salem," Alex smiled. "Sometimes the fake psychics are actually real ones in disguise."

"Speaking of drinks," Margaret's voice chimed in as she appeared beside them in a swirl of starlit silk, "the enchanted punch is at the back." Her eyes twinkled with mischief. "Though I should warn you – three glasses and you'll find yourself telling your deepest secrets to the nearest potted plant." She cast a meaningful glance at Alex that made him flush. "Last year, Nathan spent twenty minutes confessing his feelings to a fern."

Alex's heart stuttered at the mention of Nathan's name, and he suddenly found the floating chandeliers fascinating.

"Oh, and darlings?" Margaret added airily, though her eyes held a hint of genuine concern. "Do steer clear of the west corner for the next few minutes. Perseus is about to have his moment with Medusa, and the ice sculpture can be rather... passionate about historical accuracy. Last time, it took hours to defrost the guests who got too close."

In the distance, they heard the distinct sound of ice sword being drawn from an ice scabbard, followed by several elegant guests hastily relocating to safer viewing distances.

Margaret disappeared into the crowd like smoke, leaving Alex and Nathan to play tour guides for Sarah through Salem's magical aristocracy.

"That's Jeremiah Blackwood," Nathan murmured, indicating a distinguished man whose shadow seemed to move independently of its owner. "His family specializes in shadow magic."

"And the woman in silver?" Sarah whispered, scribbling mental notes.

"Diana Brightwater," Alex added, trying to ignore how Nathan's proximity made his magic flutter beneath his skin. "She communes with water spirits. Half the fountains in Salem report to her."

They moved through the crowd like this, their shoulders occasionally brushing, each casual contact sending sparks of awareness through Alex's magical senses. Nathan's cologne carried hints of winter pine and something older, something that made Alex think of frost patterns on windows and first snowfall.

But beneath the glittering surface of the evening – beneath the champagne enchantments and floating chandeliers, beneath the careful dance of old magic and older money – a current of unease rippled. The magical guests kept stealing glances at the grandfather clock, its hands ticking toward midnight with ominous precision. The protective runes worked into the crown molding pulsed stronger with each passing hour, as if preparing for something.

During brief pauses between the ethereal quartet's songs, the winter wind carried sounds through the frosted windows – what might have been carolers, might have been children's voices, might have been neither. The snow falling beyond the ballroom's towering windows seemed to dance with deliberate purpose, each flake part of some vast, cosmic choreography.

"It's almost time," Nathan said softly, his hand brushing Alex's arm in a gesture that might have been accident, might have been intention. His green eyes reflected the floating lights like captured stars. "The solstice is coming."

As midnight drew near, Margaret claimed her place at the ballroom's heart, the floating chandeliers instinctively adjusting their glow to cast her in ethereal light. Her midnight-blue gown rippled with constellations that seemed to align themselves for her speech, while the moonbeams in her hair cast a subtle corona around her elegant figure. The string quartet's final notes dissolved into expectant silence.

"My dear friends," she began, her voice carrying the weight of centuries wrapped in silk. The gathered magical elite – witches, seers, and beings that weren't quite human – leaned forward almost involuntarily, caught in the gravity of her presence. "Welcome to our thirtieth annual holiday celebration in support of Salem's children."

The room erupted in practiced applause. Alex, clapping along, leaned close to Sarah. "She means all children," he whispered, his breath stirring a few escaped strands of her elegant updo. "Magical and mundane. The Order protects everyone, whether they know it or not."

"Your generosity," Margaret continued, her gesture encompassing the room, "has enabled us to foster growth and learning throughout our community." Another wave of applause, during which several floating champagne glasses refilled themselves.

"This year's theme – 'Winter's Light in Darkness' – holds particular significance." Her eyes swept the room, lingering briefly on Alex and Nathan standing perhaps too close together, on Sarah taking mental notes, on the protective runes glowing ever brighter in the moldings. "In times of uncertainty, it is the warmth of community that guides us through the longest nights."

As Margaret wove her speech with the skill of a master enchantress, Alex felt Nathan's hand brush against his, a touch that might have been accident but felt like intention. The contact sent a jolt through his magical senses that had nothing to do with prophecies or solstices. Above them, the chandelier sprites arranged themselves to spell out words of protection in ancient languages, while outside, the snow continued its strange, purposeful dance.

"Walk with me?" Nathan's whispered request came with a gentle touch to Alex's elbow. "The courtyard's enchanted tonight. I could use some air."

They slipped away through French doors that hummed with temperature-controlling spells, stepping into Margaret's masterpiece of magical winter. Snow fell in an endless dance that never quite reached the ground, while roses bloomed defiantly through crystalline frost, their petals catching starlight in impossible ways. The air itself felt charged with possibility.

"Your grandmother's outdone herself," Alex said softly, watching their breath turn to golden mist in the enchanted atmosphere. The comment felt inadequate, a poor substitute for all the words caught in his throat.

"She always does." Nathan drew closer, his warmth more intoxicating than the enchanted punch. "Though I think this year she had extra motivation. With everything that's happening..." He looked skyward, where stars peeked through the spelled snowfall, and Alex watched the light play across features he'd memorized years ago.

"Nathan?" The tightness in Alex's chest threatened to overwhelm him. "What are you—"

"I never stopped loving you." Nathan's words tumbled out like a dam breaking. "Three years, and I never... I couldn't..." His fingers tightened around Alex's. "I just never had the courage to say it."

Alex's world tilted sideways, his magical senses singing with possibility and fear and hope. "What changed?" he managed, his voice rough with emotion.

"Seeing you at the library that day," Nathan's eyes held his with fierce intensity. "When you told me about the children, about telling Sarah our secrets... I realized that if something happened to you, if I lost you without ever saying—"

Alex didn't let him finish. He closed the space between them in a heartbeat, their lips meeting with the inevitability of prophecy fulfilled. Nathan pulled him closer, and their combined magic sparked skyward in arrays of spontaneous light, like private fireworks celebrating years of silence finally broken.

"Well!" Margaret's delighted voice cut through their moment. "It's about time!" She stood in the doorway, resplendent in her star-filled gown, while beside her, Sarah wore the triumphant grin of a reporter who'd just seen her longest-running story finally reach its headline.

Above them, the enchanted snow rearranged itself into hearts, while the roses suddenly bloomed brighter, their petals releasing tiny sparks of joy into the winter night.

The perfect moment exploded with the sound of shattering glass. The crash echoed through the courtyard like a gunshot, followed by screams that carried too much genuine terror to be part of any planned entertainment. Beneath it all, a deeper sound rumbled – like thunder, but wrong somehow, as if the sky itself was being torn.

They moved as one, spinning toward the French doors. Magic crackled to life around them – Margaret's power shimming like captured starlight, Nathan's green-gold energy dancing between his fingers, Alex's blue-white force humming with protective intensity. Sarah pressed close behind them, her reporter's instincts warring with basic survival.

The scene that awaited them stole precious seconds in pure, horrified awe.

Twelve figures stood in perfect formation, arranged like numbers on a clock face. Glass from the shattered skylight rained down around them, but none of the shards seemed to touch their robes – garments that defied natural law, seeming to be crafted from living darkness itself. The fabric writhed and twisted like smoke given form, moving to currents of air that didn't exist in our reality.

But it was their masks that captured the eye, that demanded attention even as instinct screamed to look away. Carved from what appeared to be solidified shadows, each bore a spiral pattern that moved with hypnotic purpose. The designs pulled at the viewer's gaze, drawing it deeper and deeper toward a center that promised infinity but threatened madness.

The elegant party guests had pressed themselves against the walls, their finery suddenly looking garish and artificial compared to these beings of pure darkness. Even the enchanted punch had stopped its poetry recital, the liquid cowering at the bottom of its crystal bowl.

Above them, through the broken skylight, the snow had stopped falling. The night sky beyond showed no stars at all – just an endless, watching void.

The chandelier sprites had gone dark, hiding in their crystal homes, leaving only the otherworldly glow of the intruders' robes to illuminate the scene.

"The Shepherds," Margaret breathed, her voice carrying both recognition and dread. "They've finally shown themselves."

Magic crackled through the ballroom like heat lightning, as Salem's magical elite shed their society manners for something older and more dangerous. The very air seemed to thicken with gathering power, making it hard to breathe.

"Brothers and sisters of Salem." The central figure's voice twisted reality as it spoke, each word spiraling in on itself like the mask he wore. The sound bypassed ears entirely, resonating directly in the mind. "The age of suffocating order draws to its close. We, the Shepherds of the Dark, come to herald chaos reborn."

Margaret stepped forward, and though her gown remained unchanged, she suddenly carried the presence of a warrior queen. The constellations in her dress shifted into battle formations, while the moonbeams in her hair blazed like caught lightning. "Salem cast your kind out generations ago," her voice rang with ancient authority, making the floating chandeliers chime in harmony. "Your corruption has no place in these halls."

"Old laws fade, Margaret Holloway." The spokesman's laugh rippled through multiple dimensions. "The veils thin. The children of night walk freely once more." He raised his arms in a gesture that sent reality shivering like disturbed water. "What was sealed shall be broken. What was chained shall dance free."

Alex and Nathan moved through the crowd with careful precision, years of unspoken connection allowing them to coordinate without a word. Their magic resonated together, stronger now that truth had finally been spoken between them. They took up positions at opposite sides of the room, creating a triangle of power with Margaret at its apex.

Sarah pressed herself against a wall, her reporter's notebook forgotten as she watched Salem's glittering society party transform into what it truly was – a gathering of power preparing for war. Even the enchanted roses in their crystal vases turned to face the confrontation, their petals hardening into armor.

"The prophecy is not yours to twist." Adrianna Cromwell's voice cut through the tension like a blade of pure authority. She stepped forward, her silver dress now resembling liquid moonlight. "When Kingston and Holloway blood unites, the seal shall be renewed. That is written."

"Ah, Madame Cromwell." The lead Shepherd's voice carried mocking reverence. "Still clinging to old words? The Order of Salem's time has ended." His contempt twisted the air as he spat out "Cauldron Born" like a curse. "Your borrowed power fades. The true god awakens."

"The choice belongs to us." Nathan's voice rang out clear and strong, drawing all eyes to where he stood. The jade green of his tux seemed to glow with internal light, magic radiating from him in waves.

The Shepherd's mask turned with unnatural fluidity, its spiral patterns accelerating hypnotically. "Does it?" Pure malice dripped from each word. "Are you so certain what choices were made long ago?" His laugh shattered several ice sculptures, sending razor-sharp shards skittering across the marble floor. "Why don't you ask your father, Alex Kingston?" The mask's spiral contracted like a cruel smile. "Oh, that's right... you can't."

Raw power surged through Alex, grief and fury combining into pure magical force that made the air around him crackle. Nathan's hand found his, their fingers intertwining, and their combined magic erupted in an aurora of blue-white and green-gold light that spiraled around them like protective wings.

"Now, now." The Shepherd raised his shadow-wrapped hands in mock surrender as Salem's magical elite moved into battle formations around the room. "We haven't come to fight. Not yet. We're merely..." his mask turned toward the enchanted windows where the snow had stopped falling, hanging suspended in the air like frozen stars. "Setting the stage."

The Shepherds moved as one, their robes sweeping upward in a coordinated gesture that created a maelstrom of living darkness. The vortex of shadow magic blinded everyone for one terrible moment. When sight returned, they had vanished – but their presence lingered like a scar on reality itself.

The ballroom's elegant splendor lay in ruins. Warning runes blazed crimson in the moldings, while shattered ice sculptures bled their enchanted essence into the air like dying stars. Where the twelve had stood, a spiral pattern had been seared into the marble floor, rotating counter-clockwise with inexorable purpose.

"Well," Margaret's voice cut through the stunned silence, her fingers snapping to restore her battle-ready gown to its previous elegance. "I dare say this wasn't quite the entertainment I had planned for the evening." But the attempt at levity couldn't mask the deep concern in her eyes as she watched Alex and Nathan, their hands still clasped, magic still shimming around them like aurora.

As Salem's magical elite worked to repair the physical damage and reinforce the weakened wards, Sarah's reporter instincts caught something others had missed. "Alex?" Her voice carried a note of dread. "That Christmas tree of Margaret's – wasn't there a partridge at the top?"

Alex turned, studying the towering tree with growing unease. Where the golden partridge had perched proudly just hours ago, a raven now sat, carved from what appeared to be solid darkness. Its eyes gleamed with malevolent intelligence.

Twin gasps cut through the air as Adrianna and Margaret made the connection. "'When ravens come to rest where doves once stood,'" Adrianna quoted, her voice heavy with recognition.

"The silver tears on Halloween," Alex's words tumbled out as pieces clicked into place. "And now tonight – both sabbats. Samhain was the beginning, and now Yule..." His voice trailed off as the implications settled like frost.

"It means, my dear," Adrianna's voice carried centuries of concern, "we have until Ostara to prevent what they've set in motion." She looked up through the shattered skylight where silver tears continued to fall from a starless void. "The wheel of the year turns, and with each spoke, their power grows."

The raven atop the tree turned its head to watch them, and somewhere in the distance, children who weren't children began to laugh.

"The Black Eyed Children," Sarah's voice shook slightly, though her determination remained steady. "They're not just connected to the Shepherds – they're working with them, aren't they?"

"Different faces of the same darkness," Margaret sighed, absently adjusting a moonbeam that had come loose in her hair. "The children harvest what makes us human – experiences, memories, the very essence of life." Her eyes grew distant. "The Shepherds seek something far more fundamental – the unraveling of reality itself."

"Together, they form a perfect storm," Adrianna added, her silver dress catching the light of warning runes still pulsing in the moldings. "The children weaken the fabric of humanity while the Shepherds work to tear apart the weave of existence." She gestured at the spiral burned into the marble floor, still slowly rotating. "What one begins, the other completes."

Alex felt Nathan's hand tighten in his. "And we're what stands between them and success?" The question came out softer than he intended, weighted with the understanding that had been building since that first encounter on his doorstep.

The raven atop the Christmas tree turned its obsidian head toward them, and in its eyes, Alex caught a reflection of children standing in the snow – children whose eyes matched the bird's in their perfect, endless darkness.

The gala's chaos gradually faded into the comfortable quiet of Alex's living room. A fire crackled in the hearth, its warm light competing with the soft glow of some classic Christmas movie playing on low volume. Sarah had headed home, leaving Alex and Nathan alone with the weight of the evening's revelations.

"What now?" Nathan's question hung in the air like wood smoke.

Alex sank deeper into the couch, exhaustion finally catching up with him. Nathan shifted closer, his warmth more comforting than the fireplace. "Hey," he said softly, studying Alex's face. "You look completely drained."

"I'm scared, Nathan." The admission came out barely above a whisper, as if speaking it too loudly might make it more real. "What if we can't stop what's coming?"

Artemis lifted her head from her perch on the armchair, her green eyes glowing with unusual intensity as she watched them.

Nathan's hand found Alex's cheek, the touch impossibly gentle for someone who had faced down chaos incarnate hours before. "Look at me," he murmured. "I'm here. Right here, because this is exactly where I want to be."

Alex felt himself drifting, his head finding its way to Nathan's chest. The danger wasn't over — the longest night of the year still stretched before them, pregnant with dark possibilities. But here, wrapped in Nathan's arms, he allowed himself one moment of perfect peace.

His last conscious thought was a promise to whatever powers might be listening: whatever came next, they would face it together.

The dream took him slowly at first, reality bleeding away like watercolors in rain. He found himself in a Salem he almost recognized — but wrong, twisted, as if someone had taken his hometown and stretched it just past the breaking point. Empty streets pulsed with light that had no source, while buildings loomed impossibly tall, their windows watching him with patient malice.

Black-light pumpkins marked a path through this nightmare version of Salem, their eyes tracking his movement as he followed their trail to the old library. The Victorian architecture had transformed into something that hurt his eyes to look at, its spires reaching up to claw at a sky that writhed like living shadow.

Inside, the library defied physics and reason. Endless shelves stretched into infinity, books whispering in languages that predated human tongues. And there, at the heart of this impossible space, stood Margaret — but younger, her eyes bright with knowledge that seemed to transcend time itself.

"You're close, Alex." Her voice echoed as if speaking from multiple points in space simultaneously. "But time grows short. The key exists in what was, but the lock awaits in what is."

Alex tried to speak, but dream-logic stole his voice.

Margaret's smile carried centuries of sorrow. "You will understand. But remember – every great magic demands its price. Are you prepared to pay?"

The scene dissolved, reformed. He stood at the park's edge, watching reality tear itself apart. From the resulting chasm rose something that shouldn't exist – a being of pure chaos, its form constantly shifting like smoke in wind. Only its eyes remained constant, ancient and terrible, fixed on Alex with hungry recognition.

"What has begun cannot be undone," it spoke, its voice bypassing his ears to resonate directly in his soul.

Terror froze him in place as darkness reached for him with eager tendrils. But then – warmth, golden light, hope. Nathan appeared beside him, hand extended like a lifeline.

"You're not alone," dream-Nathan's voice cut through the chaos like a blade of pure light. "Whatever comes, we face it together."

As Alex reached for that offered hand, the dream shattered into fragments of prophecy and warning: silver tears falling upward, ravens taking flight from burning trees, children's laughter echoing through empty streets, a key turning in a lock that shouldn't exist, and through it all, those hungry eyes, watching, waiting, growing stronger with each passing hour.

He woke with a gasp, still safe in Nathan's arms, but the dream's warning echoed in his mind like distant thunder.

Chapter Ten

The Warehouse

January claimed Salem like a gray shroud, holiday cheer giving way to leaden skies and bitter winds that remembered older winters. Christmas lights came down, leaving streets eerily bare despite normal activity. Even the magical community seemed subdued, as if recovering from wounds the solstice had left.

Alex stared at his monitor, trying to craft words that would explain Jeremy Martinez's disappearance without revealing the patterns only magical eyes could see. Thirty-two years old, vanished on New Year's Eve while walking his dog. They'd found the animal next morning, shivering despite taking shelter in a heated construction site, its fur rimed with impossible frost.

"Kingston." Tom Marshton's voice made Alex jump slightly. His editor stood by his desk, coffee cup in hand, looking somehow both perfectly normal and subtly wrong, like a photograph that had been edited just enough to make viewers uncomfortable without knowing why. "A word in my office?"

The temperature in Tom's office seemed to drop with each step Alex took inside, despite the radiator's valiant hissing. Ancient headlines stared down from their frames, and Alex could have sworn the text rippled when he wasn't looking directly at them, rearranging itself into messages he didn't want to read.

Tom settled behind his desk with unusual grace, his movements too precise, too calculated for his normally bearish demeanor. "Fascinating patterns emerging in these disappearances," he mused, fingers dancing across papers with deliberate purpose. "The frost, always the frost. And the timing – that delicate moment when day surrenders to night." He looked up, and something ancient stirred behind his eyes. "Rather like the old stories, wouldn't you say, Kingston? The ones mothers used to whisper about children who come out to play when the light fails?"

Alex kept his face carefully blank, though his magical senses screamed warnings. "Old stories?"

"Oh yes." Tom's smile belonged to something that had learned human expressions from careful study rather than natural practice. "Salem's history runs so very deep, especially concerning its younger residents." He leaned forward, his shadow on the wall moving a fraction of a second too slowly. "The Kingston family would know all about that, wouldn't they? Your bloodline has always been... particularly involved in local matters."

Cold fingers of dread traced Alex's spine. The temperature dropped another degree, and frost began to form in impossible patterns on the inside of the office windows. "We've been here a long time," he managed, voice steady despite the magic humming warning beneath his skin.

"Yes," Tom agreed, his eyes reflecting light that wasn't present in the room. "A very long time indeed. Long enough to know that some stories..." he gestured at the newspaper clippings on his wall, where the text was definitely moving now, "aren't just stories at all."

"Indeed. Since before the trials." Tom's smile stretched a fraction too wide. "Though not quite as long as the Holloways." He rolled the name across his tongue like a wine taster sampling a vintage. "Your friend Nathan's family has such an... impressive history of community service."

The implied threat made Alex's magic surge protectively, power crackling just beneath his skin. But before he could respond, the door burst open with deliberate force. Officer Roberts filled the frame, his usual stone-faced expression carved with unusual urgency.

"Marshton." The officer barely acknowledged Alex's presence. "Need a word. Now." Something in his clipped tone suggested more than routine police business.

"Of course, of course." Tom rose with that unsettling new grace, his hands moving with liquid precision as he adjusted his tie. The gesture looked rehearsed, as if he'd studied human movements and was trying to replicate them perfectly. "We'll resume our... discussion later, Kingston. I'm finding your perspective on local matters increasingly fascinating."

Alex made his way to the door, trying to ignore how the temperature seemed to drop with each step. A sound like children's laughter echoed through the office – or perhaps through his mind – impossible to pinpoint, as if it originated from everywhere and nowhere simultaneously.

He glanced back from the doorway. Tom and Roberts stood in close conversation, their expressions intense, but it was their shadows that caught his eye. The dark silhouettes on the wall moved half a second behind their owners, and sometimes made gestures all their own.

Moonlight painted silver paths across Alex's bedroom floor, winter-pale and watching. Artemis claimed her spot at the bed's foot, her purrs carrying that particular resonance they'd taken on since Halloween night – pure protection wrapped in feline contentment, like safety given voice.

Alex settled against the headboard, grateful for his room's familiar comfort after the day's wrongness. Nathan's presence had begun weaving itself into these private spaces – toothbrush paired with his own, preferred shampoo in the shower, reading glasses catching moonlight on the bedside table. Small anchors of domesticity that helped reality feel solid when shadows moved wrong.

"I'm telling you," he called toward bathroom sounds of running water and Nathan's nighttime routine, "it wasn't just what he said about your family's 'community service' – it was how he said it. Like he was savoring some private joke."

"He can't know about our world." Nathan's voice carried doubt despite his words. Water stopped, and he appeared in the doorway wearing Alex's old Salem State shirt, worn soft with memory. "I mean, yeah, Grandmother's been Salem's biggest donor for decades, but—"

"But he knows something." Alex shifted to make room as Nathan claimed his side of their bed. Artemis's purr deepened to include them both in its protective sphere, her magic recognizing family. "The frost patterns, the children after dark – he described them like someone who's seen them up close."

Outside their window, winter pressed cold fingers against glass.

"There's more." Alex turned fully toward Nathan, unease prickling along his skin. "Their shadows – Tom's and Roberts' both. They moved wrong, like... like they were thinking for themselves."

Nathan's hand stilled on Artemis's fur, tension threading through his frame. "That's not possible." His voice carried the weight of old warnings. "Shadow manipulation needs decades of study, unless..."

"Unless what?"

"Unless something touched them." Nathan's words dropped to barely above whisper, as if speaking truth might make it more solid. "Something that remembers what existed before light. Something that lives in pure chaos."

Artemis's head snapped up, ears pivoting toward the window with preternatural focus. They followed her gaze, but saw only moonlight dancing with the protective runes Alex had carved months ago – back when their biggest worry had been keeping normal shadows at bay.

"We need to tell Sarah." Alex settled back against Nathan's chest, drawing comfort from his warmth. "She's been tracking the disappearances, seeing patterns we might have missed. After what happened at the gala..."

"Tomorrow." Nathan pulled him closer, pressing a kiss to his temple. His smile carried love tinged with protective fear. "Right now, just... let me hold you."

Artemis abandoned her post beside them, moving to the window with silent grace. She settled into her guardian stance, tail twitching with ancient purpose, green eyes fixed on darkness with the unblinking focus that reminded Alex why cats had been magic's first guardians, long before humans dreamed of spells.

They found their familiar nighttime position, a puzzle solved through practice – Nathan's arm draped protectively around Alex's waist, their breathing falling into perfect sync. Outside, winter pressed hungry fingers against warded glass, but their bedroom remained a sanctuary of shared warmth and whispered promises.

"We'll sort this out." Sleep softened Nathan's voice, but couldn't hide his protective edge. "Tomorrow brings Sarah's research, Grandmother's wisdom, answers waiting to be found..."

"Mmm." Alex melted deeper into Nathan's embrace, letting love's certainty chase away the day's shadows. "Though I'm betting Margaret cares less about supernatural conspiracies and more about when you'll make this arrangement official."

"God." Nathan's laugh rumbled through both their chests as he pressed drowsy kisses to Alex's temple. "She's probably already transformed my old room into some ancient library. Subtle as a brick through a window, that woman."

At the window, Artemis's eyes blazed emerald green, tracking something that moved through deeper shadows – small figures whose eyes reflected nothing, because they had learned to swallow light long ago.

Morning light filtered through Alex's kitchen windows, catching dust motes that danced like tiny stars. Three coffee cups steamed on the ancient table while Artemis prowled the room's perimeter, her guardian instincts never quite at rest.

"I keep thinking about yesterday." Sarah wrapped her hands around her mug, reporter's instincts warring with disbelief. "Tom's been odd lately, sure, but involved in all this?" She turned to Nathan, who was inhaling toast like he'd forgotten breakfast existed. "What's your take?"

"Theoretically possible." Nathan swallowed hastily at Alex's pointed look. "But connecting your editor to ancient dark forces feels like a stretch. Though..." He paused.

They spent the next half hour building and discarding theories, each possibility feeling simultaneously too fantastic and not fantastic enough. The morning grew older as their coffee grew colder.

"Oh!" Sarah's eyes suddenly lit with that particular fire that meant she'd found something. "Speaking of research – I think I know what that key opens." She pulled her notebook from her bag, flipping to a page dense with her precise handwriting.

"Why do I feel like I'm not going to like this?" Alex's stomach tightened with familiar dread.

"Because you won't." She laid out photocopied newspaper articles, pointing to faded type. "The serial numbers on the brass key? They match a warehouse owned by Augustus Blackwood."

Nathan's coffee froze halfway to his lips. "Blackwood?" The name carried generations of weight. "As in—"

"One of the founding five, yeah." Alex ran a hand through his hair, pieces clicking into place. "Morganna Blackwood sits on the council now – youngest member in centuries, actually. Took her seat two years ago." His brow furrowed. "But Augustus? That name's never come up."

"So." Sarah closed her notebook with practiced finality. "Address is on Thompson Street, down by the old harbor. Figured it's worth checking out, unless you two have better lunch plans?"

Alex caught Nathan's eye across cooling coffee cups, silent understanding passing between them. Artemis chirped a warning from her window perch, but they were already gathering coats against January's bite.

The warehouse district sprawled along Salem's forgotten shoreline, a graveyard of industry where century-old brick rose like ancient monoliths against pewter sky. Alex's car crawled down streets that hadn't seen regular traffic since shipping moved to deeper harbors, wheels crunching rock salt and memories.

"There." Sarah pointed through windshield fog at a building that seemed to absorb light rather than reflect it. Three stories of weathered brick and blind windows, its cornices decorated with symbols that might have been architectural flourishes, might have been warnings. Loading dock doors hung askew on rusted tracks, while fire escapes clung to brick like metal ivy.

"Well," Nathan's voice carried forced lightness, "at least it looks exactly as haunted as we expected."

They parked in the building's vast shadow. Up close, the brickwork revealed patterns too precise to be accidental – protection runes worked into industrial design, wards disguised as decorative cornices. Everything covered by decades of grime and seasalt, yet somehow still humming with dormant power.

Their footsteps echoed through vast emptiness, sounds bouncing off bare brick and rusted support beams. Winters past had left their mark – broken windows, water-stained floors, debris scattered like forgotten memories across concrete.

"Bit underwhelming for an ancient magical warehouse," Alex whispered, though his magical senses hummed warning. "I was expecting at least one eldritch horror to jump out by now."

"There." Nathan's voice carried quiet urgency. "Third floor." A strange glow filtered down through skeletal rafters – not electricity, not sunlight, but something that made their magical senses prickle with recognition.

The metal staircase protested each step with sounds that suggested imminent collapse. "If we die on these stairs," Alex muttered, gripping the questionable railing, "I'm haunting whoever approved this building's safety code."

Three flights brought them to a hallway where darkness pressed closer, held at bay only by that strange light bleeding under a single door. The office beyond stood empty except for one impossible thing: a brass lamp burning on a desk that hadn't seen use in decades, its light falling on a door set into the far wall.

The door's surface bore no handle, no modern lock – just a single keyhole that might have been Victorian, might have been older. The brass key in Alex's pocket grew warm, as if recognizing its purpose after long sleep.

"Well," Sarah's whisper carried equal parts excitement and dread, "I guess we know what that key opens."

Above them, winter wind howled through broken windows like children's laughter, while somewhere in the building's shadows, eyes that reflected no light watched and waited.

The office door's hinges screamed protest, the sound ricocheting through empty space like breaking glass. They froze, waiting for something to answer that awful cry, but only hollow silence pressed back.

The small office felt wrong – dimensions that didn't quite match its external footprint, shadows that retreated too quickly from their flashlight beams. Nathan studied the impossible lamp, its light pulsing slightly like a heartbeat. "This shouldn't be burning," he murmured, magic detecting something ancient in its flame. "No power, no fuel source, no—"

"Guys." Sarah's voice drew their attention to the inner door. Even from several feet away, they felt its cold radiating outward – not winter's bite, but something deeper, older. Alex approached carefully, running sensitive fingers across its surface while his magical senses probed deeper.

"What exactly are you doing?" Sarah's attempt at humor couldn't quite mask her nervous energy.

"Checking for wards." Alex's fingers traced patterns only he could feel. "Old families never left anything important unprotected, but..." He frowned. "I'm not sensing any barriers. Almost like..."

"Like it's waiting for us," Nathan finished quietly.

The brass key slid into the lock with terrible purpose, metal recognizing metal with an audible click. Alex hesitated one heartbeat before turning it, prophecy hanging suspended between action and consequence.

The door swung inward, revealing a chamber that shouldn't have fit within the warehouse's dimensions. A round table dominated the space – not furniture but something older, an altar wearing modern disguise. An oil lantern cast living shadows across scattered artifacts that made their magical senses recoil.

"What in hell..." The words escaped them in perfect unison, their breath visible in suddenly frigid air.

"Alex." Nathan's voice carried quiet dread as he studied the table's surface. "This isn't just a meeting place. These patterns – it's a ritual space."

Children's laughter echoed through empty floors below, the sound bouncing off brick and steel until its source became impossible to locate. Sarah hugged herself against rising chill. "Whatever we're doing here, let's do it fast."

Alex's attention caught on something that seemed deliberately unremarkable – a torn scrap of paper that almost begged to be overlooked. His fingers trembled slightly as he read the faded words:

"R- The Old Quarry---"

The rest had been torn away with surgical precision, but that hollow laughter rising through the building suggested they'd found exactly what they were meant to find.

"We know you're here..." The children's voices wove together, coming from everywhere and nowhere. "We've been waiting, Alex Kingston..."

They backed toward the staircase, artifacts forgotten as darkness pressed closer. The lamp's flame guttered, casting their shadows strange against walls that seemed to lean inward.

Alex's car cut through Salem's dimming streets, leaving the warehouse's watching darkness behind. Winter clouds pressed low and heavy, pregnant with snow that waited like prophecy to fall.

"The note mentioned the old quarry," Alex's knuckles stayed white on the steering wheel. "R....who is that?"

"Finally, an actual lead." Sarah's pen scratched across her notebook, the sound grounding them in normalcy. "Even if it feels like we're being led exactly where someone wants us to go."

Evening painted Salem in watercolor grays by the time Sarah headed home. Alex and Nathan found refuge in their bedroom's warmth, Artemis claiming her space between them like a purring guardian.

"The quarry might be worth exploring." Nathan's voice carried quiet purpose as he traced protection runes in the air above their bed. "Though Sarah's right – this feels less like investigation and more like following breadcrumbs."

They made plans for Valentine's Day, trying to pretend it was just another date, just another adventure. But as darkness claimed their room and sleep drew them under, both felt prophecy clicking into place like tumblers in an ancient lock.

Above them, winter clouds finally released their burden, snow falling in perfect spirals that might have been patterns, might have been warnings.

In Salem's forgotten harbor, where salt-worn warehouses kept centuries of secrets, twelve figures gathered in a chamber that rejected physics' basic laws. Reality bent around their meeting place – a space that existed as both vast cathedral and cramped tomb, its geometry flowing like water in ways that hurt mortal minds to witness. Shadows gathered in corners that shouldn't exist, while angles curved in directions that had no names in human mathematics.

A single kerosene lantern cast the room's only illumination, its flame burning an impossible shade of violet-black that seemed to drink light rather than create it. The fire moved wrong, flickering in patterns that suggested consciousness, casting shadows that sometimes moved before their owners did.

The twelve stood in perfect formation, their robes woven from material that might have been fabric, might have been solidified darkness.

They gathered around a table of ancient oak, its surface carved with spiraling patterns that writhed like living things when caught in direct sight. Objects of power lay arranged across the wood with deliberate precision: a bell jar housing what appeared to be solidified shadow, its contents occasionally pressing against the glass like a caged animal; a compass whose needle danced to magnetic fields from other dimensions; a mirror that reflected visions of places that couldn't exist in any sane reality; and at the center, a book bound in material that drank light like a dying star.

"The prophecy unfolds." The words spiraled from one figure's hood, twisting through the air like smoke given voice. "Each piece falls into its predetermined place."

"Indeed." Another shadow-wrapped form shifted, darkness flowing around them like liquid night. "Kingston and Holloway, drawing ever closer, their power growing with each shared breath." A sound like cruel laughter rippled through the impossible space. "Yet their understanding remains... inadequate."

"Balor stirs." The speaker's finger traced the table's spiral patterns, reality rippling in its wake like disturbed water. "The first seal weakens. The children's games serve their purpose well – each disappearance, each harvested soul adds to our reservoir of power."

The violet-black flame danced, briefly revealing their true shadows on the wall – forms that rejected human geometry, shapes that shouldn't exist in euclidean space.

"The Order's understanding of chaos is... quaint." Amusement twisted through the speaker's spiral-voice. "They see only entropy, only destruction. They fail to grasp that true chaos is infinite possibility – every choice occurring simultaneously, every reality overlapping, every moment eternal."

"And when the first seal breaks?" This voice carried youth's hunger, sharp and eager.

"Reality will... soften." A gesture turned the air transparent where their hand passed, offering glimpses of other times, other Salems, other possibilities. "The boundaries between what is and what could be will blur."

"Balor's essence will seep through," another continued, "like darkness through cracks in dawn, like dreams through the edges of waking."

"What of the Kingston boy and his Holloway lover?" The female voice carried edges of glass and shadow. "Their union is complete. Should this concern us?"

"By the time they understand, it will be far too late."

The flame surged, casting their shadows huge against the walls – shadows that moved with independent purpose, suggesting wings and teeth and geometries that human minds couldn't process without breaking.

"And our children?" Someone asked from the darkness. "They continue their collection?"

"They gather what we require." The words twisted through the air. "Each disappeared soul, each stolen life weakens the barriers further. When the first seal breaks..."

"We will have enough." The female voice rang with certainty. "Enough power, enough chaos, enough harvested essence to ensure that what shatters can never be rebuilt."

Outside the building – which appeared abandoned to mortal eyes – winter descended with unnatural purpose. Frost formed in spiraling fractals across every surface, while shadows slithered with conscious intent. Above, ravens circled in perfect silence, their wing-beats cutting eldritch symbols against the cloud-veiled moon.

"Soon," the first speaker's voice bent reality around its edges. "Soon the true game begins, and Salem will remember what chaos meant before order chained it."

The lantern guttered out, but the darkness that rushed in was not empty. It moved with purpose, thought with ancient hunger. And in its depths, eyes older than time itself opened –

eyes that remembered the void before form, before structure, before possibility crystallized into singular reality.

Chapter Eleven

Valentines and Keystones

January melted into February, bringing with it both winter's deepening chill and the warmth of new love. Alex Kingston found himself navigating two parallel realities: the growing supernatural threat hanging over Salem like storm clouds, and the unexpected joy of falling deeper in love with Nathan Holloway.

The breakthrough came on a bitter January evening, when frost painted Alex's windows with warnings they were learning to read. They'd been studying the mysterious note for what felt like the hundredth time, its cryptic messages burning themselves into their dreams, when Nathan suddenly straightened from his slouch over a local history tome.

"Alex." The excitement in his voice cut through the study-induced haze. "Look at this." His finger traced an aged photograph – Salem's founders day celebration, circa 1923. "The lapel pins they're wearing. That symbol..."

The marking matched the one from their parchment perfectly, like a key they hadn't known they were looking for. That discovery sent them tumbling down a rabbit hole of century-old secrets and hidden bloodlines. Sarah's reporter's instincts combined with Nathan's deep knowledge of Salem's true history proved to be a devastating investigative force.

As their research deepened, so too did Alex and Nathan's connection. Marathon research sessions inevitably ended with them tangled together on Alex's couch, Nathan's heartbeat providing a rhythm that finally allowed Alex real rest. Mornings began softly now – shared coffee and gentle kisses that made even the weight of prophecy seem bearable.

But reality had a way of asserting itself. The Black Eyed Children's presence grew stronger as winter tightened its grip on Salem. Each new sighting sent ice through Alex's veins, each disappearance adding to the growing sense of dread. Something ancient stirred beneath the city's foundations, its malevolence manifesting in impossible storms and shared nightmares that left the town's residents gasping awake at 3 AM.

Through it all, Nathan became Alex's anchor. When the horror of their discoveries threatened to pull him under, Nathan was there with steady hands and unshakeable faith. "We're going to stop this," he would say, voice carrying absolute conviction. "Together." The word carried echoes of prophecy and promise both.

As Valentine's Day approached, Alex found himself caught between two urgencies – the desire to celebrate this unexpected gift of love, and the pressing knowledge that time was running out. The final piece of their puzzle remained elusive, dancing just beyond their grasp like the shadow of a child disappearing around a corner.

It was Nathan who proposed the compromise, his practical nature shining through even in romance. "Let's combine date night with detective work," he suggested, eyes twinkling. "Dinner first, then we'll explore those old mining tunnels everyone's forgotten about."

Alex couldn't help but laugh, heart swelling with affection. "Only you could make hunting eldritch horrors sound like a romantic evening out."

Valentine's Day arrived with unexpected clarity, the sun breaking through weeks of oppressive clouds. Alex woke to his phone's gentle chime:

"Happy Valentine's Day! Looking forward to our very unconventional date tonight. Something feels right about those tunnels – maybe we'll finally find what we're looking for, and I can take you somewhere normal next time. Like a movie, where nothing tries to eat our souls. Love, N."

Warmth bloomed in Alex's chest despite the February chill seeping through his windows. As he moved through his morning routine, he couldn't shake the feeling that tonight would shift something fundamental in their journey.

He fired off a quick text to Sarah, confirming their post-expedition meet at Rosie's. Her response came immediately: "Be careful down there. And try to actually enjoy the date part before diving into certain doom."

Alex's fingers brushed the small box hidden in his desk drawer. Inside lay a silver pendant, its surface etched with protective runes that had taken him weeks to perfect. Not exactly typical Valentine's fare, but then again, nothing about their relationship had followed the usual script. He just hoped it would help keep Nathan safe through whatever darkness lay ahead.

Artemis watched him prepare to leave with distinct disapproval, clearly unimpressed that Nathan hadn't provided her morning tribute before heading to work. "I know, I know," Alex soothed, filling her bowl. "He'll make it up to you with the fancy treats."

As he stepped out into the deceptively bright morning, the pendant a comforting weight in his pocket, Alex felt the subtle shift in the air that usually preceded major discoveries. The final piece of their puzzle was close – he could feel it humming in his magical senses. But each revelation they'd uncovered had carried its price, and he suspected this one would demand the highest toll yet.

Still, with Nathan by his side, the weight of prophecy felt manageable. Whatever secrets the tunnels held, whatever price fate demanded, they would face it together.

The winter sun cast his shadow long against the snow, and somewhere in that shadow, something moved independently, like a child playing a game only they could see. The longest night of winter had passed, but as Alex was learning, sometimes the deepest darkness waited in broad daylight.

The sun slipped toward the horizon as Alex and Nathan approached the old quarry, their shadows stretching across snow-crusted ground like grasping fingers. The spot had once been popular with teenage couples seeking privacy, but tonight, knowing what might lurk in the abandoned mine beneath their feet, romance felt like a thin veneer over something ancient and hungry.

"Some Valentine's Day, right?" Nathan's attempt at lightness couldn't quite mask the tension in his voice. "Most couples are at nice restaurants right about now."

Alex squeezed his hand, drawing comfort from the contact. "I'm with you. That makes it perfect." The words carried more weight than simple romance – they echoed with prophecy and promise both.

They shared a brief kiss that tasted of coffee and concern before turning to the task at hand. The mine's entrance lay half-hidden behind winter-dead brambles, barely visible in the dying light. As they pushed through the thorny growth, Alex felt that familiar prickle along his magical senses that usually preceded discovery or danger – sometimes both.

"Wait." Alex pulled out the pendant before they could go further. "I want you to have this. I know it's not exactly traditional Valentine's fare, but..." He held out the silver disk, protective runes catching the last rays of sunlight.

Nathan's expression softened as he took the pendant, immediately slipping it over his head. The magic within it hummed in harmony with his own. "It's perfect," he said softly. "Though you realize this means I'm never taking it off."

They summoned magical light with practiced ease, blue-white and green-gold spheres illuminating their descent into darkness. The tunnel air grew steadily colder, their breath forming ghost-shapes that lingered too long before dissolving. Walls wept with moisture, hosting colonies of phosphorescent fungi that pulsed in patterns that seemed almost deliberate.

"Alex." Nathan's whisper carried equal parts wonder and dread. His fingers traced symbols carved into the rock face – marks that seemed to shift slightly under his touch. "These markings..."

"Like a first draft," Alex finished, a chill crawling down his spine that had nothing to do with the temperature. "The original version of whatever ritual the Shepherds are trying to complete."

Above them, the last light of day vanished, and somewhere in the darkness ahead, something that might have been a child's laugh echoed off ancient stone.

The tunnel opened into a vast cavern that swallowed their magical light like a hungry thing. Through the thick darkness, they could make out impossible rock formations and the remnants of what might have been structures – or might have been something else entirely, worn down by centuries of patient darkness.

"Alex." Nathan's voice carried equal measures of wonder and dread. "This is it. The original site. Where everything began."

A rumble interrupted them, deep and wrong, like the earth itself was stirring from ancient sleep. Dust and stone fragments rained down, striking the ground with sounds that seemed deliberately paced, almost musical.

Nathan's fingers dug into Alex's arm. "What—"

The rumble grew, and with it came a sound that made Alex's magical senses scream warnings – children's laughter, but wrong, twisted, echoing from everywhere and nowhere, as if the very rocks were remembering sounds they should never have heard.

"We need to move." Alex pulled Nathan toward where they'd entered. "Now."

But their escape route had already been claimed. Three small figures stood between them and freedom, their eyes perfect circles of darkness that reflected their magical light like black mirrors, endless and hungry.

"Welcome, Alex Kingston." Their voices wound together in impossible harmony, bypassing ears to resonate directly in the mind. "We've been so patient, waiting for you."

Nathan's hand shot up, green-gold energy blazing toward the children. The blast struck stone as they shifted like smoke, their laughter taking on a cruel edge. "Your magic cannot touch us," they sang in terrible unison, smiles spreading too wide across small faces. "We are older than your kind's simple tricks."

The pendant around Nathan's neck suddenly flared to life, protective runes pulsing with azure light. The children hissed in unison, taking an involuntary step back.

"Holloway blood," they spat, their voices carrying something that might have been fear. "It carries echoes of the first binding. But it cannot save you. Not now. Not when the hour approaches."

Alex spotted a narrow passage and yanked Nathan toward it, their feet finding purchase on ancient stone as the sounds of pursuit echoed behind them – footsteps too light, laughter too dark.

They burst into a chamber that felt older than time itself. At its center stood an altar of black stone, its surface carved with symbols that matched their collection of clues – the key, the parchment, the map. But here, in their original form, the markings seemed alive, pulsing with terrible purpose.

The children's laughter grew closer, bouncing off walls that had witnessed the birth of Salem's darkest secrets.

"Alex." Nathan's voice cracked with recognition. Following his gaze, Alex's eyes locked onto something that made his magical senses hum like struck crystal.

There, nestled in the altar's center, lay a stone no larger than his palm. Its surface bore markings of impossible precision – parallel lines flanking a perfect circle, within which nested the ancient symbols of cauldron and triple goddess.

"What are we looking at?" Alex murmured, drawn forward despite himself. The stone seemed to call to him, its magic resonating with something deep in his blood. Each symbol pulsed with an inner light that shouldn't have been possible in the chamber's darkness.

The children's laughter grew closer, bouncing off ancient walls with terrible purpose. Nathan's eyes darted around the chamber, panic rising as he realized they'd trapped themselves. "Alex, we need to move. NOW!"

Alex's fingers closed around the stone just as a wave of power exploded through the chamber. The surge of magic felt like being caught in a storm's heart – reality twisted, folded, compressed. Everything spun into a void that threatened to crush them, the pressure building until breathing became impossible, until thought itself began to fade—

Then, with a sound like reality hiccuping, they crashed into existence in Alex's living room. Artemis yowled in surprise, her fur standing on end as she leaped straight up from her favorite cushion.

"I'm sorry," Nathan gasped, bent double and breathing hard. Sweat beaded on his forehead, his skin pale from magical exertion. "Teleportation was my last resort. Takes too much power, but I couldn't see another way out."

Alex opened his hand, revealing the stone. In the normal light of his living room, the symbols seemed to shift and dance, telling stories in a language older than words. Artemis padded closer, her green eyes fixed on the artifact with unusual intensity.

The stone hummed against his palm, its magic intertwining with his own like it had been waiting centuries for precisely this moment.

Rosie's Diner glowed with warm light against the gathering night its windows fogged slightly from the contrast between the cozy interior and the mid February chill. Sarah sat across from

Alex and Nathan in their usual booth, barely touching her slice of apple pie as she listened to them recount what happened in the mine.

"So, this stone," she said looking at it after Alex had finished, "What is it?" Her curiosity getting the better of her, as she leaned in for a closer look, examining the pattern carved into it's surface.

"I'm not exactly sure," Alex added shoving another piece of pie into his mouth, realizing that him and Nathan, hadn't eaten yet. "It was almost as if it was calling to me."

Rosie appeared at their table with fresh coffee, her pale blue eyes twinkling as she took in their linked hands. "About time," she said, filling their cups. "The amount of pining I've had to watch in this diner... I was about ready to lock you two in the storage room until you figured it out."

"Honey, half of Salem has been watching this drama unfold. Some of us just had better seats than others." She winked and moved away to tend to other customers, leaving behind the distinct impression that she knew more than she was letting on.

A sudden gust of cold air filled the room, as the diner's door opened. A mother and young child entered, shaking off the evening chill. The child couldn't have been more than seven or eight, wrapped in a puffy winter coat and wearing light-up sneakers. All three of them tensed, watching until they were sure it was just a normal family getting dinner, not something darker wearing the shape of innocence.

"We need to figure out what the significance of this stone is," Sarah said once the mother and child were settled at a distant booth. "These disappearances... they're escalating."

As they began to compile their knowledge, sharing theories and observations, the diner's warm light seemed to push back the gathering darkness outside.

Chapter Twelve

The Lighthouse

March crept into Salem on waves of endless rain, washing winter's remnants into storm drains and leaving something darker in its wake. MISSING posters became part of the city's unofficial wallpaper – Rachel Smith's bright school photo outside the grocery store, Michael Patterson's baseball portrait curling in the wet wind, Sarah Thompson's ballet picture watching from her mother's bookshop window. Each face a reminder of what lurked beneath Salem's surface.

Alex was walking Sarah through their latest findings that dreary Tuesday afternoon when his phone cut through the newsroom's familiar bustle. Unknown number. They shared a look weighted with months of experience before Alex answered, putting it on speaker.

"Alex Kingston!" The distorted voice carried an unsettling note of approval. "Well done."

"Who is this?" Alex demanded, though something in the voice tugged at his memory. "What do you want?"

A pause, filled with static that might have been laughter. "Who I am matters less than what comes next." The voice seemed to shift as it spoke, like smoke changing shape. "The final piece awaits where land meets sea, where light cuts through the darkest night."

"Where land meets sea," Sarah repeated under her breath, her reporter's instincts already churning. "Where light cuts through darkest night..." Her fingers drummed against her desk, a habit that surfaced whenever she was closing in on a story.

"Bring your allies," the voice continued. "Bring the stone. Midnight. The fate of more than Salem hangs in the balance."

The line died with a finality that felt deliberate.

"What the hell—" Alex started, but Sarah was already lost in her laptop, her fingers flying across the keys with possessed intensity. He recognized that look – the one that meant she'd caught a scent.

"That's it!" She shot up from her desk, drawing startled looks from their colleagues. "Sorry," she mumbled, sinking back down.

"Maybe try not to draw too much attention?" Alex suggested dryly.

Sarah leaned in close, her voice dropping to an excited whisper. "I solved it. The riddle." She spun her laptop toward him. "Derby Street Lighthouse."

The screen showed a weathered white marble structure rising from rocky shores, its face etched by decades of salt wind and winter storms. The article beneath detailed its history: "Constructed 1871, built upon foundations of unknown origin. Architectural anomalies include unprecedented design elements and, most notably, spiral patterns carved into its base that predate the structure itself."

"Sarah," Alex said slowly, "that lighthouse is twenty miles up the coast."

The coastal road unspooled before them like a ribbon of wet ink, Alex's headlights cutting through fog thick enough to feel. Nathan sat beside him, occasionally squeezing his hand when the tension grew too heavy, while Sarah leaned forward from the backseat, her reporter's instincts already humming. As they wound through Salem's oldest quarters toward the coast, the January sky hung so low and heavy it was impossible to tell where clouds ended and sea began.

"There." Sarah's voice cut through the car's nervous silence. "Up on the rise."

The lighthouse stood like a pale giant against the darkness, its beam carving perfect circles through the night. Alex felt his magical senses prickle as he pulled into the gravel lot, stones crunching beneath his tires with deliberate intensity. The whole setup screamed 'trap,' but they were well past the point of playing it safe.

"Stay here," Alex told Sarah, who for once didn't argue. She'd seen enough supernatural showdowns lately to know when to hang back.

He and Nathan swept the perimeter, magic ready beneath their skin. Finding nothing immediate threatening, Alex gave Sarah the all-clear.

"Any sign of our mystery caller?" she asked, joining them in the salt-heavy air.

"Nothing yet." Nathan's voice carried tension. "But something's wrong here. Can you feel it?"

Alex could. The air felt charged, like the moment before lightning strikes. Nathan's pendant pulsed with soft light, responding to whatever power saturated this place. The lighthouse beam kept its steady rhythm, but each sweep seemed to illuminate something different in the fog.

The door's creak cut through the night like a blade. A figure emerged, haloed by impossible blue light spilling from within. Alex and Nathan moved in perfect sync, magic sparking between their fingers – but then the figure stepped into the moonlight, and Alex's world stopped turning.

He knew that face. Older now, lined with years of worry, blonde hair threaded with silver, but those eyes – Alex saw them every morning in his mirror. His magic guttered like a candle in wind.

"Dad?" The word came out broken, a child's voice in a man's throat.

James Kingston stood before them, impossibly alive, looking at his son with an expression that carried ten years of compressed emotion. "Hello, Alex." His voice was exactly as Alex remembered, yet somehow different. "It's been a long time."

For a long moment, only the wind moved, carrying salt and secrets across the space between father and son. Then Alex surged forward, a decade of grief and questions driving him. His hands found his father's shoulders, gripping tight enough to prove this wasn't another dream, another trick.

"How?" The word carried too many questions to count. "Where have you—" Alex's voice cracked. "Ten years, Dad. Ten years."

James laid a weathered hand on Alex's arm, the touch carrying a hesitation that spoke of time's cruel distance. "I know you have questions, son." His eyes held shadows Alex didn't remember from childhood. They flickered to Nathan and Sarah, who stood frozen in their own tableau of shock. "But we need to get inside. Time grows short, and there's so much you need to understand."

They followed James through the lighthouse door, Alex's mind spinning like the beacon above them. His father – alive, present, real – had been behind everything? The messages, the clues, the breadcrumb trail that led them here?

The lighthouse's interior defied expectation. Ancient symbols carved into age-worn walls pulsed with ethereal blue light, their patterns suggesting meanings just beyond comprehension. Yet among these arcane markings sat modern technology – monitors displaying data streams, computers humming with purpose. The blend of old and new created an atmosphere that made Alex's magical senses buzz with recognition and warning simultaneously.

James guided them to a circular chamber at the tower's base. "Please," he gestured to a ring of chairs that seemed to echo the spiral patterns they'd been chasing for months. As they settled in, James remained standing, his gaze touching each face before finally resting on Alex. In the blue-tinged light, father and son's matching eyes reflected generations of Kingston magic.

Above them, the lighthouse beam kept its steady rhythm, each sweep illuminating different secrets in the gathering dark.

"I owe you an explanation." James's voice carried years of carefully guarded secrets. "Especially you, Alex." His eyes held his son's, matching blue reflecting shared pain. "Everything that's happening now, my disappearance – it all traces back to one moment."

He drew a deep breath, like a man preparing to relive his worst nightmare. "Ten years ago, I stood exactly where you are, Alex. Young, certain, absolutely convinced I understood the prophecy." A bitter smile crossed his face. "Too arrogant to see what was right in front of me."

His pacing traced patterns that echoed the symbols on the walls. "I thought I had everything under control. The founder's stone, the Holloway family's support—"

"The founder's stone?" Sarah's reporter instincts caught the detail. "You mean..."

James reached into his pocket, withdrawing an object identical to the one they'd discovered in the mining tunnel. "The very same. Though this one's power was spent long ago."

"You mentioned the Holloways," Nathan's voice carried a hint of recognition.

James turned to Nathan, and something like old grief crossed his features. "Your uncle Richard was more than just an ally. He was my best friend." The words seemed to physically pain him. "We performed the sealing ritual together, convinced we could strengthen the barriers." His voice dropped lower. "But we were wrong. The entity was too strong, the seal already compromising. And then..."

He fell silent, the lighthouse beam sweeping past windows to cast strange shadows across his face. "Then I discovered the true cost of stopping it. The price that had to be paid."

James turned to Alex, his eyes bright with decades of contained grief. "I misread everything. The combined power of myself and my best friend – two bloodlines mentioned in the prophecy – it wasn't enough to mend the seal. Not even close."

"So you found another way." Alex's voice barely carried above the lighthouse's ambient hum, but the words landed like stones in still water.

"A willing sacrifice." James's words seemed to physically pain him. "Pure blood, untouched by darkness. And not just anyone – it had to be someone bound to Salem's soil."

The implications crashed through the room like thunder. Alex felt the ground tilt beneath him, Nathan's hand in his the only anchor in a world suddenly gone sideways.

"You were eleven." James's voice cracked. "I couldn't... I couldn't leave you and your mother alone. Richard..." He swallowed hard. "Richard volunteered."

The blue light pulsed slower now, as if the very walls were listening. "We performed the ritual, but we'd only understood fragments of the prophecy." Bitter self-recrimination colored every word. "By the time I realized Richard and I weren't the ones it spoke of – not entirely – it was too late."

"'One child of storm, one child of flame,'" Nathan's voice filled the silence, weighted with new understanding. "'When joined shall break or mend the chain, that binds the realms of light and shade – upon their choice, all fates are laid.'"

James nodded slowly. "Our choice, our actions – they didn't strengthen the seal. They fractured it." His eyes grew distant, remembering. "In an instant, I was thrown into the void between worlds, lost in endless nothing."

The lighthouse beam swept past again, and in its light, they could see the toll those years in the void had taken – marks that went deeper than mere physical age.

Nathan's grip on Alex's hand tightened as the pieces aligned: two bloodlines, two generations, two chances to either save or doom everything.

James's gaze moved between Alex and Nathan, something like hope kindling in his exhausted eyes. For the first time since they'd entered the lighthouse, the weight of his decade-long burden seemed to lift slightly. "But this time," his voice carried a warmth that made Alex's heart clench, "this time there might be another way. A chance to right my wrongs."

Alex leaned forward, torn between desperate hope and hard-earned caution. "What are you saying?"

"The ancient texts," James reached into his coat with reverent care, "they speak of a power greater than sacrifice. The willing union of Kingston and Holloway blood, joined not through violence or necessity, but through choice." His eyes softened. "Through love."

The paper he withdrew looked impossibly old, its edges worn soft as fabric, the ink having long ago seeped into the very fibers. As he smoothed it against his knee, Alex could feel the magic radiating from it like heat from a flame.

"'In the time of the thirteenth moon,'" James read, his voice taking on the cadence of ancient ritual, "'when shadows dance in morning's light, two souls entwined might save or doom, all that was wrong shall be made right.'"

The lighthouse beam swept past, making the words seem to shimmer on the page.

"'The union sealed by love or fate, shall birth a power none can tame, to heal the world or seal its fate, when ancient blood ignites the flame.'"

"Is that—" Nathan's voice caught, recognition dawning in his eyes.

"The final piece." James smiled, real hope lighting his face for the first time. "The part of the prophecy we didn't have before. The part that changes everything."

Nathan's fingers tightened around Alex's, their shared magic humming in response. "You're telling us..."

"Yes." James's voice carried wonder and certainty. "Your connection — it's not coincidence. It's what we've been searching for all along."

"Oh my god." Sarah straightened, her reporter's mind assembling the puzzle in real time. "That's it, isn't it? Your relationship, your love — it's the union of bloodlines the prophecy spoke about!"

A small laugh escaped Alex. "Well, I guess I owe Margaret an apology. She did try to tell us."

Alex turned to Nathan, finding his own mix of awe and disbelief mirrored in those green eyes he'd fallen for. "Dad?" His voice carried a child's need for confirmation. "Our love — it could really be strong enough to seal this thing?"

James's weathered face softened. "Love freely given and returned is one of the most powerful forces in any reality. When that love bridges two ancient magical bloodlines?" He shook his head in wonder. "Its power is beyond measuring."

"But practically speaking," Nathan's logical mind kicked in, though his voice trembled slightly, "how would this work? Is there a specific ritual?"

James moved to one of the monitors, bringing up an intricate circular design that made their magical senses hum with recognition. "This is the original seal, created when the entity was first bound. These parallel lines?" His finger traced the pattern. "Kingston and Holloway bloodlines."

"It matches the founder's stone," Sarah breathed, leaning closer.

"Exactly." James's enthusiasm was catching. "The cauldron and triple moon – Cerridwen's symbols, representing her power binding it all together."

"Hold on." Sarah's investigative instincts surfaced. "It can't be as simple as them just being in love. There has to be more."

"There is." James's expression sobered. "The ritual requires you to channel your combined energy directly into the seal. You'll be exposed to the entity's influence." His voice dropped. "And success isn't guaranteed."

Alex and Nathan shared a look that spoke of years of trust, of love built slowly and surely, of a connection that went deeper than magic.

"We'll do it," they said together, their voices harmonizing like they'd rehearsed it.

Pride and fear warred on James's face. "I hoped you'd say that. But you need to understand – if anything goes wrong, if your connection wavers for even a moment..."

"We could lose everything," Alex finished quietly.

Nathan's hand found his again, warm and sure. "Or we could save everyone."

The lighthouse beam swept past, illuminating their joined hands, and for just a moment, their combined shadows showed something ancient and powerful – a glimpse of what they might become together.

"Not to be the pessimist here," Alex's voice cut through the moment of hope, "but the Shepherds won't exactly sit back and watch us fix their plans. And the Black Eyed Children..." He left the thought unfinished, the memory of their last encounter still too fresh.

James's expression hardened, shadows deepening in the lines of his face. "They'll try to stop us. With everything they have." He ran a hand through his silver-streaked hair, a gesture so familiar it made Alex's heart ache. "That's where we'll need help. You and Nathan will have to focus entirely on the ritual. We'll need others to hold the line."

They spent the next hour planning, strategy mixing with hope and fear in equal measure. Margaret's name came up repeatedly – her power, her knowledge, her connection to both families making her invaluable.

As they finally made their way back to Alex's car, the lighthouse stood sentinel behind them, its beam cutting through the darkness with renewed purpose. Through the windshield, they watched it grow smaller in the rearview mirror, but its light seemed to follow them, a reminder of promises made and battles yet to come.

Sarah broke the thoughtful silence from the backseat. "You know Margaret's going to be insufferably smug about being right all along."

The tension broke as they all laughed, the sound carrying equal parts nervousness and determination. Above them, the clouds finally began to break, revealing stars that seemed to shine just a bit brighter than usual.

The lighthouse's beam faded into the distance, but its promise remained: there was still light to be found in the darkness, still hope to be kindled from love.

The days following their lighthouse revelation brought changes that rippled through Salem's magical community, most notably at the Holloway mansion. Margaret, while insufferably pleased about being right regarding Alex and Nathan's destined connection, had turned her triumphant energy toward her newest project: rehabilitating James Kingston.

"Absolutely not." Her voice had carried that particular tone that had cowed several generations of Salem's magical elite when James had tentatively suggested finding his own place. "I have more than enough room, and more importantly—" she'd fixed him with a look that could have frozen flame, "—I have ten years' worth of lectures about hubris and proper planning that you're going to sit through while I make sure you remember how to eat regular meals."

Nathan's old room had been transformed with suspicious speed, suggesting Margaret had been preparing for this possibility longer than she'd admit. The space now balanced comfort with functionality – a proper bed sharing space with research materials and magical texts. Alex strongly suspected his father had been deliberately maneuvered into Margaret's sphere of influence, but watching James slowly recover his color and vitality under her forceful care, he couldn't bring himself to object.

Chapter Thirteen

Death and Discovery

At the Salem Gazette, disappearances had become their own terrible routine. Missing persons reports filled Alex's inbox with grim regularity, each one following a pattern he couldn't publish: the unexplained frost, the children's laughter, the shadows that moved wrong. Their wall of photographs grew weekly – faces of all ages now, not just children, each vanished between day and night, each leaving only questions and impossible cold behind.

The air itself felt different, as if reality had grown thin from too many holes poked through its fabric. Magic users felt it most keenly – that sense of something vast and hungry pressing against increasingly fragile barriers, watching through eyes that had never been human.

Officer Menendez slumped in the chair beside Sarah's desk, his usually crisp uniform showing wear from too many double shifts. Dark circles under his eyes spoke of nights spent chasing shadows that moved wrong. Alex pretended to focus on his screen while listening, his magical senses noting how even the officer's own shadow seemed uncertain.

"Seventeen since New Year's." Menendez's voice carried exhaustion and something darker. "And those are just the confirmed cases." His hands spread in helpless gesture. "We get calls about strange children, but by the time we arrive..." He trailed off, professional mask cracking.

He leaned closer, voice dropping to barely above whisper. "The shadows aren't right anymore. Even at high noon, they fall wrong. Move when they shouldn't." His fingers drummed nervous patterns on Sarah's desk. "Put that in an official report and they'll have me doing psych evaluations until retirement."

"The witnesses all describe the same things?" Sarah's pen hovered over her notebook, though they all knew what details would make the final article.

"Cold spots. Children's laughter. And those eyes..." He stopped, straightening his tie with hands that trembled slightly. "Look, off the record? My daughter swears she saw them watching her school playground. Now I drive her myself, every morning. Some of the other parents too – not that anyone's talking about why."

Alex caught Sarah's pointed look across their desks. They'd seen it too – reality growing thin around Salem's edges, shadows behaving like living things rather than mere absence of light.

"The victims' ages?" Sarah prompted gently, though they already knew what was coming.

"It's everywhere now." Menendez rubbed his eyes. "Started with pets, moved to children, but lately? We've got missing persons from six to sixty-five. No pattern except..." He trailed off, seemingly wrestling with what to reveal.

"Except?" Sarah's reporter's instincts caught the hesitation.

"They all saw children first. Strange kids asking to play or needing help. Even the adults." Age seemed to settle on him like a physical weight. "My daughter's school has a buddy system now. Nobody walks alone. But how do you protect people from something that looks like it needs protecting?"

His voice dropped lower, cracking slightly. "The families are the worst. They keep hoping we'll find something – anything. But it's like these people just... stop existing. Like they were never here at all."

After Menendez left, Sarah turned to Alex, her notepad untouched. "They're ramping up. More victims, more frequently. And these shadow distortions..."

"I know." Alex's eyes drifted to Tom's office, where their editor worked behind glass walls. His shadow stretched across the floor at an impossible angle, occasionally twitching in ways that had nothing to do with Tom's movements. "Dad thinks they're building to something. Each disappearance, each stolen soul adds to their power. They're counting down to something."

Outside their window, a group of schoolchildren walked past in careful pairs, their teachers watching with haunted vigilance. Their shadows, Alex noticed, stayed firmly attached – almost too firmly, as if they'd been deliberately anchored against something trying to pull them loose.

Early afternoon light filtered weak and watery through Salem's cloud cover as Alex's car wound through residential streets. Each house they passed seemed to watch them, windows like worried eyes tracking their progress. The Thompson home waited ahead – another intact family about to join their growing wall of grief.

"Third one this week," Sarah whispered, her reporter's notebook heavy with similar interviews. Her fingers traced the edges of pages filled with patterns she couldn't publish, connections she couldn't explain. "They're getting bolder."

"Or more desperate." Alex's knuckles whitened on the steering wheel as they turned onto Cherry Street. Colonial revival homes stood sentinel, their perfect facades hiding neighbors who had learned to look away when children vanished.

The Thompson house stood like a snapshot of interrupted life – pristine white clapboard and black shutters maintaining a facade of normalcy while subtle signs spoke of tragedy: curtains drawn against afternoon light, untouched mail spilling from the brass box, a child's bicycle frozen in time against the porch railing, its chain gathering rust. The sound of Alex and Sarah's footsteps on the walk seemed too loud in the unnatural quiet.

Susan Thompson answered their knock with the particular emptiness Alex had come to recognize in those left behind – that hollow look of grief suspended by hope that wore people down like winter wind on stone. She led them into a living room where normal life had stopped mid-sentence: homework forever half-finished on the coffee table, a jacket tossed casually over a chair awaiting a return that hadn't come, family photos showing a bright-eyed girl with auburn braids and a smile that hurt to look at now.

"She started talking about Lily two weeks before..." Susan's fingers twisted together in her lap like worried birds. "We thought it was normal – she's eight, imaginary friends happen. But there were signs we should have..." Her voice cracked on the weight of retrospect.

"Signs?" Sarah's voice carried professional gentleness, her notebook open but untouched. Some stories needed to be heard before they could be written.

"Her room wouldn't warm up." Susan's eyes darted to the corners of the room, checking shadows that seemed to deepen at their mention. "We'd crank the heat, but the cold... it felt alive. And the shadows moved wrong. Too dark, too..." She searched for words. "Too purposeful."

"Purposeful?" Alex kept his voice carefully neutral.

"Like they were watching. And her drawings..." Susan stood abruptly, moving to a desk scattered with children's artwork. "She used to draw normal things – our house, flowers, her friends. But then..."

The pictures made Alex's magical senses recoil. What should have been innocent crayon drawings carried wrongness in every line: children with eyes like holes in reality, shadows stretching against natural law, spiral patterns that seemed to twist when viewed directly.

"The night before," Susan's voice dropped to a whisper, "we heard her laughing after bedtime. She said Lily wanted to play. The room was so cold we could see our breath, and the shadows on the wall..." She shuddered, remembering. "They looked like children dancing, but wrong – like watching a dance from another world trying to mimic ours. We told ourselves it was just the nightlight, but..."

A knock at the front door cut through her words. Susan almost seemed relieved at the interruption, hurrying to answer it.

Dr. Elias Moore swept into the Thompson's living room like he owned the laws of physics, his presence making reality shift uncomfortably around him. Despite March's lingering chill, he wore only tweeds over Oxford cloth, as if cold were something that happened to other people. Salt-pepper hair stood wild from repeated agitated combing, while wire-rimmed glasses magnified eyes that burned with barely contained fervor.

"Mrs. Thompson." Academic precision clipped each word, but something darker hummed beneath his cultivated tone. "Thank you for allowing this intrusion. These temperature anomalies you reported – fascinating patterns. And the shadow behaviors..." His enthusiasm felt wrong against the room's grief.

He halted mid-stride, finally registering Alex and Sarah's presence. "Ah." His smile didn't quite fit his face. "The Salem Gazette's finest. Kingston and Chen." Those intense eyes studied them with unsettling focus. "Your coverage of these incidents has been... remarkably precise. Almost as if you understand exactly what to look for."

Something in Moore's emphasis set Alex's magical senses screaming. Those sharp eyes behind wire rims held knowledge that went deeper than academic theory – the kind of understanding that came from seeing things humans weren't meant to witness.

"Dr. Moore's from the university." Susan Thompson's voice carried forced normality, her fingers worrying the tissue in her lap. "He studies paranormal phenomena..." She trailed off, clearly rethinking the wisdom of inviting him inside. Even the room's shadows seemed to lean away from his presence.

"Similar incidents spanning centuries," Moore cut through social pretense like a blade through silk. His intensity filled the living room's careful normalcy – family photos watching from walls, a half-finished puzzle on the coffee table, evidence of life before everything shattered. "The patterns remain remarkably consistent – new childhood companions appearing, localized temperature drops, shadows rejecting physical law."

His fingers drummed against a leather notebook that seemed to drink light rather than reflect it. "Tell me about Lily, Mrs. Thompson. Every detail matters."

"I..." Susan's maternal instinct to help warred with growing unease. Her eyes darted between Moore's fever-bright gaze and the relative safety of Alex and Sarah's presence. "She dressed old-fashioned, like from historical photographs. And her eyes..." Her hand fluttered to her throat, protective. "Sarah called them 'special' eyes. Like looking into space with all the stars gone."

Moore's pen scratched across his notebook with unsettling eagerness, while somewhere in the room's deepening shadows, something small shifted just out of sight.

Moore's interrogation stretched time like taffy, each question making the room's shadows grow longer. Alex and Sarah exchanged silent warnings across the Thompson's carefully maintained living room, their reporter's masks growing thinner with each probe that cut too close to truth.

"And your thoughts on all this, Mr. Kingston?" Moore's attention swiveled with predatory grace. Something ancient stirred behind his academic facade, making Alex's magical senses spike warning.

"It's... complicated." Alex forced casual dismissal into his voice, playing the skeptical journalist. "Shadows moving on their own, children with unusual eyes – sounds more like urban legends than news." The lie tasted bitter, but Susan Thompson's grief deserved better than becoming someone's research project.

Moore's stare dissected him layer by layer, those wire-rimmed glasses magnifying eyes that had seen too much, understood too well. "Come now." His smile showed too many teeth. "Surely someone of your... background has developed some theories about these patterns?"

"Dr. Moore." Alex cut in, watching Susan retreat further into herself with each question. "Perhaps we should continue this discussion elsewhere? Mrs. Thompson has been more than generous."

"Yes, quite right." Moore straightened with unnatural grace, his eyes lingering on children's artwork that seemed to move when viewed directly. "Mrs. Thompson, invaluable data. We must understand what we're dealing with if we hope to stop it."

Ice crawled down Alex's spine at the phrasing. Not 'find them' or 'save them' – but 'stop it,' as if the victims were merely data points in some greater academic pursuit.

Outside, March air caught Moore's tweed as he fell into step beside them, his enthusiasm bordering on fever. "Mr. Kingston, Ms. Chen – perhaps we might collaborate? I've tracked these patterns for years." His glasses caught sunlight wrong. "Your articles suggest... unique insights that could prove valuable to my research."

"My office," he added, smile stretching slightly too wide. "Tomorrow afternoon? We have so much to discuss."

Before they could frame polite refusal, Moore vanished into his waiting car with liquid grace. As he pulled away, temperature plummeted until their breath clouded in suddenly arctic air. Shadows stretched across Cherry Street like spilled ink, taking shapes that suggested children playing games that would steal sanity from normal minds.

Alex caught Sarah's look, seeing his own unease mirrored there. Something about Moore's interest felt wrong – less academic curiosity, more predator recognizing prey.

Alex's car wound through Salem's streets, passing rows of houses where more curtains seemed drawn than usual, more porch lights left on despite the afternoon hour. The fog that had plagued the city all month curled around street corners in patterns that occasionally looked deliberate.

"Okay," Sarah slammed her notebook shut with unusual force as they pulled away from Cherry Street. "What the hell was that about? Because Dr. Elias Moore gave off way more than just standard creepy-academic-studying-tragedy vibes."

"You caught that too?" Alex took a corner too sharp, knuckles white on the steering wheel. "The way he talked about the disappearances – like he was collecting specimens instead of investigating missing people."

"He knew things, Alex." Sarah rifled through her earlier notes, reporter's instincts on high alert. "Those questions about spiral patterns, the timing of the temperature drops... We deliberately kept those details out of our articles."

"Exactly." Alex checked his rearview mirror, half-expecting to see Moore's intense gaze following them. "No normal paranormal researcher should know those connections. Unless..."

"Unless he's part of this." Sarah sat up straighter. "Wait – your dad said the Shepherds have had people in Salem for years, right? Watching, waiting?"

"A professor would be perfect cover," Alex finished her thought. "Access to historical records, legitimate reason to study the weird and unexplained, tracking patterns through time..." He frowned. "But something about him felt off. Different from the Shepherds at the gala."

"Different how?"

"The Shepherds had this... spiral energy. Everything about them curved inward, like their masks. Moore felt..." Alex searched for words. "Colder. More precise. Like he was hunting something specific."

Sarah was already deep in her phone. "I'm digging into his background. Academic history, publications, his time in Salem..." She stopped suddenly. "Alex. Look."

They were passing Pioneer Village, its colonial buildings stark against the pewter sky. Ravens lined every surface like dark sentinels, their eyes tracking the car's movement. Between buildings, two small figures stood unnaturally still, watching their passage.

"Speaking of your dad," Sarah said, clearly trying to break the tension. "How's the forced residency at Margaret's going? Nathan mentioned something about her threatening to hex his coffee black if he tried to move out?"

A small smile cracked Alex's tension. "She's been... intense. But the good kind. Self-appointed rehabilitation director. Yesterday she had him cornered for an hour, lecturing about proper magical maintenance while forcing some kind of restoration tea down his throat."

"And you? How are you handling having him back?"

Alex watched fog curl around prematurely lit streetlamps, considering his answer carefully.

Margaret's conservatory had become their war room by default, its magical flora providing better protection than any technological security system. Enchanted tea flowed endlessly, helping clear minds clouded by their supernatural encounters. Nathan had slipped in after his library shift, settling naturally beside Alex. Their proximity created its own magic – small patterns of light that caused Margaret's roses to bloom out of season.

"Elias Moore." James paced between floating plant displays, his restored vitality evident in his restless energy. "The name is familiar, but I don't know much about him. He has written papers on Salem's supernatural history, leyline theories, childhood paranormal experiences..."

"Nothing unusual for someone in his position," Margaret observed, directing the teapot with a casual flick of her finger. "Standard academic fare."

Sarah had claimed one of Margaret's overstuffed chairs, her ever-present notebook balanced on her knee. "But why stay separate from the Shepherds? Why not show himself at the gala if they're working together?"

"Because they're not." James stopped abruptly, revelation clearing his features. "Not directly, at least. The energy Alex described – that cold, precise focus – that's something entirely different."

Margaret's posture shifted, her earlier casualness falling away. "You're suggesting he's just another academic chasing results?"

"The Thompson interview felt like a dissection," Alex added, the memory making him tense. "He wasn't trying to find Sarah – he wanted to understand what took her. Like she was a data point instead of a missing child."

"So what's our play?" Sarah's pen hadn't stopped moving. "Moore, the escalating disappearances, all of it?"

"We watch him." Margaret set her cup down with quiet authority. "While he thinks he's studying us." A smile crossed her face that belonged more to a predator than a grandmother. "I know certain people in academia who might be... persuaded to share details about our curious professor."

"And the disappearances?" Alex felt Nathan's hand find his under the table, their magic humming in harmony. "They're speeding up. Whatever's coming, it's getting closer."

James moved back to their circle, shadows of old guilt crossing his face as he watched his son's fingers intertwined with Nathan's. Above them, the conservatory's enchanted vines shifted uneasily, responding to the tension building in Salem's very foundations.

The nameplate on Dr. Moore's office door seemed ordinary enough, but the frosted glass window rippled like disturbed water when viewed straight on. Alex's knock echoed down the university hallway with unnatural persistence, as if the sound itself was reluctant to fade.

"Enter." Moore's voice carried that same fever-pitch intensity from the Thompson house.

The office beyond the threshold rejected academic normality. Bookshelves crawled up every wall, their contents shifting like living things when not directly observed. Ancient texts whose languages shouldn't exist sat beside standard scholarly works, their spines marked with symbols that made Alex's magical senses recoil.

Display cases housed objects that straddled the line between mundane and wrong – a child's toy casting impossible shadows, a compass whose needle danced to magnetic fields that didn't exist, drawings that moved in the corner of vision. The air tasted of dust and something colder, something that predated written language.

Moore hunched behind a massive oak desk drowning in organized chaos: star charts marked with calculations that ignored astronomical law, photographs of spiral frost patterns, and children's drawings that echoed the Thompson girl's final works too closely for comfort.

"Ah, Mr. Kingston." Moore glanced up, eyes magnified to unsettling proportion behind wire-rims. "I rather thought you might come. Yesterday's conversation left quite a few threads dangling, didn't it?"

Alex slipped into his reporter's mask, the one that had served him through countless normal interviews before his world tilted supernatural. "Your theories about patterns in the disappearances caught my attention. Always looking for fresh angles on ongoing stories."

"Is that so?" Moore's smile stayed carefully confined to his mouth. He gestured to a chair whose wooden frame bore carvings that whispered of centuries. "And which aspects particularly... resonated with you?"

"The temperature anomalies, for starters." Alex settled into the chair, trying to ignore how the patterns seemed to shift beneath his fingers. "And the shadow behavior you mentioned. Have you found similar cases historically?"

Something like genuine excitement lit Moore's face, though it felt precisely calibrated. "Oh yes. Salem's quite rich with such incidents. Children vanishing after meeting strange new friends, localized cold spots, shadows that reject physics." He withdrew a leather journal that radiated age. "I've documented cases back to the colonial period."

"Really?" Alex leaned forward, playing up journalistic interest while his magical senses mapped the room's wrong angles. Reality felt thin here, like tissue paper stretched too tight. "Any patterns in timing?"

"Fascinating you should ask." Moore's journal opened to reveal meticulous documentation, each entry marked with symbols that echoed the lighthouse's ancient warnings. "There are cycles. Periods of intensity followed by dormancy. Though lately..."

"The pattern's shifting?"

"Accelerating." That unsettling gleam returned to Moore's eyes. "More frequent, broader victim range, bolder manifestations. Almost as if..." He studied Alex's face with clinical precision. "Almost as if whatever's behind it no longer feels the need for subtlety."

"And what do you think is behind it all, Dr. Moore?"

"Come now, Mr. Kingston." Moore's smile widened a fraction too far, showing teeth that seemed too numerous. "We both know your articles only scratch the surface. Just as we both know your interest in my research extends beyond mere journalism."

The office temperature plummeted. Shadows began to move independently in the display cases, while the children's drawings stirred like disturbed insects, their black-eyed subjects turning to watch with crayon-rendered hunger.

"I'm not sure what you mean." Alex kept his expression neutral despite every magical instinct screaming danger.

"No?" Moore leaned back, his shadow moving a heartbeat behind him. "Perhaps we should discuss your family's history in Salem. The Kingston line has such... fascinating connections to certain historical events. Particularly those involving the boundaries between perceived reality and actual truth."

Alex felt his magic stir defensively but held it in check. "You've done quite a bit of research on local families."

"Oh, I've researched many things, Mr. Kingston. Many things indeed." Moore's voice took on that clinical coldness. "Did you know that these children aren't simply taken? They're... experienced. Their essence absorbed into something older and hungrier than human minds were meant to comprehend."

The office dimmed though no lights had changed. Under Alex's fingers, the chair's patterns writhed into familiar spirals that echoed the lighthouse's ancient warnings.

"Interesting theory," Alex managed, fighting the urge to flood the room with protective magic.

"Not theory." Moore's smile remained fixed while his eyes suggested knowledge that should have driven him mad. "Observation. Just as I observe how your articles track patterns invisible to normal journalists. How you know exactly which questions to ask... and which to avoid."

The game had shifted, Alex realized. This wasn't investigation anymore – it was confrontation. But what role did Elias Moore truly play in their cosmic chess match?

"A good journalist follows evidence," Alex said mildly, watching shadows pool in the office corners like spilled ink. "These cases have certainly presented some... unusual patterns."

"Unusual." Moore rolled the word around like wine at a tasting. "Such careful word choice. Like your articles – dancing so precisely around truth without acknowledging it." He lifted a child's drawing. "Rather like these, wouldn't you say? Truth hiding in plain sight, waiting for those who know where to look."

The drawing moved in his hands, crayon figures shifting like stop-motion animation, black eyes tracking Alex with hungry purpose.

"Children have active imaginations," Alex offered, voice steady despite the dropping temperature. "Especially processing trauma."

"Do they?" Moore set the drawing down, but it continued its subtle dance. "Or do they simply see what adults have trained themselves to ignore? The spaces between choices, the moments where reality... splits."

A book crashed from the shelves, its impact echoing far too long. Neither man moved to retrieve it.

"Tell me, Mr. Kingston," Moore's voice grew colder, more focused. "When you interviewed the Thompson family, did you notice their daughter's shadows? How they formed games no human child would know how to play?"

The office shadows had condensed to near solidity, temperature low enough to turn breath visible. On Moore's desk, every crayon drawing had oriented toward Alex, their subjects watching with endless void-dark eyes.

"I investigate all aspects of my stories thoroughly." Alex kept his voice steady despite the magic crackling beneath his skin like bottled lightning.

"Oh, I'm quite sure you do." Moore leaned forward, his shadow stretching impossibly behind him. "Just as I thoroughly understand what I study. The patterns, the players, the pieces moving on this cosmic board..." His voice dropped to a whisper. "The prophecies that might not mean what everyone assumes."

The fallen book had opened itself, pages turning in a nonexistent wind. Text spiraled across each page, matching the lighthouse's ancient markings with unsettling precision.

"Tell me, Mr. Kingston," Moore's eyes now definitely glowed with internal light, "when did you realize you were playing their game? And more importantly..." His smile stretched inhumanly wide. "When did you start to suspect that the game you think you're playing isn't the real game at all?"

The office air had become almost solid with magical tension and conscious shadows. Their standoff balanced on a knife's edge – until reality itself... twisted.

Space folded between the bookshelves, creating a spiral that hurt to look at directly. From this impossible geometry stepped a robed figure, their mask carved from living darkness, its patterns flowing like liquid chaos.

"You overstep, Moore." The Shepherd's voice spiraled around itself. "This is not your game to play."

Moore's calculated facade shattered into fury. "I was here first! Years of research, of watching, of understanding—"

"Understanding?" The Shepherd's laugh made reality ripple. "You understand nothing. You're just another piece, moved exactly where needed."

Alex rose slowly, magic gathering at his fingertips, but Moore's attention snapped to him.

"Stay there, Kingston." He pulled something from his desk that seemed to drink light. "Our discussion isn't finished."

"Actually, it is." Alex dropped all pretense, releasing a wave of protective magic that pushed back the gathering shadows.

The Shepherd moved with impossible grace. "Finally, some honesty! Show us what the young Kingston can do."

Chaos magic exploded through the office. Books took flight, their text rearranging into floating spiral patterns. Frost crystallized across every surface, forming familiar lighthouse markings.

Alex barely got his shield up before Moore's device activated, sending out pulses of anti-light that created holes in reality. His magical barrier crackled where the pulses hit, requiring constant reinforcement.

"Fascinating." Moore watched with academic fervor despite the chaos. "The resonance patterns between Order and Chaos..."

"This isn't your research project!" The Shepherd's gesture bent reality, creating a vortex that threatened to consume everything.

Alex countered with one of Nathan's stabilizing spells. The competing magics clashed spectacularly, making Moore's equipment smoke and spark.

"Enough!" The Shepherd's voice became ancient, suggesting something infinitely older speaking through them. Shadows solidified into dark tentacles that whipped toward Alex.

Drawing on his connection with Nathan – a constant warm harmony in his magic now – Alex created pure light that severed the shadow constructs. But Moore's device pulsed again, disrupting the spell.

"The interaction of opposing forces," Moore muttered, taking notes even as reality warped around him. "The interference patterns of multiple magical paradigms..."

"Fool." The Shepherd's mask spiraled faster. "You think you're studying them? They've been studying you, using your obsession to—"

Alex seized his chance, combining Margaret's binding spell with his father's reality-anchoring technique. The magic struck true, temporarily forcing normal physics on the space.

The Shepherd staggered, their robes suddenly subject to gravity. "Clever," they admitted, their voice losing its spiral quality. "But futile. The game is already won, Kingston. Your moves were decided long ago."

Their final gesture sent dark energy crashing into Moore. Reality folded like origami, and they stepped through, leaving only echoing children's laughter.

The office settled, though frost remained and shadows stayed too deep. Among scattered books still showing fading spiral text, Alex knelt beside Moore's still form. But the professor was already gone, his expression frozen in a mixture of academic fascination and dawning horror – one more victim in a game far larger than he'd understood.

Chapter Fourteen

The Apporaching Storm

Alex's teleportation landed with a sound like reality catching its breath, scattering loose papers across Margaret's living room. He stumbled, still supporting Moore's lifeless weight.

Margaret had been mid-lecture, gesturing at James with a teacup as she explained why his system for organizing ancient texts was "endearingly incorrect." Their relaxed moment shattered – her tea took flight in defensive formation while James threw up a shield that made the air shimmer.

"Alexander Kingston," Margaret recovered first, her cup settling back onto its saucer with pointed dignity. "What have I said about materializing unannounced in other people's—" She stopped abruptly, finally registering Moore's still form. "Is that—"

"He's dead." Alex's voice cracked. "The Shepherds... they were waiting in his office. It was a trap, but I don't think it was meant for me."

"Dead?" James lowered his shield, moving forward to help Alex with the body. "Start from the beginning."

"I went to talk him, like we planned." Alex sank into the nearest chair, adrenaline giving way to exhaustion. "But he knew things, Dad. Things he shouldn't have known. About us, about the prophecy." He ran a shaking hand through his hair. "Then reality just... folded, and one of them stepped through."

Margaret's expression had gone sharp with calculation. "The Shepherds killed their own agent?"

"That's just it," Alex looked up at them both. "I don't think he was their agent at all. The way they spoke to him... it was like he was another piece on the board. One they'd finished using."

The days after Moore's death blurred together, time bending around preparation and prophecy. Margaret's conservatory became their war room – ancient texts spread across every surface, protection spells humming in the greenhouse glass, while Sarah's investigative notes wove through centuries of magical history. James and Nathan pored over ritual requirements, their combined knowledge building framework for what was to come.

But on March 19th, as Ostara's dawn approached with inexorable purpose, Alex simply... vanished.

They searched Salem's shadows for hours – Nathan's magic calling to his partner's like beacon to flame, Margaret's locator spells spinning useless in ancient streets, Sarah checking every place that held meaning in their tangled story. Even the Black Eyed Children seemed absent, as if holding their breath along with the rest of Salem.

As false dawn painted the sky in shades of coming spring, James suddenly straightened, memory clicking into place. "I know where he is." His voice carried quiet certainty that made them all turn. "There's only one place he could be – the same place I went, when I faced this choice."

The lighthouse. Of course. Where else would Alex Kingston go to watch darkness gather before dawn?

Above them, stars began fading one by one.

The lighthouse beam cut perfect arcs through pre-dawn darkness, each sweep a heartbeat marking time's slow march toward morning. Alex gripped the railing's cold metal, letting its ancient rhythm ground him while his thoughts spiraled like the seabirds wheeling below. Salt wind carried prophecy's weight, heavy with promise and threat alike.

Each flash of light painted snapshots of what waited – Nathan's eyes bright with love and steel determination, void-dark children watching from lengthening shadows, Salem herself balanced on destiny's knife edge. His town, his heart, his fate, all turning like the lighthouse beam through endless night. Everything they'd fought for, everything they'd lost, everything still hanging in balance before dawn's judgment.

"Some view, isn't it?"

His father's voice made him jump. James stood haloed in the doorway's light, silhouette both achingly familiar and strangely new – a ghost made flesh, wearing ten years of void-touched absence like a second skin.

"The lost find their way here," James said softly, moving to join his son at the railing. "When choices weigh heaviest, when destiny feels too large to carry alone. I stood right here, that last night, watching these same waters and wondering if I was strong enough for what came next."

"Dad." The word caught like sea spray in Alex's throat. "How did you find me?"

James settled beside him at the railing, both Kingston men watching light wage eternal war with darkness across endless water. For several heartbeats, they just existed together – father and son sharing space after a decade of void-touched absence, while above them stars surrendered one by one to coming dawn.

"Used to come here myself." James's voice carried soft memory. "When the weight of it all got too heavy. Something about this view..." He gestured at the horizon where silver met black. "Way the beam cuts through darkness, steady as heartbeat. Helps put cosmic troubles in perspective."

He turned, and Alex saw tears catching lighthouse light. "Need you to know something, son. How proud I am – of the man you've become, the strength you've shown. The love you and Nathan share..." Words failed him momentarily. "And how sorry I am, for all these years lost."

"Why didn't you..." Alex's voice cracked on years of questions. "Just one word, one sign you were alive somewhere..."

James's sigh held a decade's worth of regret. "Thought I was protecting you both – you and your mother. Keeping distance meant keeping you safe." His hand found Alex's shoulder, tentative at first before settling with remembered purpose. "I was wrong. Watching you these past months, seeing you face what I ran from... you're stronger than I ever was, Alex. Braver than I dreamed of being."

The beam swept past again, catching tears on both their faces.

Something broke in Alex then – a dam holding back ten years of absence. He pulled his father into fierce embrace, feeling James's surprised intake of breath before strong arms wrapped around him in return. A decade of missing pieces clicked together as they held each other, every unasked question finding answer in shared heartbeat.

"Missed you so much, Dad." The words muffled against James's coat, carrying the weight of a thousand empty holidays, a thousand unshared moments.

"My boy." James's voice roughened with emotion, arms tightening as if afraid Alex might vanish. "God, I missed you. More than I have words to tell."

They separated slowly, both making show of studying the horizon while wiping eyes. The beacon swept past again, but this time Alex felt its strength rather than its solitude – light against eternal dark, order standing fierce against chaos's hunger.

"We end this." Alex's voice found steel beneath grief. "Together, all of us. Whatever comes."

Pride and love transformed James's face as he studied his son. "Yes." His smile carried certainty. "Kingston and Holloway blood finally joined as it was meant to be." His hand squeezed Alex's shoulder, touch carrying generations of purpose. "Time to finish what our ancestors began."

Above them, stars pulsed in rhythm with the lighthouse beam, as if the very night held its breath waiting for dawn's judgment. Somewhere in Salem's depths, children who had never been children paused their ancient games, sensing prophecy about to turn its final page.

At the top of the lighthouse stairs, James suddenly paused, his hand going to his chest. Alex watched as his father fumbled beneath his shirt, drawing out a simple gold chain.

"Alex." James's voice carried the weight of years. "I want you to have something." He unclasped the chain, revealing a wedding ring that caught the lighthouse beam. "Your mother gave me this on our wedding day. I've kept it close ever since."

Alex's breath caught at the sight of the simple gold band, worn smooth by years of constant touch.

"Dad, I can't—" he started, overwhelmed by the gesture's significance.

"You can." James's smile held gentle certainty. "Some might say this thing between you and Nathan happened too fast to be the key to everything. But real love..." He shook his head. "Real love doesn't always need time. Sometimes it just is."

He pressed the ring into Alex's palm, closing his son's fingers around it. "You and Nathan deserve the chance at happiness that I had to leave behind."

"Dad..." Alex's voice cracked as he stared at the ring.

"I want you to have this." James's voice roughened with emotion. "Not just as a piece of your mother and me, but as a symbol of the love that's going to save us all – yours and Nathan's."

His hands found Alex's shoulders, blue eyes meeting matching blue. "I need you to know how incredibly proud I am of the man you've become. Your strength, your heart, your willingness to fight for what matters... you're everything I could have hoped for in a son, and more."

Warmth bloomed in Alex's chest – a lifetime of longing for his father's approval finally fulfilled. "Thank you," he managed, barely above a whisper.

Their hug lasted longer this time, making up for years of missed embraces. When they pulled apart, both blinked back tears.

"Now," James cleared his throat, lightening the moment, "I'm not saying propose to Nathan this second. But when you know it's time – and you will know – you'll have a ring ready."

Alex laughed, the sound surprising them both. "Maybe we should save the world first?"

"Well," James's grin matched the one Alex saw in mirrors, "nothing says 'marry me' quite like preventing an apocalypse together."

As their chuckles faded, Alex felt something shift inside him. The weight of their task remained, the danger still loomed, but now it balanced against something stronger – hope, love, and the unshakeable knowledge that he wasn't alone. He had Nathan, his father, his friends.

The ring settled against his chest as he slipped the chain over his head, feeling right – like a prophecy fulfilling itself in small ways before the big moment.

"Come on," he said, new purpose in his voice. "Let's go save the world."

They descended the lighthouse stairs together, leaving behind the steady sweep of the beacon. But Alex carried his own light now – family, legacy, and love burning bright enough to face whatever darkness waited below.

Chapter Fifteen

Into the Darkness

The door to Margaret's mansion burst open, Alex and James rushing into a room thick with tension. The others huddled around Sarah's laptop screens, their faces illuminated by data that spelled approaching doom.

"What's happening?" James read the room's energy instantly.

"They're moving." Nathan's voice carried barely controlled fear. "The Shepherds are mobilizing across Salem. Whatever they're planning, it's starting."

Sarah's fingers flew across her keyboard. "Black Eyed Children sightings everywhere in the last hour. They're done pretending – it's like they want to be seen now."

Alex's eyes found Nathan's across the room, their connection humming with shared understanding. The moment they'd been dreading, preparing for, had finally arrived.

James swept to the central table, unrolling an ancient map of Salem that seemed to pulse with its own energy. "They'll converge here." His finger landed on the city's heart. "Where the veil runs thinnest. Where they'll try to complete Balor's awakening."

"Then that's our target." Alex felt his father's ring warm against his chest, a reminder of everything at stake. His voice stayed steady despite the fear coursing through his veins.

Nathan moved to his side, their fingers intertwining with practiced ease. "Together," he whispered, their magic harmonizing at the contact.

James watched them with fierce pride. "You two will need to perform the sealing ritual at the convergence point. The rest of us..." He glanced at Margaret and Sarah. "We'll hold back the Shepherds and their children as long as we can."

"The Order's been notified." Margaret's voice carried centuries of authority. "Adrianna's people will protect the town's non-magical residents. Keep reality stable for those who can't know what's really happening."

Above them, thunder rolled without clouds, and somewhere in Salem's shadows, children began to sing.

"But how will we know what to do?" Nathan's voice carried the weight of prophecy and doubt.

James's smile held a flash of his old mischief despite the gravity pressing down on them. "Trust each other. Trust what you feel. The knowledge runs in both your bloodlines – when the moment comes, you'll know."

As they gathered supplies, a strange calm settled over Alex. Fear still churned beneath his skin, but something stronger rose to meet it – a bone-deep certainty that this was his path, their path, written in magic older than Salem itself.

The mansion shuddered suddenly, foundation stones groaning. Outside, the sky pulsed with sick light that shouldn't exist.

"It's starting." James's voice turned to steel. "The entity's pushing against the weakening seal. We move now!"

They burst into the night, piling into vehicles with practiced urgency. Reality warped around them as they drove, the world bending like hot glass as Balor strained against ancient bonds. Salem's skyline shimmered beneath a dome of impossible energy, dark figures moving within like sharks beneath ice.

Alex white-knuckled the steering wheel, stealing glances at Nathan beside him. Memories flashed through his mind – their first meeting, shared coffee and hidden glances, quiet moments when the world narrowed to just them. Now here they were, racing toward a confrontation that would decide everything.

Black Eyed Children materialized in the road ahead, their void-dark eyes fixed on the approaching cars with hungry patience.

"Hold on!" Alex floored the accelerator. The spectral figures burst apart like smoke as the car plowed through, reforming behind them with terrible purpose.

They skidded into the town square, leaping out into chaos. Townspeople fled from shadows that moved with conscious malice, while at the center, a vortex of dark energy pulsed like a wound in reality.

"There!" James's voice cut through the mayhem, pointing to the storm's heart. "That's your target!"

Alex caught Nathan's eyes one last time – a look that carried love and determination and promises of tomorrow. Their hands found each other with practiced ease, magic humming between them like struck crystal. Together, they plunged into the maelstrom that would either save or doom everything they held dear.

The ring pressed against Alex's chest, warm with purpose, as behind them, children's laughter echoed from too many directions at once.

Battle erupted behind them as James, Margaret, and Sarah engaged the darkness, but Alex and Nathan pushed forward toward their true purpose – the ritual that would either save Salem or surrender it to chaos.

The vortex's heart held an impossible quiet. The chaos of fighting fell away, leaving them alone in the eye of the storm. They faced each other, fingers interlaced, as reality itself seemed to hold its breath. Ancient power stirred in Alex's blood, singing in harmony with their joined magic. Nathan's pendant blazed like a captured star, pulsing in rhythm with their synchronized heartbeats.

"Ready?" Alex's voice barely carried above the energy humming around them.

Nathan's eyes held universes of love and steel determination. "With you? Always."

The words came to them like remembered music – an incantation older than Salem, older than the first whispered prophecies. They spoke as one, their voices weaving together as light bloomed beneath their feet, spreading ancient patterns across the trembling ground.

But something vast and hungry pushed back against their efforts. Balor had noticed them now, its ancient malevolence pressing against the barriers between realities. Alex felt its attention like a physical weight – endless chaos recognizing the threat of their ordered love.

The vortex twisted around them, reality bleeding at its edges as two forces as old as existence itself clashed: chaos incarnate against the pure, structured power of love freely given. In this moment, at this center point of everything, two young men bound by prophecy and choice stood together against the void.

The ring against Alex's chest burned with purpose, while Nathan's pendant threw out rays of defiant light. Around them, children's laughter echoed with increasing desperation as the final battle for more than just Salem's soul began.

The ancient words hung in the air like frost, thrumming with power. Alex and Nathan stood within the vortex's heart, hands clasped, eyes locked, as intricate patterns of light bloomed beneath their feet. The seal's design spread outward in complex webs of energy, each line pulsing with their combined magic.

For one perfect moment, the world seemed to pause. Power coursed through them like lightning seeking ground, their love made manifest in pure energy. This was it – the moment when

Kingston and Holloway blood would finally unite, sealing chaos away forever.

Except... nothing happened.

The light pulsed once, twice, then began to fade. The intricate patterns dimmed to ghostly traces, mere echoes of what should have been their triumph. The vortex continued its hungry dance around them, undiminished.

"I don't understand." Nathan's voice cracked with confusion and rising fear. "This should have worked. Why isn't it working?"

Alex dropped to his knees, studying the fading seal. The parallel lines representing their bloodlines remained stubbornly separate, a void between them where unity should have bloomed.

"Something's wrong." His fingers traced the gap. "The lines won't join. Our bloodlines aren't merging like they should."

Battle raged around their bubble of failure – magical explosions, desperate shouts, and the hollow laughter of children who had never been children. Nathan knelt beside Alex, his touch carrying tremors of fear.

"How is that possible?" His voice barely carried above the chaos. "We love each other. We're together. Isn't that what the prophecy meant?"

Dark energy lashed from the vortex like a striking snake, missing them by inches. Balor pushed harder against reality's thinning walls, growing stronger with each passing moment.

"Again," Alex grabbed Nathan's hands. "We try again. Maybe we missed something in the words, or—"

But their second attempt felt wrong from the start. The power hummed beneath their skin, but disconnected, like instruments playing slightly out of tune. Something vital remained just out of reach.

"Alex! Nathan!" James's voice cut through the chaos, strained with effort. "What's happening? The seal's not taking!"

Alex met his father's desperate gaze across the battlefield. "It's not working! The bloodlines won't unite!"

Understanding dawned on James's face, quickly hardening to determination. "Hold on!" He started toward them. "Just hold your ground. I'm coming!"

But dark-robed figures materialized to intercept him, wielding shadows like living weapons. Alex watched helplessly as his father was driven back, fighting with desperate intensity against the Shepherds' relentless assault.

The ring pressed cold against Alex's chest as reality continued to warp around them, and somewhere in the chaos, children's laughter took on a triumphant edge.

We have to help him!" Nathan lurched toward James, but Alex caught his arm.

"Wait." The word cost him everything to say. "We can't leave the seal. If we move now, we lose what little hold we have left."

They stood frozen between duty and desperation, watching their loved ones fight against impossible odds. Through the chaos, they glimpsed Sarah and Margaret – the witch wielding spells like lightning while the reporter swung an iron fireplace poker with terrifying efficiency, back-to-back against children whose smiles held void-dark hunger.

"Alex." Nathan's voice cracked on his name. "What do we do?"

The ring burned cold against Alex's chest, its promise of legacy and love feeling suddenly hollow. He met Nathan's eyes, seeing his own fear and helplessness mirrored there. Their connection, usually so strong it made magic sing, felt fragile as spider silk.

"I don't know." The admission tasted like ash. "I thought we were enough. Our love, our connection – it was supposed to be the key." His fingers found Nathan's, squeezing tight. "But something's missing, and I can't..."

The vortex convulsed around them, reality shuddering like a dying thing. Then came a sound that froze their blood – a roar from somewhere beneath reality itself, ancient and hungry and finally, finally waking up.

Balor stirred in its prison of order, and they were painfully, terribly out of time.

Alex gripped Nathan's hands tighter, desperation crystallizing into determination. "We keep trying. Whatever we're missing, whatever's wrong – we figure it out now."

"Together." Nathan's voice carried their shared promise, though fear threaded its edges.

They began the incantation again, pouring everything they had – love, will, destiny – into ancient words. But Alex couldn't shake the feeling that something crucial danced just beyond their grasp, something that had been obvious all along.

The vortex vanished between one breath and the next. Sudden silence pressed against their ears, more terrifying than the chaos had been. They stood frozen, hands locked together, as dust settled around them like snow.

"Did we..." Nathan's whisper sounded too loud in the quiet. "Did it work?"

Alex's heart sank as he studied the ground. The seal's pattern remained, ghost-pale and unchanged, their bloodlines still separated by that impossible gap.

"No." The word tasted like failure. "We're still missing something vital."

Sarah and Margaret emerged from the settling dust, battered but alive. "Alex! Nathan!" Sarah's voice carried desperate relief. "Are you okay? Tell me the ritual worked."

Before Alex could confess their failure, something cut through the air that made his magic recoil. It started as a rumble beneath their feet, building into laughter that seemed to come from everywhere and nowhere – not the hollow mirth of Black

Eyed Children, but something older, darker, infinitely more malevolent.

"Oh, it worked." The voice dripped ancient amusement, bypassing their ears to resonate directly in their minds. "Just not as you hoped, precious Children of Cerridwen."

Nathan's fingers tightened around Alex's. Sarah and Margaret moved closer, forming a protective circle that felt painfully inadequate against what waited in the darkness.

"What was that?" Sarah's reporter's steadiness cracked slightly.

"I think," Alex said slowly, "we just met the God of Chaos. Or at least, his voice."

The laughter came again, making reality shiver around them. "Clever child." Mockery frosted each word. "But not clever enough, it seems. Your pathetic attempt at sealing has only fed my strength."

Alex's mind spun through possibilities, each worse than the last. How could their failure have fed the entity's strength? What crucial piece had they missed in the prophecy's puzzle?

Then a worse thought struck him like lightning. "Dad?" The word came out barely above a whisper. "Where's my father?"

They turned as one, really seeing the battlefield for the first time. Where James had last stood fighting against the Shepherds' shadow magic, only scorched earth remained.

"They took him." Ice formed in Alex's veins as understanding crashed over him. "The Shepherds grabbed him in the chaos."

"Oh god." Sarah's reporter's mind connected the dots first. "James knows more about the seal than anyone alive. If they're trying to fully wake this thing..."

"They'll use him to do it." Nathan's voice carried grim certainty, his hand finding Alex's again.

Margaret's face hardened into something ancient and dangerous. "Then we move. Now. Before they can complete whatever ritual they have planned."

The entity's laughter echoed around them again, and in its sound, they heard James screaming.

Alex felt something harden inside him, despair crystallizing into purpose. "We find him. Now. We can't complete the seal until we figure out what we're missing anyway, and I won't leave him with them."

"But they could be anywhere." Sarah's reporter's instincts kicked in despite her exhaustion. "Where would they—"

The entity's voice rolled through reality again, cutting her off. "Seek the place where it all began." Each word twisted space like a knife. "Where the veil first tore, and the traitor stirred her cauldron. But hurry, children. Time slips away like water through desperate fingers."

The presence receded, leaving behind silence that pressed against their skin like ice.

"The mining tunnels." Nathan's grip on Alex's hand tightened. "Valentine's Day – all those symbols, the altar. Everything we saw..."

"The convergence point." Understanding lit Alex's eyes. "Where the entity's power runs strongest. Where it all started."

"Then that's our target." Margaret's voice carried steel. Her garden-party elegance had given way to something older, something that remembered when magic ran wild and raw.

They rushed for Alex's car, but dread coiled in his stomach like a living thing. The entity wasn't just ahead of them – it had been herding them toward this moment all along. His father's life balanced on choices they hadn't even made yet.

"Hold on, Dad," Alex whispered, feeling James's ring pulse cold against his chest. Behind them, something that wore a child's shape began to draw spiral patterns in the air with silver tears.

The night pressed closer, hungry for what came next.

Alex floored the accelerator, Salem's outskirts blurring past. Hope warred with the echo of the entity's laughter still rolling through his mind, each mocking note a reminder of what waited ahead.

The mining tunnels gaped before them like a wound in the hillside, partially collapsed from decades of abandonment. Wind whispered through the entrance, carrying sounds that might have been echoes, might have been children playing games that had never known daylight.

"Well, that's not ominous at all." Sarah's attempt at humor fell flat against the tunnel's watching darkness.

Alex and Nathan shared a look, remembering their Valentine's night discovery that felt like years ago now. Light bloomed in their hands, joined by Margaret's silver-white glow. "Stay close," Alex warned, memories of their last venture here pressing cold against his skin.

Their magical light seemed pathetically small against the absolute dark. The air grew thick and heavy as they ventured deeper, their footsteps echoing back wrong, as if something else walked just behind them.

"Anyone else feel like we're being watched?" Sarah's whisper carried more than just nerves.

Alex knew exactly what she meant. The darkness had weight here, presence. Whispers teased the edges of his hearing – too quiet to understand, too persistent to ignore. The shadows between their lights moved with purpose, reshaping themselves when viewed directly.

The tunnel split and split again, each choice offering new ways to get lost in this labyrinth of ancient stone and older secrets.

"How do we know which way?" Frustration edged Nathan's voice. "They could be anywhere down here."

Alex closed his eyes, reaching for some sense of his father. Something brushed his consciousness – not James, but a woman's voice, ancient and familiar though he'd never heard it before. *Left*, it whispered.

"This way." His eyes snapped open, pointing left with complete certainty. He couldn't explain how he knew, but something pulled him forward like a lodestone finding true north.

Behind them, small footprints appeared in the tunnel dust, though no children had passed this way in decades.

The tunnels drew them deeper, passages constricting to narrow throats before opening into caverns vast enough to swallow their light. Ancient symbols emerged from the darkness as they passed – spirals that seemed to move when caught in peripheral vision, runes that whispered meanings older than language.

The walls felt alive, watching their progress with patient malice. Shadows danced at the edge of sight, always retreating when confronted directly. Their lights caught glimpses of markings that shouldn't exist – patterns that suggested the miners hadn't been the first to delve these depths.

"Wait." Margaret's light swept the ground. "Look at this."

Fresh footprints marred the tunnel's dust – multiple sets all heading deeper into the earth's wounds. Some looked human. Others... didn't quite match any known anatomy.

"We're getting close." Sarah's hope carried an edge of fear.

Their brief relief shattered at the next turn. Three identical tunnels gaped before them, each throat of darkness promising different flavors of horror. The walls here bore more elaborate markings – spirals within spirals, each telling stories that hurt the mind to contemplate.

"Alex?" Nathan's voice carried quiet desperation.

Alex closed his eyes, reaching for that earlier certainty, that pull toward his father. But the tunnels felt wrong here, reality thin and stretched like old fabric. Only whispers answered, speaking words that might have been names, might have been prayers.

"I can't..." Frustration cracked his voice. "The connection's gone. Something's blocking—"

A scream shattered the darkness – distant but unmistakable. James's voice, twisted with pain that echoed wrongly off stone that remembered older screams.

"Dad!" The word burst from Alex before he could stop it.

He plunged down the central passage, the others racing to keep up. Their wild lights caught fragments of horror – mining equipment long abandoned and symbols that glowed with hungry purpose.

Behind them, small footsteps appeared in the dust, following with terrible patience.

James's scream echoed closer, bouncing off stone that seemed to drink the sound. Alex's foot caught something in the darkness, sending him sprawling. His magical light winked out like a dying star.

"Alex!" Nathan was at his side instantly, warm hands finding him in the dark.

As they helped him up, Alex's fingers brushed what had tripped him – something too smooth, too cold to be natural stone. He knew what it was before Nathan's light found it, but seeing it still stopped his breath. The founder's stone lay corrupted, dark veins pulsing beneath its surface like infected blood.

"How did..." Sarah's whisper carried equal parts awe and dread. "Why would they leave this here?"

Another scream cut through the tunnels, closer now and wrong – like something was using James's voice to make sounds a human throat shouldn't produce. Dark energy rolled through the passage like a physical wave, nearly taking their feet from under them.

"God." The word fell from Alex's lips as horror dawned. "We're too late. They've started."

The whispers that had stalked them rose to a fever pitch, and ahead, sickly light pulsed in rhythm with the stone's dark veins. Whatever ritual the Shepherds had begun, it fed on James's pain, each scream another step toward whatever waited in the void beyond reality.

Alex clutched the corrupted stone, its surface fever-warm against his palm. The ring around his neck grew colder with each step deeper into the earth's wounds, as if recognizing the proximity of something that remembered when order first caged chaos.

Behind them, children's laughter echoed from too many directions at once.

They followed the corrupted stone's fever-warmth deeper into earth's bones, guided by sickly light that grew stronger with each turn. The whispers had become a chorus now, voices speaking words that existed before language, seeming to leak from the very stone around them.

"Close now." Margaret's voice barely carried above the tunnel's watching silence. "Eyes sharp."

The passage widened, rough walls smoothing into worked stone older than Salem's first foundations. Ancient symbols pulsed with their own light – patterns Alex recognized from the lighthouse, from the prophecy, from nightmares he couldn't quite remember upon waking.

"There." Sarah pointed toward orange light flickering ahead, its color wrong against the tunnel's absolute dark.

They crept forward, matching their steps to the rhythm of chanting that vibrated through the ground like a dying heartbeat. Nathan's hand found Alex's in the dark, fingers intertwining with practiced ease.

"Whatever comes next," Nathan whispered, his touch grounding Alex against rising fear, "we face it together."

Alex squeezed back, drawing strength from their connection. They doused their lights, letting the chamber's sick glow guide them forward through stone that remembered older rituals.

The cavern that opened before them stretched impossibly vast, its ceiling lost in shadows that moved with purpose. Pillars thick as ancient trees rose into darkness, each carved with symbols that hurt the mind to read directly. At the chamber's heart, a dais of black stone waited like an open wound, ringed by circles that glowed with power older than order itself.

Twelve robed figures swayed in perfect unison around the altar, their chanting building toward something terrible. James lay motionless on the black stone, while above him stood a thirteenth figure in elaborate robes, wielding a staff that pulsed in rhythm with the founder's stone's corruption.

The ring against Alex's chest grew colder with each breath, as if recognizing the proximity of something that remembered when chaos wore flesh.

"Dad." Alex's whisper caught in his throat, fingers whitening around the corrupted stone.

The leader's staff rose like a conductor's baton, chanting building toward something terrible. Circles etched in ancient stone blazed with light that shouldn't exist, casting shadows that moved independent of their sources.

"We have to move. Now." Sarah's urgency carried the weight of every disappearance they'd failed to prevent.

Alex felt destiny pressing down like physical weight. Everything – every revelation, every loss, every moment since those first black eyes appeared at his door – had led them here. He caught Nathan's gaze, saw his own mix of terror and steel reflected back.

"We use what we've got." Alex raised the founder's stone, dark veins pulsing against his palm. "Our magic, whatever power this thing still holds. Maybe we can't complete the seal, but we can sure as hell disrupt their party."

Nathan's hand covered his on the stone, their magic harmonizing instantly. "Together," he said, the word carrying the weight of prophecy.

They rose as one, ready to step into whatever waited in that ancient chamber. But before they could move, the chanting cut off like a severed throat. Silence rushed in, broken by laughter that bubbled up from earth's bones – a sound that remembered when reality had no rules.

The leader turned, hood falling back to reveal a face that twisted something in Alex's memory. Black eyes, endless as the void, stared back at them. When he spoke, his voice carried echoes of every scream these tunnels had ever heard.

"Welcome, children." His smile belonged to something that had never worn human flesh. "We've been so looking forward to this reunion."

Every robed figure turned in perfect unison, their eyes matching their leader's bottomless dark. The founder's stone burned fever-hot against Alex's palm, pulsing in rhythm with his racing heart.

The ring around his neck grew cold enough to burn as reality held its breath, waiting to see which way the prophecy would fall. Behind them, small footsteps stopped their patient approach, and above, in darkness that moved with purpose, children's voices began to sing a song that had never known daylight.

The final page of their story waited to be written, and the ink would be paid for in blood and chaos.

Chapter Sixteen

The Truth Revealed

Silence filled the chamber like smoke, heavy and choking. The robed figures stood unnaturally still, their void-dark eyes fixed on the intruders with hungry patience. From his place on the dais, their leader studied them with calculating amusement, like a cat watching cornered mice.

"I have to say," his voice carried impossible resonance, "you've surprised me. Though perhaps I shouldn't be shocked – Kingstons and Holloways have always been ruthlessly stubborn about their principles."

"We stand against any threat to the natural order." Margaret's voice cut through the chamber's weight, carrying centuries of authority. But as she studied the leader's face, something familiar tugged at ancient memory. Something in the way he held himself, in features twisted by whatever darkness he'd embraced.

"What have you done to my father?" Alex's demand echoed off stones that remembered older betrayals.

The leader's laugh held no joy, only the cold mirth of chaos given voice. "Really, Margaret? You don't recognize your own flesh and blood?"

Nathan staggered as if struck. "Uncle Richard?" The name fell from his lips like a prayer he'd never meant to speak.

"What twisted game is this?" Margaret's voice cracked for the first time, power warring with maternal instinct.

The leader pulled back his hood, revealing Richard Holloway's face – older now, marked by a decade of dark magic, but unmistakably Margaret's lost son. "Oh Mother," he smiled with too many teeth. "Did you really think I'd died that night? That I'd sacrificed myself for James's foolish attempt at heroism?"

"You fool." Margaret's words carried decades of grief suddenly transformed to rage. "I raised you better than this. The dark arts consume everything they touch."

Richard spread his arms wide, robes rippling with symbols that hurt the mind to read directly. "Welcome," his voice echoed with something ancient and hungry, "to the true heart of the Shepherds of the Dark."

"You're trying to destroy Salem!" Sarah's reporter's voice cut through the chamber's weight.

Richard's void-dark eyes flashed. "Such a limited perspective. The entity you fear isn't our enemy – it's our salvation. For generations, we've worked to harness its power, to elevate humanity beyond the prison of order."

"By stealing children?" Nathan's words carried generations of protective magic. "By destroying lives?"

"Necessary steps." Richard's smile showed too many teeth. "Steps your ancestors," he gestured to Alex and Nathan, "were too weak to take. But tonight changes everything. James's unwilling contribution and the corrupted stone will finally complete what began centuries ago."

James stirred on the altar, pain twisting his features. Richard's gaze swept their small group like a predator choosing its next meal. "Perhaps introductions are in order. Some faces you might recognize."

The figure to his right lowered their hood, revealing Dr. Eleanor Blackthorn's familiar features. Alex felt Sarah stiffen beside him – they'd interviewed the Historical Society curator dozen of times, never suspecting.

"Dr. Blackthorn has ensured our town's true history remains... properly documented." Richard's words dripped dark amusement. His attention shifted left, smile widening impossibly. "And of course, our most valuable asset at the Salem Gazette. Tom, join us properly."

Horror crashed through Alex as their editor lowered his hood. Tom Marshton – his mentor, his guide through journalism's twisted paths – stood among their enemies.

"Tom?" Sarah's whisper carried broken trust. "God, no."

"I'm sorry, Sarah." Tom's familiar gruff voice carried something ancient and hungry now. He moved to Richard's side with fluid grace that didn't match his bearlike frame.

"Mr. Marshton has been essential." Richard's hand settled on Tom's shoulder like a claiming mark. "Keeping certain stories buried, guiding your investigation exactly where we needed it."

The betrayal hit Alex like physical pain. Every late night at the paper, every story edit, every piece of advice – had it all been manipulation?

"You'll understand eventually, Kingston." Something flickered behind Tom's newly darkened eyes – regret or triumph, impossible to tell. "The Shepherds' vision extends beyond Salem, beyond this reality. What comes next... it's bigger than all of us."

"You're starting to understand." Richard's approval dripped venom. "The Shepherds' roots run deeper than Salem's foundations. We've infiltrated every institution, every seat of power." His laugh echoed off ancient stone, a sound that had forgotten how to be human. "Even your precious Order of Salem never saw us moving in their own shadows."

Black Eyed Children materialized from darkness like smoke given purpose, their void-dark eyes fixed on the small group with infinite patience. The chamber's shadows deepened, responding to their presence.

Alex's mind spun through layers of betrayal, through the horrifying scope of what they faced. But Nathan's hand found his, magic harmonizing between them like struck crystal. Sarah and

Margaret's presence steadied him, their combined strength a counterweight to rising despair.

"Doesn't matter how many masks you wear." Alex's voice carried unexpected steel, magic crackling between his fingers like captured lightning. "What you're doing ends here."

Something flickered across Richard's face – annoyance rippling his calculated amusement. Darkness gathered around him like a living cloak. "Such conviction, Alex. But you're too late. The ritual feeds on your father's life force, awakening what should never have been bound."

His staff pulsed with sick light, symbols writhing across its twisted surface. "You have a choice, Alex, Embrace your true heritage, accept the god of chaos's gifts..." His smile showed too many teeth. "Or share James's fate. The power waiting beyond order's prison exceeds anything you've imagined. All it asks is that you release these childish notions of right and wrong."

The corrupted stone burned against Alex's palm, responding to the power building in the ancient chamber. He caught Nathan's eyes, finding steel determination there, then glanced back at Sarah and Margaret's unwavering faces. In this moment, facing a secret society that had pulled Salem's strings for generations, choice crystallized into certainty.

"Never." The word carried generations of Kingston conviction. "Whatever power chaos offers, the price is too high. We'll find another way."

Richard's carefully crafted mask cracked, revealing something ancient and hungry beneath. "Foolish boy." His snarl echoed off stones that remembered older betrayals. "You've chosen your side. Now watch as we build a new world on the ashes of your precious order."

At his gesture, the robed figures resumed their chanting, while Black Eyed Children glided forward with terrible grace. The chamber itself seemed to tremble, dark energy crackling through air grown thick with possibility.

James stirred on the altar, pain twisting his features. Alex's heart clenched at his father's groan.

"Stop this." Nathan's voice carried quiet authority. "Whatever power you think you'll gain, it's not worth destroying everything."

"You've lost the right to make demands, nephew." Richard's amusement frosted into something darker. His staff pulsed with sick light. "Time to end this tedious family drama."

The children moved with liquid purpose while robed figures tightened their circle, shadows stretching wrong beneath their feet.

"Nathan." Alex's whisper carried desperate hope. "The stone – if we try the ritual here, at the source..."

Nathan's hand covered his on the corrupted stone instantly, their magic harmonizing like struck crystal. Power surged between them, pure and fierce.

Richard's void-dark eyes widened. "Stop them!"

But before the Shepherds could close their trap, blue-white light erupted from the stone, pushing back darkness with temporary brilliance. The barrier wouldn't hold long, but in this moment of borrowed time, Alex felt prophecy crystallize into possibility.

In their bubble of borrowed time, Margaret caught her son's gaze. "Richard." Her voice carried decades of maternal ache. "It's not too late. Whatever this thing promises, it's lying. Help us end this."

Something flickered behind Richard's void-dark eyes – a ghost of the man he'd been, there and gone like smoke. "You still don't understand." Fury frosted his words. "The power we're unleashing will remake everything. If you won't join willingly, your sacrifice will serve just as well."

His staff rose like a conductor's baton, darkness coiling around him like living smoke. The Black Eyed Children resumed their liquid advance while the Shepherds' chanting built toward something terrible. Reality itself seemed to bend, responding to forces that remembered when chaos wore flesh.

The corrupted stone burned against Alex's palm, pulsing in harmony with the chamber's sick energy. Nathan's pendant blazed in answer, their combined magic humming like struck crystal.

"Whatever comes next," Nathan's voice carried steel beneath its softness, "I love you."

As Richard's power gathered, as James writhed on the altar between worlds, as reality threatened to tear – Alex felt the weight of prophecy bearing down. Everything they'd fought for, everything they loved, balanced on this moment's knife edge.

The chamber trembled, ancient stone groaning under forces it was never meant to contain. Their world teetered on the brink of transformation, waiting to see which way prophecy would fall.

Just as Richard's staff crackled with killing power, a voice cut through the chaos like a blade of pure authority.

"Enough."

Margaret Holloway stood somehow taller, her silver hair catching light that shouldn't exist. Power radiated from her in waves, causing the Black Eyed Children to retreat like smoke before wind. Even the Shepherds hesitated, sensing something ancient and implacable in her presence.

She strode through their barrier of light, each step carrying centuries of determination. "You disappoint me, Richard."

"Mother." Her son's face twisted with rage and something deeper – a child's fear of maternal judgment. "Still clinging to your outdated ideals? The world we're creating has no room for such weakness."

Margaret's laugh held no warmth. "New world?" Her power filled the chamber like storm clouds gathering. "You're a child playing with forces you can't begin to understand."

"You're too late!" Richard's voice carried triumphant madness. "James's life force feeds our god even now. Not even you can stop what's coming."

Margaret's eyes narrowed to dangerous slits. "We'll see." Power crackled around her like bottled lightning. "Alex, Nathan – the stone and pendant. Channel everything you feel. Love runs deeper than chaos ever could."

As magic surged between the young men through stone and pendant, Margaret faced her son. "Shall we settle this properly, Richard? Show me what darkness has taught you."

His answer came as a bolt of void-dark energy. Margaret deflected it with elegant precision, ancient stone shrieking as it took the hit instead. What followed defied description – Margaret, whom Alex had known only as Nathan's elegant grandmother, moved like living mercury. Mother and son traded spells that bent reality, light warring with darkness in a duel that spoke of decades of building tension.

The chamber erupted. Shepherds and their hollow-eyed children surged forward, emboldened by their leader's rage.

"Alex, Nathan, now!" Sarah's warning cut through chaos.

Alex's magic burst forth, sending robed figures tumbling like scattered pins. The founder's stone blazed between them as they began the incantation again, its light growing until it rivaled the sun.

Margaret and Richard's battle reached impossible intensity. She matched him blow for blow, drawing on generations of

Holloway power. But with each exchange, darkness fed him strength, twisting him further from the son she'd known.

"Can't you see?" Richard deflected her attack, void-dark energy coiling around him like smoke. "The old ways die tonight! Our true god rises, and Salem will be its cradle!"

"Power built on pain is no power at all." Margaret's voice held steady despite the sweat on her brow. "It's poison, Richard. It will devour everything you are."

Through the chaos, Alex noticed something strange around his father. The dark energy cocooning James pulsed irregularly, weakening whenever the founder's stone flared.

"Nathan!" Hope sparked in Alex's chest. "Look – we're disrupting it!"

"Then we hit it harder." Nathan's determination sang through their joined magic.

They poured everything into the stone – love, fear, hope, destiny. Nathan's pendant blazed in harmony, the artifacts resonating like struck crystal. Light exploded from both, painting the chamber in impossible radiance. For one eternal moment, everything froze – sorcerers mid-spell, Shepherds caught between steps, Black Eyed Children suspended like insects in amber.

As vision returned, Alex's heart stuttered. The corrupted stone had shattered, its pieces scattered like dark stars. But between their outstretched hands hovered something new – a perfect sphere of blue-white energy that sang with pure possibility.

Richard's roar of fury shattered the moment.

Time stretched like taffy as darkness erupted from his staff, writhing tentacles of void-energy striking with serpent speed. The orb of light pulsed between them, defiant against approaching shadow.

"Alex!" Nathan's desperate reach came too late.

Darkness struck like a physical thing, tearing them apart. Alex slammed into ancient stone, air exploding from his lungs. Nathan hit the ground hard near the chamber's edge. Their beautiful sphere of light flickered once, twice, then winked out of existence.

"No!" Margaret's cry held a mother's anguish.

Alex fought to stand, vision swimming as he searched for Nathan. He found him across the vast space, stirring weakly, his pendant now dark as dead stars.

Richard's laughter echoed off walls that remembered older betrayals. "Did you really think it would be that simple?" He stalked forward like a predator scenting blood. "That love alone could stop what we've spent generations building?"

The Black Eyed Children flowed forward like smoke given purpose, while the Shepherds' chanting built toward something terrible.

"It's done." Richard raised his staff, darkness coiling around him like living smoke. "The seal shatters, our god wakes, and Salem becomes ground zero for a new world order."

Alex struggled toward Nathan, but his body betrayed him, legs folding beneath him. Through blurred vision, he watched Sarah reach Nathan's still form, saw Margaret standing fierce against growing darkness. Everything felt distant, like a nightmare he couldn't wake from.

James convulsed on the altar, void-energy feeding through him into something vast and hungry. "Dad." The word fell from Alex's lips like a prayer.

Richard turned, eyes now perfect circles of darkness, his smile too wide for his face. "You fought well, nephew. But the game was rigged from the start."

Something roared beneath reality itself, shaking the chamber's ancient foundations. Cracks spider-webbed across the floor, leaking mist that moved with purpose.

"Feel it?" Richard's voice carried terrible joy. "The true god rises. Salem burns first, then the world."

Alex searched desperately for any hope, any chance of salvaging this catastrophe. But darkness grew like a living thing, Richard's laughter harmonizing with that impossible roar while Nathan lay still as death. The seal they'd tried to forge lay shattered like their chances of survival.

The chamber shuddered again, stones raining from above as whatever waited in the void pushed harder against reality's thinning walls. In this moment of absolute defeat, with Richard's triumph echoing off ancient stone and chaos pressing close,

Alex Kingston faced a terrible truth: everything they'd sacrificed, everything they'd fought for, might not have been enough.

Chapter Seventeen

Shadows Ascended

The chamber convulsed, ancient stone weeping dust and debris. Alex forced himself upright, every nerve screaming from his impact with the pillar. Through settling chaos, Margaret Holloway stood like the eye of a storm, silver hair writhing in magical wind as she faced her fallen son.

"You haven't won yet." Her voice cut through the chamber's hungry growls. "While I draw breath, you'll not unleash this madness on our world."

Richard's laugh held nothing human. "Then let's fix that particular problem, Mother."

He moved like smoke, staff trailing void-dark power. Margaret's hands rose, blue light crystallizing into a barrier that sang with generations of Holloway magic. Their powers collided in a fountain of impossible colors, reality warping where order met chaos.

For one eternal moment, Margaret held – face carved from steel, channeling power that remembered when magic ran wild and raw. Then her barrier shattered with a sound like breaking stars.

Darkness took her, lifting her like a puppet with cut strings before slamming her into ancient stone. She crumpled, terrifyingly still, as above them silver tears fell upward with increasing urgency.

Alex struggled toward Margaret, toward Nathan, toward anything that might turn this tide. But his body refused to cooperate, magic crackling through his nerves like broken glass.

Richard turned, triumph twisting his features into something inhuman. "Watch carefully, Alex Kingston. Watch the old guard fall. Your precious order crumbles, and nothing can stop what comes next."

A laugh rolled through the chamber – deep, wrong, a sound that remembered when reality had no rules. The same voice that had haunted their nightmares since this began.

James rose from the altar with puppet-string movements, each gesture an insult to natural law. When he turned, Alex's heart stuttered. His father's familiar eyes had transformed into perfect circles of void-dark nothing. The voice that emerged belonged to something that had never worn flesh.

"Finally." Balor spoke through James's mouth like ill-fitting clothing. "Eons of waiting, ended."

"Dad?" Alex's voice cracked on that single syllable. "Please..."

The thing wearing his father's face turned. For one heartbeat, something flickered in those bottomless eyes – a flash of James

Kingston fighting his way through darkness. Then void swallowed it whole.

"Your father fed my awakening well, child." Amusement frosted each word. "His shell serves a greater purpose now."

Richard prostrated himself before his twisted god. "Great One. We welcome you to this realm."

Those terrible eyes regarded Richard with ancient hunger. "You've earned your reward, faithful servant."

Darkness seeped from spider-web cracks in ancient stone, coiling around James's feet like living smoke. Black Eyed Children gathered close, their empty gazes fixed on their master with terrible devotion. The Shepherds fell to their knees before chaos incarnate.

Sarah scrambled back to Alex's side, leaving Margaret's too-still form. "What now?" Fear made her whisper sharp.

Alex surveyed their catastrophe. Margaret crumpled against ancient stone. Nathan motionless in shadow. The founder's stone scattered like dark stars across the chamber floor – their last hope shattered with it. Everything they'd fought for, every sacrifice made, had led to this moment of absolute failure.

His eyes found Nathan again, heart screaming to reach him. But chaos incarnate filled the space between them, making inches stretch to miles.

"Ah." The thing wearing his father's face turned those void-dark eyes on Alex. "The last conscious heir of our opposing bloodlines. How perfect that you should witness everything you love crumble while your other half lies broken."

James's arms rose, darkness crackling like captured lightning. "Watch closely as I unmake your precious Salem. The world follows after."

Reality convulsed. Fresh cracks spiderwebbed across ancient stone, leaking mist that moved with terrible purpose. The chamber's very foundations seemed to remember what they had been before order gave them shape.

Through the entity's laughter, through Richard's triumphant sneer, through darkness gathering for its final push into daylight, Alex Kingston faced impossible odds. His father lost to chaos, Nathan beyond reach, their allies fallen – what hope remained?

The answer lurked just beyond grasp, but one truth burned certain: while breath filled his lungs, while any chance of saving Nathan existed, surrender remained impossible.

Sarah's grip anchored him to now, her presence a reminder that he wasn't completely alone. "Whatever insane plan you're cooking up," she whispered, "I'm in."

They faced the nightmare together, two small figures against a tide of ancient darkness. The entity's stolen eyes found them, cruel amusement twisting James's familiar features.

"How precious." Its voice mixed James's tone with something that remembered when chaos wore flesh. "Salem's last defenders, standing brave before their own extinction."

A blur of movement caught Alex's eye. The Black Eyed Children flowed toward them like smoke given purpose, moving with terrible grace.

"Sarah, move—" His warning came too late.

They swarmed around them, small hands cold as grave dirt clutching at clothes and skin. Alex fought against their grip, but trying to strike them was like punching mist. Their touches left frost-burns on his soul.

Sarah's scream cut through chaos – a sound of pure terror as they dragged her across ancient stone, her feet barely brushing ground. Alex lunged after her, but darkness solidified between them, a wall of pure void forcing him back.

Richard's laughter echoed off watching walls as they delivered Sarah to James's possessed form. "Beautiful work, my little harbingers." His voice dripped satisfaction. "Such a precious offering."

The thing wearing his father's face cupped Sarah's chin. She tried to pull away but something held her still, horror freezing her features as those void-dark eyes studied her like a specimen.

"Yes." Its voice remembered when chaos wore flesh. "This one burns bright. Her essence will feed us well."

"Take me!" Alex slammed against the barrier, desperation cracking his voice. "I'm the one you want!"

Amusement flickered in those bottomless eyes. "Why choose? Your time approaches, young Kingston. But first..." It turned back to Sarah. "Let's savor this appetizer."

Darkness coiled around her like living rope. Sarah thrashed against it, terror warring with defiance. "Alex," she gasped as void claimed her. "Don't you dare give—"

The rest vanished as darkness lifted her, wrapping her in terrible light. The entity raised James's hands like a conductor before orchestra.

"Perfect." Its hiss carried ancient hunger. "Such sweet life force. We grow stronger."

Alex's knees hit stone as strength finally failed. He surveyed their absolute defeat: Margaret and Nathan still as death, Sarah feeding chaos itself, his father lost to ancient evil. He, Alex Kingston, their last hope, knelt powerless as reality prepared to remember what it had been before order gave shape to dreams.

True despair finally claimed Alex Kingston. This was their end – not with heroic sacrifice or noble last stands, but with whimpers in the dark. Every struggle, every sacrifice, had led to this moment of absolute failure. The entity would devour Sarah, then them all, before unmaking Salem and the world beyond.

"Finally understand?" Richard's voice cut through spiraling despair. "This is defiance's reward. You could have joined us, helped shape the chaos to come. Instead, watch everything you love feed our god's hunger."

Alex's nails bit crescents into his palms. He wanted to scream rage against darkness, wanted to die fighting like stories promised heroes should. But what meaning had defiance now? What could one broken witch do against chaos incarnate?

Sarah's essence drained away like water through cupped hands. The entity swelled with stolen life while reality shivered around them, remembering what it had been before order gave it shape. The bitter truth settled like ashes on Alex's tongue: they had lost. The final battle ended not with bangs but whispers.

In this moment of complete defeat, Alex closed his eyes. If oblivion waited, he would meet it remembering love. Nathan's smile on lazy mornings. His father's laugh before darkness claimed him. Sarah's fierce loyalty. Margaret's quiet strength. Everything precious chaos would soon unmake.

"I'm sorry," he whispered, tears cutting cold tracks down his cheeks. "I wasn't enough."

The entity's laughter rolled through the chamber like thunder before rain. Alex Kingston waited for darkness to claim him, unaware that destiny had one final card to deal.

The ring against his chest grew warm.

Then he heard her – that same ancient voice from the tunnels, but clearer now. "Hearken, my child." Her tone carried warmth unlike Balor's cruel thunder. "All is not lost." Alex's thoughts reached back: *What do I do?* "You are my creation, my Cauldron Born. This fight ends as I will it. Rise."

Alex's eyes opened to new purpose. Through pressing darkness and failing hope, something stirred against his skin. His fingers found James's ring, still hanging from its chain. The sensation started subtle, barely noticeable through chaos, but grew stronger with each heartbeat – like something ancient trying to wake.

Memory flashed bright as lightning: the lighthouse, his father's voice carrying hidden meaning: *"When the time comes, you'll know. And you'll have a ring ready."*

The ring pulsed warm against his palm as understanding crashed through him. All the pieces aligned, showing what they'd missed all along.

"The bloodlines," he whispered, revelation dawning. "It was never about two separate powers working together. That's why Dad and Richard failed – they misread everything."

His gaze found Nathan's still form across the chamber. The entity's laughter, Richard's mockery, even Sarah's peril – everything faded against this new certainty burning in his chest.

Strength he shouldn't still possess flooded his limbs as he surged upright. The entity turned James's possessed face toward him, confusion flickering through void-dark eyes.

"Where do you think you're running, little Kingston?" Its voice remembered when chaos wore flesh.

Alex didn't waste breath answering. He dove across the chamber, dodging Black Eyed Children's grasping hands and

Shepherds' desperate grabs. Nothing mattered except reaching Nathan.

"Stop him!" Richard's command came too late.

Alex slid to his knees beside Nathan, cradling his head with trembling hands. "Nathan." Urgency made his whisper sharp. "Please. We're not finished yet. I need you."

The ring slipped onto Nathan's finger like destiny finding its mark – bloodlines binding in the most ancient way possible. Alex sealed it with a kiss that carried prophecy and promise both.

For one eternal moment, nothing changed. The chamber's chaos faded to white noise as Alex held his breath, counting Nathan's too-slow heartbeats. Time stretched like pulled taffy while prophecy waited to see which way fate would fall.

Then – so subtle he might have imagined it – blue light bloomed from the ring. It spread like dawn breaking, traveling up Nathan's arm in rivers of pure power. Answering warmth flooded Alex's chest, as if some ancient thread had finally connected their separate stories into one shared tale.

Nathan's eyelids fluttered like moths testing lamplight.

"That's it." Alex's whisper carried generations of love. "Come back to me. We've got a world to save, and I can't do it alone."

As Nathan stirred toward consciousness, as that blue glow strengthened like rising tide, hope burned bright in Alex's chest for the first time since entering these ancient depths. They weren't finished. Whatever darkness waited, whatever chaos threatened – they would face it together, bloodlines finally united as prophecy had always intended.

The ring blazed brighter, its light remembering when magic ran wild and raw, when love could reshape reality itself.

In the chamber's depths, children who had never been children fell silent, sensing something vast and ancient stirring – not chaos this time, but order born of freely given love. The final chapter of their story waited to be written, not in darkness, but in light.

Chapter Eighteen

Rising Light

The ring's soft blue light pulsed in perfect harmony with Alex's heartbeat. The chamber held its breath, chaos suspended as Nathan's eyelids fluttered against returning consciousness. Even the shadows seemed to wait.

"Nathan." Alex poured love and urgency into the whisper. "Come back to me."

Nathan's eyes opened slowly, unfocused at first before finding Alex's face. Recognition sparked like struck flint. "Alex?" His voice came rough as stone. "What..."

A roar of pure fury shattered the moment. The entity wearing James's flesh had noticed the change. "NO!" Thunder rolled through its stolen voice. "This cannot be!"

Blue light bloomed stronger, wrapping them both in its protective glow. Nathan's gaze caught on the ring, understanding dawning like sunrise. "Alex, is this—"

"Yeah." Alex's smile carried more hope than fear for the first time since entering these depths. "Think I finally figured out what we were missing."

Determination hardened Nathan's features as their fingers interlaced. "Together?"

"Always."

They rose as one, their joined power flaring like captured stars. Black Eyed Children recoiled from its radiance, their empty eyes showing fear for the first time. The darkness draining Sarah's essence wavered, thinning like smoke in strong wind. She gasped, color returning to her face.

Richard stalked forward, rage twisting his features. "You think this changes anything?" His snarl carried desperate edge. "Our god is awake! You're too late!"

But the entity staggered in James's stolen body, its perfect darkness flickering. For a heartbeat, Alex glimpsed his father's true eyes fighting through void. "What is this?" Its voice lost its thunder, uncertainty creeping in. "What have you—"

The entity froze mid-sentence, recognition dawning like winter sunrise. "No," it breathed, true fear entering its ancient voice. "It cannot be. Her power... Cerridwen."

Alex and Nathan stepped forward as one, their combined power blazing like captured dawn. Their hands rose in perfect sync, magic harmonizing between them like struck crystal.

"No." Richard's arrogance cracked, showing fear beneath. "It's not possible!"

Together they began to cast, their circle manifesting in pure blue light. Black Eyed Children struck its barrier like moths hitting flame, thrown back by power older than their hunger. Their empty eyes showed something new: uncertainty.

"You fools!" Richard's staff pulsed with desperate darkness. "You can't stop what's already begun!"

His attack rebounded off their circle, darkness amplified and returned threefold. The staff shattered like struck ice, sending Richard sprawling across ancient stone.

Their voices wove together, calling the watchtowers. Earth answered from the North with trembling stone. East's wind whipped their hair like storm-song. South's fire danced in their joined magic. West's waters sang in their blood. Elements that remembered when magic ran wild and raw responded to love's summons.

Balor howled through James's stolen voice, the sound shaking reality's foundations. Sarah dropped from void's grasp as dark tendrils dissipated like smoke in strong wind.

Margaret stirred to consciousness, wonder dawning as she witnessed prophecy unfold. Alex and Nathan's voices rose stronger, invoking Cerridwen herself – she who had bound chaos when the world was young, she who had created the Cauldron Born.

As they began the incantation one final time, both knew with bone-deep certainty: this was how it was always meant to be. Not separate powers working together, but love freely given creating something entirely new.

"The seal." Margaret's voice carried wonder despite her weakness. "They've done it. The bloodlines are truly one."

"I WILL NOT BE DENIED!" The entity's roar shook ancient stone. "EONS OF WAITING END NOW!"

Darkness lashed out but dissolved against their shield of pure light. Alex and Nathan stood unwavering, focused on James's possessed form.

"Dad." Alex's voice rang with certainty. "Fight it. We're here."

James's body convulsed unnaturally, the entity's ancient voice warring with human tones. "A-Alex..." James fought through chaos. "S-son..."

"That's it." Hope made Alex's words stronger. "We can end this. Together."

Nathan's grip tightened. "Mr. Kingston, your son is the bravest soul I've ever known. I swear by everything I am, I'll stand beside him always."

The ring blazed like captured starlight, sending waves of pure power through the chamber. Black Eyed Children wailed as their forms began unraveling. The Shepherds collapsed as darkness abandoned them.

"No." Richard stumbled back, terror replacing arrogance. "This isn't possible!"

James writhed at the chamber's heart, light and shadow warring across his skin. Alex and Nathan shared one look, understanding flowing between them. The risk was enormous – failure meant losing everything, including James. But as reality trembled around them, choice crystallized into certainty.

"Nathan." Alex's voice steadied them both. "From that first moment, I knew you'd changed my world forever. Through all this darkness, you've been my light."

"And you've been mine." Nathan's eyes held universes. "You taught me what real courage means."

Their joined power pulsed brighter with each word, weaving ancient patterns through reality itself.

"I vow to stand with you," Alex continued, "through whatever comes. In shadow and light, in battle and peace."

"Until death and beyond." Nathan's grip anchored them both. "Two bloodlines made one, two hearts beating in time."

Blue light spiraled around them, forming symbols older than written language. The very air hummed with possibility.

"NO!" Richard hurled void-dark power in desperate rage.

Their barrier caught his attack, held it suspended between order and chaos, then returned it threefold. He flew backward, crashing against ancient stone as his own darkness claimed him.

An inhuman scream filled the chamber as James convulsed one final time. Darkness poured from his eyes and mouth, coalescing into something vast and hungry that remembered when chaos wore flesh.

"Dad!" Alex moved instinctively, but Nathan held firm.

"Wait," he breathed. "Look."

The shadow swelled until it consumed half the chamber. Thunder cracked as two massive eyes opened within the void, burning red like dying stars.

"FOOLS." Reality trembled at its voice. "YOUR MORTAL MAGIC IS NOTHING. I AM ETERNAL. I AM VOID ITSELF."

Frost crystallized on ancient stone as temperature plummeted. The few remaining Black Eyed Children pressed against walls, their empty eyes fixed on chaos unveiled.

"We're not afraid of you." Alex's voice cut through darkness like a blade of light.

"Our love," Nathan's words harmonized with his, "burns stronger than any void."

The entity's eyes narrowed to burning slits. "THEN COME, CHILDREN OF CERRIDWEN. LET US SEE HOW LOVE FARES AGAINST OBLIVION."

Darkness surged toward them like a tide of night. Alex and Nathan raised their hands as one, their joined power meeting void head-on. Light and shadow clashed at the chamber's heart, reality warping around their point of contact.

The entity's laughter shook ancient stone, but they stood unwavering, their blue-white radiance defiant against endless dark. Something shifted in Nathan then – power flooding through him like a broken dam. The ring blazed on his finger as understanding crystallized into certainty.

Pure light erupted from their joined hands, piercing void-dark matter. Each strike made chaos recoil before surging back stronger.

"IMPOSSIBLE." The entity's voice held new tension. "NO MORTAL CHANNELS SUCH POWER."

They attacked in perfect sync – Nathan's azure bolts weaving with Alex's golden light in a dance that illuminated every shadow. But ancient darkness answered with terrible fury, spreading across ceiling and walls like living ink. Ice formed in the very air they breathed.

"I HAVE DEVOURED WORLDS," it roared. "CONSUMED CIVILIZATIONS. YOUR LIGHT IS NOTHING!"

A tendril of pure void caught Nathan, sending him sliding across frost-slick stone.

"Nathan!" Alex was at his side instantly.

"I'm okay." Nathan's voice strained as Alex helped him up. "But we need to end this. We can't maintain this level of power much longer."

"Together then." Alex's grip tightened. "Like we promised."

They stood as one, voices joining in ancient words: "Lady Cerridwen, goddess of three, on this night your children call to thee. Mother, Maiden, Crone..."

The entity howled – was that fear threading through its fury? Darkness thrashed against growing light as something vast and ancient stirred beyond reality's walls.

For one eternal moment, light warred with void at the chamber's heart. Reality bent around their clash, ancient stone groaning under forces it was never meant to contain.

Nathan felt his strength ebbing, the price of channeling such power taking its toll. But Alex's presence anchored him, their shared determination carrying them past mortal limits.

"Almost there," Alex ground out, face pale with effort.

"Through darkness your light is shown... Lady stir your cauldron well, sing your song and cast your spell..." Their voices wove together as ancient words gained power.

The entity's form began to contract, its burning eyes flickering against relentless light. Hope sparked in Nathan's chest – then chaos gathered itself for one final, devastating strike.

Darkness lashed out faster than thought. "ALEX!" Nathan's scream tore from his throat as void-force sent his love crashing into ancient stone. Alex crumpled, terrifyingly still.

"FOOLISH CHILDREN." The entity's triumph rolled like thunder. "DID YOU THINK LOVE COULD MATCH CHAOS?"

Nathan's world narrowed to Alex's motionless form. But through rising despair, Margaret's whisper reached him: "The union... it's not complete. You know what must be done."

Understanding blazed like dawn. Nathan gathered Alex in trembling arms. "Come back to me," he breathed against cold lips. "We're not finished yet."

Their kiss sparked power through the chamber. The ring blazed, the founder's stone sang, and reality itself held its breath. Alex's eyes flew open, blazing golden – but not just Alex looked out through them.

When he spoke, two voices emerged: his own and something ancient that remembered when magic ran wild and raw. "IMPOSSIBLE." Balor's roar carried the first notes of fear.

But it was happening. Their bloodlines finally, truly merged. Golden light spiraled around Alex while azure power wreathed Nathan. As one being, they faced chaos incarnate.

Their combined power lanced toward void – perfect fusion of gold and blue-white, Kingston and Holloway magic made manifest in pure love. The entity howled as light pierced shadow. Its darkness unraveled, drawn back into its ancient prison by power older than chaos itself.

A new seal blazed into ancient stone – not separate lines now, but a single pattern speaking of two bloodlines perfectly joined. Silence fell like blessing until James stirred, confusion melting into pride as he saw his son and son-in-law standing victorious.

"Dad!" Alex's voice carried only his own tones now as they rushed to James.

His father's weak smile carried worlds of love. "You did it. You actually did it."

"Guys!" Sarah's sharp call broke their reunion. "Look!"

Richard stirred in the corner, making Alex and Nathan snap to defensive stances. But as his eyes opened, something had changed. The darkness that had twisted his features was gone, leaving only confusion and something like fear.

"What... where am I?" His voice carried none of its former power. "What's happening?"

James pushed himself upright, leaning on Alex for support as he studied his old friend. "The entity," he said carefully, "must have been controlling him all along. With chaos sealed away..."

Margaret hobbled toward her son, using a makeshift cane fashioned from debris. She examined him with piercing intensity, then – *SMACK* – cracked him across the head with surprising speed.

"You absolute IDIOT!" Years of worry transformed into maternal fury. "How DARE you—" She continued berating him while Richard stared up at her, thoroughly confused and thoroughly cowed.

Alex tried to hide his laugh in a cough, earning an elbow from Nathan and a knowing look from his father.

They made their way out slowly, supporting each other through winding tunnels that felt smaller now, less threatening. Dawn greeted them as they emerged – Salem's first true sunrise in what felt like years.

Alex and Nathan paused at the mine's mouth, hands linked, watching light paint their town in gold. Below them, Salem stirred to normal life, blissfully unaware of how close chaos had come to unmaking everything.

"We actually did it." Nathan's whisper carried wonder and exhaustion in equal measure. His thumb brushed over the ring that had changed everything.

Alex squeezed his hand, feeling their magic hum in harmony. They'd closed one chapter, but standing here in dawn's light, watching their town wake to a safer world, they knew their real story was just beginning.

Behind them, Margaret's lecture continued unabated, while Sarah documented everything in her reporter's notebook, carefully editing out the parts the world wasn't ready to know.

The ring glowed softly in the morning light, content in having served its purpose in love's triumph over chaos.

Chapter Nineteen

A New Beginning

Spring sunlight poured through Margaret's windows, highlighting dust motes and battlefield grime on her sitting room's exhausted occupants. They'd barely had time to collapse into various chairs before Margaret started forcing restorative tea on everyone.

Sharp knocking cut through their collective daze. Alex hauled himself up, muscles protesting every movement. He opened the door to find Adrianna Cromwell's knowing smile.

"Well." Her eyes took in his disheveled state with barely concealed amusement. "It seems prophecy chose correctly after all." Behind her stood Eleanor Kingston, who immediately shifted into grandmother mode.

"Alexander James Kingston." She clicked her tongue. "Couldn't even wash your face before receiving company?"

Alex led them toward the sitting room, but Eleanor froze in the doorway. James offered a tired smile. "Hello, Mother."

"James?" The name came out barely above a whisper. "But... you're dead. We mourned you."

Adrianna's attention caught on Richard, nursing both his head and his dignity where Margaret had thoroughly adjusted his attitude earlier. "Indeed." Her voice carried centuries of authority. "It seems we have two resurrections to discuss. Along with what I suspect are numerous violations of Order protocol."

They spent the next hours recounting everything – the Black Eyed Children, the corrupted stone, the final battle beneath Salem. Adrianna listened with practiced neutrality, though her eye twitched slightly at each broken rule. Eleanor alternated between staring at her returned son and shooting concerned looks at her grubby grandson.

"Well," Adrianna finally said, accepting a fresh cup of Margaret's tea, "I suppose saving reality itself earns some latitude regarding regulations." Her stern expression cracked into something warmer as she studied Alex and Nathan. "Though next time, perhaps inform the Order before performing ancient rituals?"

Nathan caught Alex's eye across the room, both fighting grins. There would be paperwork and meetings and probably several lectures about proper magical procedure. But for now, they were together, they were alive, and they had tomorrow to look forward to.

The ring glinted on Nathan's finger, catching morning light like a promise kept.

Life in Salem settled into a new normal in the months following that night beneath the earth. The town's rhythms continued unchanged, its people either unable or unwilling to remember the darkness that had nearly claimed them. Whether this convenient forgetting came from the entity's defeat, human nature's talent for denial, or the Order's liberal application of memory charms remained unclear.

For Alex and Nathan, reality had taken on a dreamlike quality. Their house on Salem's outskirts became a perfect blend of their lives – Nathan's carefully tended magical herbs sharing space with Alex's organized chaos of half-written stories and supernatural research. The founder's stone sat in a place of honor above their fireplace, while protection runes glowed softly in their window frames.

James threw himself into hunting down the remaining Shepherds, with a newly-reformed Richard at his side. Despite Margaret's protests, James had reclaimed his old house. "Can't let it sit empty while Alex and Nathan have their own place," he'd explain for the hundredth time. Richard, however, remained under his mother's roof – though whether this was punishment or protection remained amusingly unclear.

The Salem Gazette gained a new editor after Tom Marshton's abrupt resignation. His letter cited stress and exhaustion, though he couldn't quite remember why. His enthusiastic recommendation of Alex for the position came with similar holes in memory. Sarah stepped naturally into Alex's old role, her reporter's instincts now sharpened by an understanding of Salem's deeper truths.

The Black Eyed Children vanished like morning mist. Whether banished with their master or simply waiting in deeper shadows, no one knew. But Alex and Nathan kept watchful eyes on darkness, just in case.

Summer settled warm and golden over their backyard six months later. Nathan knelt in his garden, fighting a losing battle with particularly stubborn roses while Alex typed nearby, Artemis prowling between them.

"I swear she's cheating." Nathan glared at his imperfect blooms. "Grandmother's roses CANNOT be that perfect without magical intervention."

Alex glanced up from his laptop, affection softening his smile. "Your natural ones have more character."

Artemis pounced on a toy mouse that occasionally moved itself, her guardian nature now more interested in play than protection. The ring on Nathan's soil-covered hand caught sunlight like a promise kept.

"Better clean up." Nathan brushed dirt from his knees. "Sarah's waiting for dinner."

"Speaking of." Alex watched Artemis's toy scurry under furniture of its own accord. "She's becoming quite the magical scholar."

"Margaret's thrilled." Nathan conjured light patterns for their cat to chase. "Finally someone properly excited about pre-colonial grimoires. Though giving her access to the restricted archives..."

"Could be interesting?" Alex finished, remembering their own adventures started with similar curiosity.

Above them, summer clouds painted Salem's sky in perfect peace.

Reality had shifted since that night in the quarry – not in world-shattering ways, but in gentle adjustments that suggested better balance between chaos and order. The fog lifted from Salem's streets, leaving the town more comfortable in its own skin.

Spring twilight painted everything in soft focus, blurring lines between magical and mundane. Their house stood warm against deepening evening, protection runes glowing softly in window frames. Artemis watched their departure from her usual perch, green eyes gleaming as she maintained household wards. Her enchanted mouse toy performed its own miniature patrol beside her.

They drove through streets that held deeper meaning now. Pioneer Village had lost its ominous edge, its shadows no longer holding hungry children. The quarry, though officially closed, occasionally pulsed with harmonious energy that made magical practitioners smile without knowing why. Even the lighthouse seemed to cast a warmer beam across darkening waters.

Their conversation drifted toward Sarah's possible news and Margaret's likely dramatic reaction, comfortable in the peace they'd helped create. But neither noticed the figure watching their car disappear around the corner, its smile never quite fitting its face.

Shadows moved around it with purpose that suggested neither chaos nor order – something new, something waiting. Reality bent slightly in its presence, as if unsure how to categorize this fresh anomaly.

The next game would start subtle – whispers and suggestions, patterns invisible until players were too deeply involved to step away. The figure's smile widened, showing teeth that had never been human. "A new game," it breathed to evening air. "With rules of my own making."

Street lights flickered once. When they stabilized, the figure had vanished, though its shadows continued their purposeful dance. Reality settled back into normal rhythms, pretending nothing unusual had occurred.

But ancient powers stirred beneath Salem's surface, preparing games that would make chaos entities seem straightforward. Sarah waited at Rosie's Diner with news that would change everything again, while at town's edge, wolves howled at a moon that shouldn't yet have risen.

The ring on Nathan's finger caught twilight like a promise, unaware that some promises carry unexpected price tags.

www.ingramcontent.com/pod-product-compliance
Lightning Source LLC
LaVergne TN
LVHW031938200125
801714LV00002B/2/J